Shot in the Dark

SHOT IN THE DARK

A MEN OF THE SECRET SERVICE ROMANCE

TRACY SOLHEIM

TULE
PUBLISHING

DEDICATION

This one is for the Tule girls. Meghan Farrell Fuhrmann, thank you for always having a smile on your face even when I'm telling you my book is going to be late. *Really* late. Sinclair Sawhney, thank you for helping me to keep my characters authentic and for always making my stories better. And, Jane Porter, thank you for creating a community where authors can come, let their hair down, and find their love of writing again. You are my hero.

CHAPTER ONE

A SINGLE GUNSHOT rang out, shattering the quiet tranquility of the remote African watering hole. The ground beneath the vehicle where Josslyn Benoit was standing began to shake violently when the small herd of elephants she and her team were observing stampeded back into the bush. Hundreds of birds rose up from the savanna, forming a dark cloud overhead, the frenzy of their wings nearly deafening.

Their sound wasn't loud enough to drown out the second gunshot, however.

From her perch in an open-air Land Rover, concealed behind a grove of elephant grass and two towering river bush willow trees, Josslyn peered through her binoculars as a cow stumbled. Blood trickled down the female elephant's chest. A third shot cracked through the air, hitting the wounded animal in the hind end. Josslyn grabbed hold of the seatback as the earth shook again when the elephant stumbled before finally falling to the sand. A young calf circled wildly behind the fatally wounded elephant, its anguished wails resonating throughout the bush.

"I thought you said there wasn't any hunting permitted here?" Josslyn hissed at their guide.

"Them be poachers, miss." He shrugged, clearly un-fazed by the illegal actions of his countrymen.

"Poachers?" Trevor Kearn, the representative from Global Wildlife Conservation who was traveling with them, sounded almost giddy. "Hugh, keep that camera rolling. If we can get this on film, it will go a long way to strengthen our argument that legalized hunting has done absolutely *nothing* to stem the poaching trade here in Zimbabwe."

The big Scottish cameraman grunted in exasperation. Still, he combat-crawled to the edge of the tall grass to get a better shot.

The pitiful cries of the baby elephant cut through the thick afternoon air like a machete, the sound making Josslyn's stomach roll. As a scientist, she understood the circle of life. But that didn't mean she had to like it. Or the role her fellow humans played in it.

A band of ragtag tribesmen emerged from the bush on the opposite side of the watering hole. Josslyn was relieved to see that only one of them was armed. He was carrying a high-powered military-grade rifle with a telescopic sight, perfect for shooting accurately over long distances. She abhorred poachers and hunters, but she despised guns and everything related to them more. Still, she reasoned with herself, in this situation, a single gun was preferable to the men poisoning the entire herd in order to steal the ele-phants' tusks.

"They don't look very friendly," Alyssa whispered.

Josslyn was instantly regretting putting the biology grad

student in harm's way.

"They're poor and they're desperate to feed their families," Josslyn explained quietly, not bothering to hide her disgust at the situation. "Their government is charging hunters exorbitant fees to come here to track big game, but none of that money ever reaches the hands of these tribesmen. That leaves poaching as their only option for survival."

"I need a shot of them hacking out the ivory tusks with the machete," Trevor whispered to Hugh. "The more gruesome it is, the better we can make our case that this has to be stopped."

An Australian surfer turned animal rights' activist, Trevor lived for these types of confrontations. At one point in her life, so had Josslyn. But as the shine wore off her relationship with Trevor, so too had her desire to constantly embarrass her family by doing something radical and dangerous.

One of the tribesmen withdrew a lethal-looking blade from his side. Alyssa sucked in a sharp breath next to Josslyn. The baby calf kept its distance from the poachers but continued its frantic pacing and wailing. Another of the tribesmen gestured at the calf. Josslyn's heart began to beat faster. The locals poached the elephants as a last resort to feed their families. They wouldn't kill for no reason. Especially a calf that had the potential to grow tusks in the future.

"Just take the damn tusks and leave the baby alone," Josslyn muttered through her clenched jaw.

These particular men had other intentions, however. The one with the rifle aimed it at the despondent calf.

Alyssa gasped.

Trevor swore.

"No!" Josslyn shouted just as the gun discharged.

Five pairs of eyes turned their way, including those belonging to the man holding the gun.

"Now you've done it, lass," Hugh exclaimed as he jumped back into the Land Rover.

Their guide was furiously trying to get the engine to turn over. Hugh pushed Alyssa down to the floor of the vehicle. Trevor was bouncing up and down still swearing at the men.

"You bastards," he yelled. "We've got all that on film. We're going to find out who's behind this ring and when we do you'll be hit with so many sanctions, you won't be able to wipe your asses much less buy bullets to hunt a defenseless animal!"

"Get down, you two," Hugh ordered, yanking Josslyn behind one of the padded seats.

The Land Rover jerked to life just as another shot from the rifle echoed over the water. Trevor continued to rail at the poachers before suddenly clutching his chest and sinking to his knees. A dark stain was already spreading across his T-shirt by the time Josslyn reached him.

"Trevor!" she shouted over the crunch of the tires and the rush of the wind.

The Australian grimaced at her touch. "The asshole shot me!"

"Well no surprise there," Hugh muttered as he pulled the first aid kit from under the passenger seat. "You practically dared him to do it."

"He killed that baby elephant for no reason!" Trevor let out a low moan when the Land Rover practically went airborne over a ridge in the unpaved road. "Listen, Hugh. Don't let my death be in vain. Tell me you got images of what those brutes did?"

Hugh exchanged a look with Josslyn before rolling up a sweatshirt to put beneath Trevor's head.

"You're not going to die," the Scotsman gruffly reassured him.

Josslyn tried to summon up the same amount of confidence as their cameraman. The fact was there were fifty miles of rough, unpaved road between them and competent medical help. A wave of guilt had her rocking back on her heels. If only she hadn't yelled out like that, the poachers would have never known she and her team were watching, much less filming. Trevor would still be smiling the cocky smile that made smart women stupid.

Growing up, her father frequently warned her about keeping her emotions in check. Easy for him to say. He'd been a stoic surgeon. She, on the other hand, had a natural talent of not thinking before speaking. Making matters worse, lately there always seemed to be a hot microphone nearby when her tongue went rogue. Still, she never let her emotions get in the way of her staunch defense of the little guy. Even if in this case the *little guy* was a three-thousand-pound wild animal.

Alyssa tore at Trevor's T-shirt, frantically applying pressure with gauze she'd pulled from the first aid kit. "The bullet hit his shoulder," she said with remarkable calm considering their circumstances. "We just need to keep him from going into shock. Or losing too much blood." Her face was determined when her eyes glanced up to meet Josslyn's. "I spent two summers shadowing interns in an ER. He's *not* going to die."

Trevor moaned when they hit another bump in the road. His face was pale and drawn. "Thank God they were on foot and couldn't follow us," he choked out.

Hugh exchanged a look with Josslyn. He indicated the replay monitor on the camera. She watched the video as one of the tribesmen seemed to be speaking into a walkie-talkie just before the gunman fired at Trevor.

Damn it. Josslyn looked over her shoulder, but the road was blessedly empty.

For now.

After gathering her long hair into a ponytail, she crouched down beside Alyssa, mostly to distract the young woman from the fact that Hugh was pulling a long gun from beneath the bench seat and moving to the back of the Land Rover, but also to help Trevor however she could. As a doctor of zoology, she didn't quite have the extensive medical training the rest of her family possessed, but at least she wasn't squeamish around blood.

"What can I do?"

"Move the sweatshirt from beneath his head to his feet," Alyssa commanded. "I think there's a Mylar blanket in the first aid kit. We'll need it to cover him to keep the shock at bay." The younger woman's hands were now soaked with blood from where she was applying pressure to Trevor's wound. "And I'm going to need your T-shirt."

Doing as she was told, Josslyn stripped off her shirt, exposing her skin to the harsh African sun. Hugh tossed his T-shirt to Alyssa as well. Between the two of them, they did their best to keep Trevor comfortable while the Land Rover barreled ahead, seeming to find every rut in the road as they sped toward help.

"We've got company," Hugh announced forty minutes into their mad dash.

A small dust cloud rose up along the horizon behind them. It was difficult to judge their distance, but whoever they were sharing the road with was coming at a fast clip. Josslyn glanced down at Trevor. A sheen of sweat covered his face despite the fact he was shivering beneath the blanket. Except to change out the T-shirts, Alyssa's hands never let up their compression on the wound. Her expression was fierce.

Josslyn checked the GPS screen on the dashboard. They were still some twenty miles from the capital. But twenty miles could take another hour on these roads. It was a crapshoot whether their guide could outrun whoever was chasing them. Hugh hefted the long gun into his lap.

Pulling her cell phone from her shorts, Josslyn fingered the app her brother-in-law insisted she install on her phone. There would be hell to pay, but she couldn't justify putting the others at risk. The one time in her twenty-eight years Josslyn was actually doing something worthwhile with her career, yet she still managed to potentially touch off an international incident. Her older sister's lecture was already playing out in Josslyn's head when she tapped the button.

Fifteen minutes later, the dust cloud was closing the distance on them. Josslyn could make out two Jeeps filled with military-looking personnel likely belonging to the tribal militia. Hugh turned to say something when the sound of a propeller roared overhead. She let out a sigh of relief at the sight of two Blackhawk helicopters coming their way.

"Slow down," she called to the guide as one of the choppers went on to circle the group following them.

The other helicopter landed on the roadway a half mile ahead of the Land Rover. Four United States Marines, dressed in full-battle dress uniforms leaped from the cabin before it hit the ground. Guns at the ready, they surrounded the Jeep.

Hugh and the driver quickly lifted their hands into the air. Alyssa's mouth dropped open in what was either awe or hysteria, Josslyn wasn't exactly sure.

"We need a stretcher," Josslyn shouted over the noise of the helicopter rotor. "We have an injured man here."

In a matter of minutes, the marines expertly loaded Trevor and the rest of her team onto the helicopter. The militia following them was reduced to specs on the sand as the chopper took to the air.

"Dr. Doolittle has been retrieved," the mission commander relayed to whoever was listening. "ETA five minutes."

Josslyn flinched slightly at the ridiculous code name she was assigned. Alyssa shot her a bewildered glance before leaning down to help the medic attending to Trevor.

"We were set up," Hugh muttered from where he sat on the bench beside her. "Ngoni had no intention of bringing the supplier to meet us."

"Or someone got to him," she whispered back, hoping they were both wrong.

Ngoni was eleven, a young African tribesman doing whatever he could to survive in a hierarchal economy stacked against him. Even if it meant selling exotic, endangered animals, dead or alive. Josslyn hoped he hadn't become a tragedy in her quest to get justice for the animals by exposing the international ring.

"All the same," Hugh replied. "We need to lay low for the time being."

"Nonsense. We have the perfect cover studying the African elephants' diminishing habitat," Josslyn reassured the cameraman. "Anyone could have stumbled over poachers. As far as anyone knows, today was a horrible accident. We can't stop now that we are so close."

"Don't be daft, lass," he whispered. "These thugs are nasty individuals. Animal trafficking is big business right behind trafficking illegal drugs and guns. They don't want anyone poking their noses in their lucrative operation. Especially someone with your family's connections."

Your family's connections. Those "connections" loomed over every aspect of Josslyn's life. It didn't matter that she was a top-notch zoologist. She was forever defined by the people who shared her DNA. And she didn't like it. Not one bit.

"No," Hugh continued, his tone adamant. "It's getting too dangerous to have you helping us any longer. You best go home and attack this from the other direction. Chase the clues leading to those people funding this organization."

Josslyn squared her shoulders. Saving animals was her passion, her cause, her reason for getting up in the morning. This syndicate only cared about making money. And lots of it. Whether or not an animal suffered or a species became extinct had no bearing on their illegal enterprise. The animals needed someone to stand up for them. And Josslyn never backed down from a fight—no matter her family connections.

"Our first priority is to make sure Trevor gets medical attention," she answered. "That will give us time to regroup and 'lay low' as you suggest. But I'm not going anywhere. I answer to no one but my own conscience. And my conscience won't rest until these criminals are revealed. My family thinks I'm here with the Smithsonian filming a documentary." She patted Hugh's thigh. "Everything will be fine."

Hugh gave her a look that clearly said he didn't believe her. Not that she blamed him. This wasn't the first time Josslyn found herself at the mercy of the US military and, based on past experience, there would be a long mea culpa period before her family let her forget it.

But at least this time, she was in no danger of getting her heart broken by her rescuer.

She glanced around at the men and women aboard the helicopter. Despite feeling decidedly vulnerable dressed only in khaki shorts and a black lace bra, she was relieved the crew remained stoic and professional. There would be no earth-shattering kisses this time around. She wasn't sure if she was relieved or dismayed. Josslyn stifled the urge to wave at the commander's body camera which was likely broadcasting her scantily clad image back to the States. But only because she meant what she said to Hugh about staying to see this thing through. Aggravating her family further wouldn't get her a longer hall pass.

The helicopter touched down on the rooftop of the US Embassy in Harare where a medical team was waiting to transport Trevor to a local hospital.

"I'm going with him," Alyssa announced to no one in particular.

The grad student was Josslyn's responsibility and she should order Alyssa to stay within the safe confines of the embassy until things were sorted out. But having succumbed to Trevor's charm herself once upon a time, she was fully aware of the potent effect his blue eyes and wicked dimple likely had on the younger woman. After all Alyssa had done to save him, Josslyn didn't have the heart to tell her to stay put.

"Let me find something to cover up with," she said instead. "And I'll come with you."

"Not so fast."

Josslyn froze in place, her ponytail swirling behind her as the helicopter lifted off again turning the rooftop into a wind tunnel. Spinning slowly on one heel, she turned to meet the exasperated glare of Christian Sumner, an old family friend of her brother-in-law's and a colossal pain in Josslyn's ass.

"Tell me again where they park those things," she quipped. "It must be one hell of a garage."

Christian shook his head in disgust. "Is there nothing you take seriously, Josslyn?"

She crossed her arms in front of her. Not so much as a defensive move but more to keep her nemesis from getting an eyeful of the cleavage he once so desperately wished to possess. Of course, he never really wanted Josslyn herself. Just the alliance with her powerful family that a marriage to her would bring.

"And here I thought nothing I could say or do surprised you, Christian. What are you doing here, anyway? I thought you'd gotten married and given up following me around."

He snorted before closing the distance between them. "In case you forgot, I'm now the Undersecretary of State for Africa. I don't need an excuse to be here. And I *never* followed you around."

It was Josslyn's turn to snort because both knew he was lying about the last part. "The word *under* in your title makes you sound so small and powerless."

Definitely a cheap shot given Christian's sensitivity about his five-foot-seven height, but the medics were long gone with Trevor and Josslyn needed an exit strategy from the embassy and the clutches of the American government. Christian's sudden appearance meant Hugh had been correct to worry that her time in Zimbabwe might be cut short. But she wasn't ready to leave yet. Not until she knew the names of the suppliers.

Only this time Christian was proving himself to be a formidable opponent. He didn't so much as flinch at her insult. In fact, his shoulders seemed to rise up an inch. Or two. He was on a power high and confident he had the upper hand in their current standoff. The thought put her even more on edge.

"You're in my house now, Josslyn. And you'll show both my staff and me some respect. Rescuing you and your merry band of animal rights do-gooders from angry rebel militia wasn't on anyone's agenda today. As usual, your little stunt will cost the American taxpayers a small fortune. Let's hope it doesn't cost your boyfriend his life."

Former boyfriend. Not that the change in their relationship status meant she didn't care about Trevor's survival. She did. But she also didn't want to give the man standing in front of her any more ammunition than he already had. She couldn't deny his accusations either because, well, she had been guilty of abusing her family's power a time or two. Today wasn't one of those times, though. In this operation, it was best for everyone involved if no one knew who she was. Explaining it to Christian was pointless, however. He was just another one of her family's hired watchdogs.

"As usual, it's been nice catching up with you," she lied. "If you don't mind, I'd like to go check on my team now."

"The only place you're going is back to Washington. Immediately."

His pronouncement had Josslyn halting in her steps. "Excuse me?" A trace of unease ran up her spine.

Christian's expression suddenly turned merciless as if to say "check-mate." "There's a C-one thirty taking off in fifty minutes. You're to be on it if I have to drag you on board in restraints. I'm under orders from the commander in chief. You do remember him, Josslyn, don't you?"

Damn. After using the nuclear option and calling in the marines, Josslyn knew she eventually had no choice but to go back to the States and play nice. But she'd thought she'd at least have a few days to follow up on leads and locate Ngoni. Clearly, her brother-in-law had other ideas.

Blowing out a frustrated breath, she stared past Christian, allowing the beauty of the African desert to wash over her. They were out there somewhere. Brutal men and women who would kill a baby rhinoceros for its foot, selling it later as a damn pencil holder to some sick individual around the world. She was determined to stop them, one by one if she had to. But apparently not today. Sometimes her goals felt like a mirage she'd never be able to reach. If only she could give in to her impulse to just turn on her heel and march away. She could then live her own life the way she wanted to, righting the wrongs against animals and protesting the injustice in this world.

That was easier said than done, however, when her brother-in-law was the president of the United States.

CHAPTER TWO

"WELL, DOC, WHAT'S the verdict?"
Secret Service Agent Adam Lockett tried to sit patiently in the leather exam chair waiting for the neurosurgeon to respond to his question. But his patience was in short supply. It had been nearly four weeks since the accident and, frankly, the sniper was more than ready to get back to his job commanding the Secret Service's elite Counter Assault Tactical Team. The headaches were gone—*mostly*. And he could finally tolerate the daylight again. If he was forced to endure another minute of peace and quiet in the darkness, Adam wasn't sure he wouldn't go stark raving mad. He'd never been able to sit still. Just ask any one of his teachers. And the darkness, well, he had lots of reasons to want to avoid that.

"Considering the severity of your head injury, you're progressing quite well, Agent Lockett," Dr. Mark Kozinn replied.

Adam could barely curb his enthusiasm. "So I can go back on active duty?"

"I don't see why you can't return to work."

"That's the best news I've had in weeks." Adam jumped from the chair eager to suit up and show the rest of his team he hadn't lost his aim or his mojo; he still reigned as the number-one sharpshooter in the world.

"Hold on there, Agent Lockett," White House Secret Service Director Worcester said from behind Adam. "Can you elaborate on what you mean by 'work,' Doctor?"

The adrenaline surging through Adam's chest lurched into his throat, nearly choking him. Leave it to his boss to need a freaking doctor's note before reissuing Adam's rifle. As much respect as he had for the director, the man could certainly be a major buzzkill with his strict adherence to the procedure manual.

Adam was, by nature, a man of action. He played within the rules—for the most part—but he didn't get bogged down by them. In his line of work, decisions were often made in a split second. He and his team did whatever it took to ensure the safety of the president of the United States. Even if it meant taking a bullet meant for him. Or, in Adam's case, jumping in front of a would-be assassin wielding a lead pipe.

"By all means, let me clarify." Dr. Kozinn eyed Adam warily.

Adam didn't like the look one bit. It resembled the exasperated expression his father had always worn when Adam accidentally spilled some milk. Or dropped a ball in the outfield. Or forgot to tuck in his shirt. Fill in the blank with any number of petty childhood transgressions, but the look was always the same.

"I think it would be best if you *ease* back into your duties, Agent Lockett," the doctor announced.

"But you just said—"

Dr. Kozinn held up a hand. "I said you could go back to work, but you're still not quite recovered enough to be aiming a high-powered rifle accurately, much less leading the CAT team."

"The hell I'm not! I didn't miss a target at the range yesterday," Adam argued.

He left out the fact that he'd had to wait several minutes between shots to let his eyes regain their focus, but it was the first time since the accident he'd aimed a rifle. His vision was bound to improve with practice.

The doctor shook his head, not bothering to admonish Adam for heading to the rifle range before he'd been given the okay. The look on the other man's face said it all. Swearing under his breath, Adam slumped back down into the chair.

"CTE can be debilitating," Dr. Kozinn explained as though Adam was a kindergartener and not a thirty-one-year-old trained in special ops who, despite a "debilitating" concussion, could still kick this guy's ass a thousand ways from Sunday. "Your brain needs time to heal. Exposing it to exacting tasks could be too taxing at this point."

"How long?" Adam managed to grind out through his clenched jaw. "How long do I have to sit on my thumbs in the dark?"

The doctor sighed. "I realize this has been frustrating for an adrenaline junkie like you, Agent Lockett. But there's no reason for restrictions that severe any longer. As I said, you can return to some form of active duty. In fact, it will help us better assess your cognitive skills if you're doing something constructive. I'm sure there is a job less physically demanding you can perform within the White House until you're one hundred percent." He arched an eyebrow in question at Director Worcester.

"We can certainly find Agent Lockett a detail that won't be too taxing," the director replied.

Adam swallowed a groan. The only protective detail he could think of that would qualify as not "too taxing" was babysitting the president's father-in-law, an octogenarian crippled with Alzheimer's.

"How long?" he repeated. "How long until I can return to my *actual* duties?"

"Given how well you're progressing and if you keep up your therapy, I should be able to give you the all clear at your next appointment in a few weeks," the doctor replied.

A few weeks.

It sounded to Adam like a life sentence. Especially since the president and First Lady were leaving on a two-week world tour in a couple of days. He hated having to hand over the helm of the CAT team to his rival. The idiot led by intimidation and swagger. Not only that, but he couldn't shoot worth a damn. Adam bit back a few choice swear words before reminding himself he was a survivor. He'd been through worse before and come out the other side hungrier and more focused.

Failure is never an option.

"Fine." He stood and made his way to the door. "I'll see you in two weeks, Doc."

"And I'll see you at the Crown at seven thirty tomorrow morning, Agent Lockett," the director called after him.

Adam didn't bother responding. His training as a cadet at West Point combined with years in the army's elite special forces ensured he never broke rank. Both Adam and the director knew he'd be at the White House—or the Crown as the agents referred to the presidential mansion—bright and early the following morning ready to be assigned a boring protective detail. It didn't mean he had to like it though.

❖

ADAM TOOK A long swallow from his cup of coffee. He had a feeling he'd need the caffeine to get him through the tedious day looming ahead. The sun was just beginning to peek out over the horizon on the crisp October morning, but he'd been up for over an hour, getting himself ready to return to duty by jogging the familiar route through the streets of his Capitol Hill neighborhood. It felt good to finally be able to resume most of his normal activities.

The key word being *most*.

"Hey, now that you've returned from zombie status, maybe you could open some of your mail?" His roommate since their days at West Point, Ben Segar, shoved a stack of envelopes across the kitchen counter toward Adam. "Assuming you can still read after Professor Plum bashed you on the skull with the lead pipe in the billiards room."

Adam glared at his asshole buddy. "Can still read. And

can still kick your ass."

Ben chuckled as he popped a breakfast burrito into the microwave. "I'd say we put that statement to the test, but you look so *GQ* in your suit, I wouldn't want to muss you up on your first day back."

Here was another thing that felt good—getting back to the familiar bantering with his friends. Ben and the third member of their trio of West Point brothers in arms, Griffin Keller, had been treating Adam with kid gloves for the past several weeks. While he appreciated their concern more than he'd ever let on, Adam wasn't used to the hovering and nurturing. Hell, he hadn't been mothered since he was ten. The loss of his mom had seen to the end of his childhood.

"I could take you without wrinkling the crease in my pants, but then I'd have to hang around helping you fix your glasses, and I don't want to be late for my first day on the drool detail." Adam grabbed the keys to the dull four-door sedan he'd rented until he was cleared to ride his Ducati motorcycle again. He missed the feel of straddling the sleek bike. Hell, he missed the feel of wrapping his legs around a woman, too. At least the doctor hadn't put any restrictions on sex. The pretty physical therapist in the neurosurgeon's office had been coming on to Adam for weeks. She'd be a convenient distraction while he waited out the rest of his mandatory recuperation.

"You're seriously going to ignore all those letters?" Ben asked before Adam could make a clean getaway. "Whoever they're from seems pretty adamant about getting in touch with you. They've been coming two or three a week since you were attacked."

Adam glanced down at the pile of envelopes at Ben's elbow. The top one was postmarked Leavenworth, Kansas. He had no doubt the ones beneath it were as well. The chicken scratch on the front of the letter wasn't hard to recognize. It hadn't improved any over the past two decades. More than likely, the false promises and apologies on the inside hadn't either.

"Toss 'em," Adam said without a shred of guilt.

His friend studied him speculatively. It was the touch of pity flashing in Ben's eyes that had Adam turning for the door. He was fairly certain, in Ben's capacity as the Secret Service's number one cyber asset, his housemate knew *exactly* who the stack of mail was from. Knowing how much his friend loved to solve puzzles, Ben had likely long ago put together the pieces to Adam's backstory. Adam was reminded what a solid friend the other man was for not pressing him on it.

Until today.

He didn't bother standing around trying to figure out the reason for Ben's change in tactic.

"Have fun playing with the expensive toys in your lab. I'll catch up with you tonight."

"Sure," Ben replied. "But I may be late. Griff and I are going to look at tuxedos for his wedding. Apparently, the best man is required to give some input into the decision."

"Really?" Adam looked back at Ben incredulously. "When did you get the green light as best man?"

Earlier that fall, Griffin had done the unthinkable and proposed to Marin Chevalier, the White House executive pastry chef. Adam and Ben began jokingly jockeying for the position as their buddy's best man as soon Griffin had shown them the ring. While he was disappointed to not be chosen, Adam consoled himself by the fact he'd avoided having to endure an actual shopping experience.

"What do you mean?" Ben asked. "Griffin told us about his decision the night before you left for New Orleans. Don't you remember?"

No.

The fact was, Adam didn't remember anything about the days leading up to his head bashing. Not that he was going to share that information with Ben or anyone else. The way they'd been mollycoddling him, they'd turn his amnesia into an epic situation. Adam was confident his memory would return one of these days. And if it didn't, did it really matter? He shrugged and picked up his travel coffee cup.

"I knew it." Ben slapped a hand onto the countertop. "You *do* have some residual amnesia."

Realizing too late he'd been tricked, Adam let loose a string of obscenities. "Damn it, Ben. I should have known Griff would never pick you as his best man."

"Yeah, well that remains to be seen, Humpty Dumpty," Ben said as he came around the counter, his pointer finger aimed at Adam's chest. "But you, dude, need to be honest with yourself. And the doctors. A brain injury is nothing to take lightly. You need to be taking it easy. I mean, it's not like you have that many brain cells up there anyway."

While he appreciated his friend couching his concern inside a dig, Adam had had enough of everyone telling him how he needed to be careful. He was fit enough to take care of himself, thank everyone very much. And despite not having a super-sized MIT-grade brain like Ben, Adam knew if he didn't get back to any type of work soon, his brain *would* go to mush. So the drool detail it was.

"Relax, Grandma," Adam drawled. "I'm on 'non-taxing' duty, remember? At least I'll have something in common with my protectee." He tapped his forehead. "We're both a little light on our total recall right now."

Ben rolled his eyes. "Yeah, but Dr. Benoit's amnesia is caused by Alzheimer's. Don't let yours be the result of being a dumbass."

"I'll be watching over an old man who puts his dog in a stroller when he takes it for a walk, for crying out loud. There's no chance of even a rise in my blood pressure much less any further strain on my brain." Adam gave his friend a salute before heading out the door.

◈

TWO HOURS LATER, Adam felt like his head was going to explode. Despite his earlier boast, he could feel the blood shredding the veins at the base of his skull as his blood pressure likely approached DEFCON levels. At any moment his brain would be gushing out his ears, staining the carpet of the West Sitting Hall of the White

House.

And, yet, somehow, he was able to maintain the blank expression necessary of Secret Service agents everywhere, trying to appear invisible despite the family drama playing out around him. President Conrad Manning shrugged into his suit jacket seemingly unfazed by the theatrics. First Lady Harriett Manning sat on one of the sofas next to her father, the only tell that she was aggravated, the frantic tapping of her foot.

At the center of the room, moving like a whirling dervish, amid the shower of sunshine beaming through the giant half-moon window, was the She-Devil incarnate. *Josslyn Benoit.* Adam tried unsuccessfully to blink away the image of the woman with the silky black hair, pale gray eyes, and porn-star breasts who was stomping around like a frustrated toddler in front of him. But every time he raised his lids, she was still there. And still gorgeous.

Damn it.

"I agreed to hang out with Daddy here in Washington while you two go on your little diplomatic world tour," Josslyn fumed. "I *didn't* agree to have my every step shadowed by a protective detail. The Secret Service's first priority is to protect elected officials, not me. Besides, the law allows me to refuse protection. I'm pretty sure your voters will thank you for saving them some money."

Adam swallowed back a bark of agreement. Josslyn wasn't the only one duped this morning. Somehow the drool detail had turned into the diva detail, and Adam wasn't happy about it. *Not one little bit.* He'd had his close encounter with the First Lady's wild-child half-sister two years ago. And he'd nearly been blown up in the process of saving her perfect ass from some Asian whale fishermen she and her radical friends had been protesting against.

But that was nothing compared to the torture his libido was forced to endure while the two had waited for their rendezvous with the retrieval team. Adam had quickly discovered she had the heart and soul of a warrior princess. Worse, he'd been foolish enough to kiss her. Her sassy mouth not only drove him wild with desire, but she made him want things. Things he'd never envisioned having for himself. The woman was dangerous to the part of Adam he kept locked away. Once they were rescued, he quickly made himself scarce, vowing to steer clear of Josslyn Benoit at all costs. As far as he was concerned, her wish for no Secret Service protection was his command.

Too bad his commander in chief didn't see things that way.

Josslyn stopped her pacing long enough for the president to lean down and kiss her on the cheek. "This is one issue I don't give a damn what the voters think," he said. "Your safety is my only concern here. This isn't something as simple as a photo of you in a wet T-shirt being splattered across the tabloids two weeks before the election."

Adam's palms began to sweat recalling that lusty image.

"You stepped in too many hornets' nests in Africa this week," the president continued. "Whatever you were up to put you on the radar of several extremist groups. I don't need to point out this isn't the first time you've needed to be rescued."

Adam swallowed the cough that threatened to escape. Best not to let on he knew the details of her previous adventures involving the military. There was no way she could recognize him as the operative who had recovered her that long-ago night off the coast of Japan. It had been dark on the ocean. He'd been dressed in his dark battle dress uniform with black paint obscuring his face. His name, rank and serial number were classified. And after the secrets they'd shared in the water that night, Adam preferred it stay that way.

"But it will be the last time." The president's statement left no room for argument. "I trust you ladies to have a nice day. I'll see you both at dinner." He bowed down to kiss his wife on the lips before patting the head of the little Scottish terrier taking in the scene from Dr. Benoit's lap. "You boys behave today, as well."

Giving his father-in-law's shoulder a gentle squeeze, the president headed for the stairs that would lead him to the West Wing, a line of agents and advisors following him like ants to the anthill.

"Your beau seems like a very nice man, Harry-girl," Dr. Benoit said, his Southern drawl becoming more noticeable as the Alzheimer's ate away at his brain. "But there are plenty of fish in the sea. I don't want you settling down with the first one to put a twinkle in your eye. Don't forget you're going to medical school. Don't you be letting any boy hold you back."

Josslyn flopped into one of the upholstered chairs with

a beleaguered sigh. "She *did* go to medical school, Daddy. Don't you remember? She's a pediatrician. She's *America's* pediatrician." She made air quotes around the word America's in a mocking gesture.

The lines on Dr. Benoit's forehead became more pronounced as he seemed to be scanning his memory banks for the facts. As if sensing a rise in his master's anxiety level, the little terrier shifted on the doctor's lap and began whimpering.

"Josslyn," the First Lady chastised her younger sister, "we don't ask Alzheimer's patients if they remember. It's unfair."

"Oh, right, it's just me who gets to be treated unfairly."

Before the First Lady could respond, Dr. Benoit seemed to catch both women off guard.

"This is a private conversation between me and my daughter, young lady," he shouted. "And get off the furniture. I'm sure there are some chores you should be doing instead of loitering around all day. You can start by getting me some coffee. Mine's gone cold."

Adam nearly lurched at the doctor's harsh outburst. In the five months since the First Lady's father had been living with them, Adam hadn't heard a whisper of gossip from other agents about the man ever raising his voice. In fact, Dr. Benoit was considered a sweetheart by every female agent and Uniformed Division officer at the Crown.

Josslyn stiffened in her chair before her teeth sank into her bottom lip. Whether it was to keep words or a sob locked inside, Adam wasn't sure. Knowing her personality, he'd bet on a smart retort. She didn't seem like the crying type.

"Father!" Harriett Manning began. "This is Josslyn. She's your—"

"Forget it, Harriett. It's not his fault." Josslyn sprung from the chair. "I'm happy to get the coffee."

The First Lady sought out Adam's eyes after her sister had made her way across the room and into the family kitchen.

"It seems I'm forever in your debt, Agent Lockett," she said, careful to keep her voice down. "Although I think taking a lead pipe to the head might be preferable to this detail."

You got that right.

The First Lady wrung her hands. "She'll come to her senses and toe the line. Josslyn just chafes at being hemmed in. After her mother died, Father was very busy with his surgical practice, which meant Josslyn was left in the care of his second wife's very domineering mother. The woman didn't know how to handle her granddaughter's enormous intellect any more than she did her own daughter's when she was Josslyn's age. Her solution to keeping Josslyn in line was endless lessons in cotillion and rigid social restrictions." She smiled grimly. "Needless to say, rebellion became Josslyn's drug of choice. I was too busy with my own career and raising a son to be much help. Father just spoiled her when he could. Josslyn doesn't have the political polish to think first and then speak." She shrugged. "Luckily for us, she throws herself into causes that are good for society. Deep down, she means well."

Adam wasn't sure how to respond. He'd guessed as much about her years ago. Of course, given the fit she was having over a protective detail, he didn't think Josslyn would "mean well" if she figured out Adam was the same guy she'd had a make-out session with in the middle of the Pacific Ocean.

"I'm happy to protect and serve, ma'am," he replied when it was clear the First Lady expected a response.

"Wow! If that isn't the party line, I don't know what is," the She-Devil remarked as she carried a tray with a coffee mug along with cream and sugar to the table next to her father. "I hope you'll be 'happy' standing all day in the elephant barn at the National Zoo."

Adam's jaw clenched so quickly he could feel tiny cracks beginning to form in his teeth. Did she say zoo? Adam swore under his breath. With one conk to the head he'd gone from commanding the elite Hawkeye counter-assault team to inhaling elephant shit for days on end. Suddenly sitting alone in the dark until the last of the concussion fog lifted from his brain seemed to be the wiser career choice.

"That's enough, Josslyn," the First Lady snapped. "Special Agent Lockett has a job to do, and you'll give him and the other agents on your detail the respect they deserve."

"We'll do whatever is necessary to allow the protectee to maintain their lifestyle and activities," Adam bit out.

She paused in the act of fixing her father's coffee. Smokey gray eyes framed by long dark lashes studied him carefully. "I'll bet you say that to all the girls."

The mixture of torment and anger in her eyes nearly knocked Adam off his feet. *She knew, damn it. She knew who he was.*

Harriett Manning stood abruptly, oblivious to the undercurrent arcing between her sister and Adam. "Really, Josslyn, you are unbearable today. Adam is recovering from a serious injury he suffered in the line of duty," she scolded. "So I'll thank you for losing the princess attitude."

Josslyn straightened to her full height, which wasn't very intimidating considering the top of her head came to Adam's chin. "Well, good to know the A-team will be protecting you and Conrad from the bad guys, Harriett. I'll try to keep things simple and quiet at the zoo so—Agent Lockett, is it—can recover to his full *special agent* competence level."

Adam's fists clenched at his sides. If there was anything he knew about this woman, quiet and simple were not in her toolbox.

"Josslyn!" the First Lady cried. "What has come over you?"

Dr. Benoit began murmuring agitatedly, nearly jettisoning the dog on his lap into the tray of coffee. A male nurse emerged from one of the bedrooms when the older man's murmurs turned into wails. The terrier began to yap sharply while jumping off the doctor's knees.

"Daddy," Josslyn cooed trying to calm the man. But her father flinched when his youngest daughter reached for him.

"Git away from me, girlie," Dr. Benoit scolded. "I'm not your daddy."

Josslyn stiffened again. The only part of her body moving was her throat as she swallowed roughly. The First Lady and the nurse helped the doctor to his feet.

"Why don't you take him to the solarium, Marc," Harriett Manning said to the nurse. "You'd like some time in the sunshine wouldn't you, Father?"

The dog yipped excitedly as if the question were posed to him. With the help of the nurse, Dr. Benoit shuffled to the elevator that would take them to the third floor, leaving behind an awkward silence.

"Perhaps when it's just you here with him . . ." The First Lady's voice trailed off.

"Don't," Josslyn bit out. "It is what it is."

She abruptly turned toward Adam. He was caught off guard by the brief flash of vulnerability shining in her eyes before she shuttered it. Something tugged in his chest. *Oh, hell no!* This was why he'd vowed to avoid her at all costs.

"You're a bit overdressed for a day at the zoo." She arched an eyebrow in challenge.

He ignored protocol and arched an eyebrow right back at her.

One corner of her sassy mouth turned up, the action seeming to surprise even her. "I recommend you at least change your shoes. We'll be leaving in twenty-five minutes."

Lucky for both of them, Adam still had several changes of clothes in a locker downstairs inside the Secret Service lounge. Not to mention his favorite pair of combat boots. If Josslyn Benoit thought she'd get the best of him today, she was sorely mistaken.

"I'll be ready in ten," he said.

With a flick of her hair and a swirl of her skirt, Josslyn turned and headed into the Center Hall. Adam fell into step behind her before she stopped abruptly, spinning around so that the fabric of her skirt nearly got tangled in her thighs.

"You don't have to follow me into my room, do you?"

Adam bit back a smirk. "Just to your doorway." He paused deliberately before adding, "Ma'am."

Her gray eyes narrowed and she was off again in a huff. Adam spoke into the microphone tucked discreetly in his cuff, updating Josslyn's location. The First Family and all protectees within the Crown were tracked on a computer monitor downstairs in the Secret Service director's office.

"Doolittle to the Queens' Bedroom," he relayed. He nearly chuckled at the irony of her room assignment.

Josslyn halted again. Her shoulders shook before she turned to face him. A flush stained her cheeks and she swiped at a strand of hair concealing her eyes. He tried not to notice her fine cleavage on display before him like a decadent buffet, but damn, if her deep breaths weren't drawing his gaze down like a homing beacon.

"First things, first," she drawled, bringing Adam's attention back to that sassy mouth of hers. "That code name is ridiculous. We have to come up with another one."

"You don't like your code name?" He shouldn't be engaging with her. The smart thing to do would be to tell her to take it up with the director. It would serve the man right for sticking Adam with this damn detail, anyway.

"No. I don't. How would you like to be compared to a character from a children's book?" she replied before resuming her trek to her bedroom.

"I thought everybody liked Dr. Doolittle."

She tossed a smokey-eyed glare over her shoulder at him. Adam ignored her. Too bad he couldn't unsee the cute way she wrinkled her nose.

Cute?

If his head wasn't already pounding, he'd smack himself.

"Okay, how about Pita?" he suggested before quickly admonishing himself for falling into her trap.

She came to a stop and whirled on him once again just as she reached the East Hall. "PETA? As in the People for the Ethical Treatment for Animals?" She donned a quizzical look that had her damn nose wrinkling up again. "That's good."

Adam might have felt a little burst of pride had she not looked as if she didn't expect him to have a lick of sense in his head. She took a few more steps before placing her hand on the doorknob to the Queens' Bedroom and pinning him with another one of her steely-eyed looks.

"Or, did you mean pita as in the sandwich? That wouldn't surprise me given how you've been hungrily checking out my ass."

She was so close.

Ignoring the voice in his head telling him to stand down, Adam decided to put the She-Devil in her place. "I meant P-I-T-A as in Pain. In. The. Ass."

Her eyes went wide for a moment before narrowing to slits. With a roll of her shoulders, affording him one last glimpse at the thin silver chain buried between the hollow of her breasts, she flung open her bedroom door. Before she could storm away from him, however, Adam snared her wrist in his fingers. He was way out of line, but he didn't care. Let them send him back to convalesce in the dark. He'd deal with it. But if he had to withstand the next few weeks protecting this woman, he was sure as hell going to let her know who was in charge.

"And you don't need to trouble that pretty little head of yours about the competency of your protective detail," he growled next to her ear. "Because there's not a single part of me that isn't in prime working order. Not. One."

Adam let that sink in before releasing her. Josslyn's tongue peeked out to trace her lower lip. Her breathing was a bit unsteady as she slowly raised her gaze to meet his. His junk tightened up at the challenge reflected there.

"You've got twenty-one minutes, Special Agent Lockett."

CHAPTER THREE

J OSSLYN FLOPPED BACK onto the mattress of the centuries-old canopied bed in the suite that, true to its name, had hosted actual queens. When she glanced up at the floral fabric overhead, the pattern began playing tricks on her vision, making it look as though the canopy was slowly easing down to smother her. Given how her life was going, it would be a fitting way to die.

Slamming her eyes closed, Josslyn tried to calm her breathing. She dug into her blouse, yanking at the chain anchoring her talisman to her neck. Reverently, she fingered a silver St. Luke medallion her daddy gave her the day her momma died. The metal was warm from resting against Josslyn's skin. Its edges had been worn smooth from years of sliding against her daddy's chest. He'd first put it on as a young flight surgeon in Vietnam. Josslyn's earliest memory of her daddy was his booming laugh when she tried in vain to grab at the shiny piece of jewelry with her chubby toddler fingers.

Tears burned the back of her eyes when she brought the medallion to her lips.

"You promised if I kept this with me, you'd always come back, Daddy," Josslyn whispered. "Well, I never take it off. Yet you keep slipping further and further away." She swallowed what might have been a sob.

Crying never solved anything, her daddy would always say. At least, the daddy she remembered—the one who remembered *her*. He was always so proud of Josslyn's bravery; her tenacity. *Never be one of them girly-girls your grandma is trying to turn you into.* She'd spent much of her life trying to live up to the ideals he'd laid out for her. And now the man who'd claimed she was the light of his golden years didn't even remember she existed. Just where did that leave her, exactly?

"Trapped," she murmured. "At least I can relate to how the elephants feel at the zoo."

Josslyn thumped her fists down on the bed with a growl. Of all the damn Secret Service agents in the White House, of course, she had to be assigned the Tower of Testosterone. *And the idiot pretended not to know her.* Her breath stuttered again. She'd spent the past two years fantasizing about what it would be like to come face-to-face with her rescuer again. This morning's confrontation was nothing close to what she'd dreamed. For months after he vanished, she'd bugged Conrad's chief of staff for information about the man who had saved her life. All she'd been told was his identity was classified because he worked as a sniper for president's elite protective detail. But she'd recognize those eyes anywhere. Probably because she knew the secrets behind them.

Well, he would never do as part of her detail. The arrogant man saw too much with those sharpshooter eyes of his. Most women were probably sucked in by the thick lashes—as dark as his close-cropped hair—framing bottle glass-green pupils. Josslyn, however, was not. She saw Special Agent Adam Lockett for exactly what he was. A man who could kiss a woman senseless and then vanish into thin air. If that wasn't enough, he obviously liked to wield power through the barrel of a rifle. He was the very antithesis of the ideals Josslyn championed.

And the last thing she needed right now was to have the gun-toting alpha stud shadowing her every move. Not when she had leads to chase. More importantly, she needed to keep under the radar while doing so. Making matters worse, the special agent was too damn good-looking for his own good. For anyone's good, actually. It aggravated Josslyn that she wasn't immune to his charm. She traced a fingertip along the skin on her wrist where he had touched her.

A flush of embarrassment spread over her body. Josslyn jumped off the bed. Tugging at the buttons of her blouse, she stripped the garment off in an effort to allow the air to cool her skin. She wanted to dislike the special agent on principle; she really did. But for a few hours two years ago, he'd been the only thing keeping her safe. Keeping her alive. And, truth be told, she hadn't felt more alive in another man's arms since.

And then he'd disappeared.

"Don't go there," she admonished herself as she stepped out of her skirt and pulled on a pair of khaki pants. "He was just doing his job. It didn't mean anything to him."

As spectacular as his kisses were, she'd gotten over him deserting her. *Mostly.*

Josslyn's phone buzzed, startling her out of her pity party. The incoming text had her mouth relaxing into a smile. Dax had finally cleared quarantine. At least she could focus her attention on a different alpha stud for the time being. She'd worry about ditching the Tower of Testosterone once they got to the zoo.

True to his word, Special Agent Lockett was standing sentry outside her bedroom when she emerged twenty minutes later. She wished she hadn't goaded him into changing his clothes because if he was sinfully sexy in a well-cut business suit, he looked downright edible dressed in his casual uniform. A long-sleeve golf shirt bearing the Secret Service emblem stretched tightly across his chest. The knit fabric perfectly outlined a wall of muscles she knew from experience felt as good as they looked. Gray cargo pants and a well-worn pair of combat boots that looked like he'd stolen them off a World War II veteran's feet rounded out the ensemble.

Trying valiantly not to devour the man with her eyes, Josslyn swept past him, only to have his woodsy scent wind its way beneath her nose. She marched down the stairs, annoyed that now she was tempted to turn around and inhale him. As before, he followed discreetly at her heels, mumbling into the ubiquitous microphone hidden within his clothing. And just like that, Josslyn was visualizing stripping him naked just to uncover the damn thing.

Another hot flush crawled over her skin as she stomped through the marble foyer of the North Portico entrance.

One of the marine guards silently pulled open the door for her. Aware that she was behaving like the spoiled princess the world thought her to be, Josslyn drew up short, meeting the younger man's startled eyes beneath the brim of his hat.

"Thank you," Josslyn said to him.

She never asked for the royal treatment. In fact, she wanted nothing to do with it. But right now, she didn't have much say in the matter. The least she could do was be polite to those around her.

The young marine nodded, a trace of pink staining his cheeks.

Agent Lockett chuckled behind her as they resumed walking to the black SUV waiting at the bottom of the steps.

"Well played," he murmured low enough so that only she could hear. "You're wise to cozy up to the marines considering your adventures routinely require military intervention."

She turned to glare at him, hating the sexy laugh lines fanning out from his eyes as he mocked her.

"Doolittle has exited the Crown," a woman's voice announced softly behind Josslyn.

Agent Lockett chuckled quietly again before donning the aviator sunglasses synonymous with Secret Service agents everywhere.

"Miss Benoit isn't fond of her code name," he explained to the female agent who appeared at Josslyn's shoulder.

The other woman arched a blonde eyebrow, but there was a hint of sympathy in her blue eyes. "I've yet to meet a protectee who did like their code name." She opened the back door of the SUV indicating Josslyn should get in. "I'm Agent Christine Groesch. I'll be tag-teaming with Agent Lockett on your detail."

Josslyn smiled at the other woman while quickly sizing her up. She'd obviously gotten the memo about their trip to the zoo. The agent was dressed similarly to Josslyn, wearing khakis, tennis shoes, and a light sweater. Unlike Josslyn, however, Agent Groesch had a powerful sidearm strapped to her leg. From the looks of it, the two women were close in age. Agent Groesch appeared to be capable, but she didn't project the lethal arrogance of Agent Lockett. This was clearly an agent who would do her job while minding her own business. Josslyn could work with that.

"It's nice to meet you," Josslyn said as she slid into the back seat. "I hope my day-to-day activities don't leave you too bored."

Agent Groesch's grin was sincere. "Are you kidding? I get to spend the day at the elephant house. How cool is that?"

The door quickly closed and Josslyn was disappointed when Agent Groesch took the front passenger seat next to the driver, leaving the rest of the back seat to the Tower of Testosterone. His thigh brushed against hers when he slid into the SUV. Josslyn told herself she flinched at the contact because of the Glock strapped there.

"Is it necessary to have your weapons so widely on display?" she snapped. "There will be children at the zoo, you know."

Agent Lockett kept his gaze fixed on the pedestrians meandering near the White House. "Don't worry. I haven't aimed a gun at a kid since I left Afghanistan."

His chilly response startled her. Not that she didn't deserve it because she had started it. Shame burned in her chest.

Agent Groesch cleared her throat up front. "Is there anything special we should be aware of before we get to the elephant house?"

"Yeah," Agent Lockett replied before Josslyn could. "Don't step in their poop."

The Uniformed Division officer driving the SUV laughed. Agent Groesch groaned before shooting Agent Lockett a quizzical look over her shoulder.

"Ignore him," Agent Groesch said. "He's still suffering the grumpy aftereffects from taking a hit to the head meant for the president."

Josslyn glanced over at the man seated next to her. Harriett mentioned Agent Lockett was injured in the line of duty, but she was shocked to learn that whatever injury the Secret Service agent sustained was intended for the president.

"I don't recall hearing anything about an attempted assassination," she said, surprised by the terror she felt over what could have become of her brother-in-law. "What happened?"

Slowly, he turned his head but only enough that she was faced with his hard profile. It was impossible to read his expression with his sunglasses on. He and Agent Groesch exchanged a look. Their silent communication seemed intimate, and the thought rankled Josslyn more than she was willing to admit.

They stopped at a traffic light. Agent Lockett shifted his gaze back toward the window. "If you don't hear about it, then we've done our job."

Josslyn let his words sink in. She was well aware both agents' role was to take a bullet for the president. She just never contemplated how close they came to actually doing so. But Agent Lockett was a sharpshooter on the president's advance team. It was his primary job to ensure any environment the president entered was safe. And, on occasion, he rescued animal rights protestors from the marauding fisherman.

Josslyn opened her mouth to demand more information, but she never got the chance. Instead, she found herself pressed up against Agent Lockett when the Uniformed Division officer driving the SUV swerved suddenly. Through her window, she glimpsed a white van headed straight for her side of the car.

❖

ADAM ACTED ON instinct, reaching around the seat belt to use his body to shield Josslyn from the impending impact.

He felt as well as heard her sharp intake of breath when she caught sight of the Mercedes van barreling toward them. Connecticut Avenue was congested with cars and pedestrians, leaving their driver little room to maneuver. But John was a trained professional with the agency or he wouldn't be behind the wheel. He punched the gas pedal just before the Mercedes struck them, expertly slipping between two taxi cabs coming at them from opposite directions.

Through the back window, Adam watched as the driver of the Mercedes executed his own perfect pit maneuver, spinning around to follow them through the traffic. Adam swore under his breath as he realized this wasn't a random accident. Whoever was in the van intended to do them harm. He withdrew his service weapon and unclipped the safety.

"Get down," Adam commanded, pressing Josslyn's head into his lap.

Christine was calling for backup as John steered the SUV between the vehicles in their way before making a sharp left onto N Street. The Mercedes followed suit ten seconds later.

"Metro PD will intercept us at Twenty-Third Street," Christine announced.

The Mercedes was a half block away. Adam could see two people up front, one of them brandishing a rifle.

"Ben," Adam yelled into his wrist. "Are you getting video? Who the hell are these guys?"

"The rearview camera is pretty jumpy," Ben responded into Adam's earpiece. "I'm running their images now."

The sirens from the Metro Police cruisers grew louder just as the Mercedes closed the gap. Adam positioned his finger on the control to open the back window, hoping like hell he'd get a shot off before the guy with the rifle pulled his trigger. While still a Secret Service vehicle, the SUV they were riding in wasn't as heavily armored as the Beast, the vehicle used by the president. Adam kept his other hand firmly on the crown of Josslyn's head, keeping her down and out of harm's way.

Flashing lights seemed to be coming from every direction when, just as suddenly as it appeared, the Mercedes veered into an alley and vanished from view.

"What the hell?" Adam said.

"Damn it," Ben shouted in Adam's ear. "I almost had them."

"Metro has a chopper in the sky," Christine said. "They'll keep following them."

Adam swore. "This whole block is a warren of covered back alleys and interconnected garages. It'll be like finding a needle in a haystack. Tell me you got a license plate, Ben?"

"I did," Ben replied. "But it won't be much help. It's an expired diplomatic plate. Probably stolen."

John blew out a heavy sigh after pulling over behind a row of Metro Police cruisers.

"Nice driving," Christine said to him before holstering her service weapon. "I'll go coordinate with the locals and arrange a motorcade. I don't know about you guys, but, after that, I'd rather make our trip to the zoo a party." She carefully exited the car, closing the door swiftly behind her.

"Can I get up now?"

Josslyn's breathy question came from somewhere in the vicinity of Adam's crotch. Startled that he still held her in such a compromising position, he yanked his hand from her head. She slowly sat upright. He was immediately glad of the distance between them because the sight she made had him straining against his zipper. Her eyes were wide beneath a halo of bedroom hair—likely that way from having his fingers threaded through it. Her bottom lip was dewy and pink from where she'd been chewing on it.

Damn it. He needed to get his head back in the game. One hour into his protective detail and he'd nearly involved her in a shootout. Definitely not the way to show the director he was ready to return to his command.

"Stay low," he ordered.

"There's no need to wave your gun around at me," she snapped. "I'm not some bimbo who's going to go running from the car. This isn't my first rodeo, cowboy."

Adam sighed as he clicked the safety on his gun and placed it back in its holster. "True that, sister. You've likely amassed a long list of enemies during your career protesting for animal rights. Tell me again who you pissed off in Africa?"

"*Me?*" The disbelief in her voice nearly made him laugh. "What makes you think those guys were after me?"

"Because John and I are law abiding citizens. Agent Groesch, too."

Her gray eyes were as dark as storm clouds now. "I'm a

law abi—"

Adam wagged a finger at her. "You might not want to finish that sentence. Unless you'd like me to recite a laundry list of examples to refute that statement."

She clamped her sassy mouth shut, her lips mulish, but she wisely didn't finish her argument.

"Adam." Ben's voice in his ear reminded him that they had multiple audiences. "Still nothing on the facial recognition, but I've got two other databases to try. In the meantime, the license plate reported stolen from a car belonging to the attaché of the Zimbabwe embassy last month."

"You don't say?" Adam peered over his sunglasses at Josslyn.

She crossed her arms over her chest meeting his gaze head-on.

"Metro says it's common for drug runners to steal diplomatic plates," Ben continued. "Word on the street is there was a deal gone bad last night involving the exact make and model of the SUV you're in. This could be as simple as a case of mistaken identity."

"In other words, a coincidence?" Adam and his friends didn't put much stock in fate or coincidence. Doing so could get those they protected, if not themselves, killed.

"As much as I hate to admit it, it looks that way," Ben replied. "The director says it's your call how to proceed."

Adam didn't like the idea of taking Josslyn to an area as wide open as the National Zoo without having definite confirmation of the identities and motive of the guys in the

Mercedes. Still, he didn't have a reason to keep her under lock and key at the Crown.

"Just to be safe, we'll stay within the elephant house this morning," he said to Ben. "Let me know as soon as you come up with anything."

Christine was climbing back into the SUV when Adam signed off with Ben. "Where, to?" she asked.

"The zoo," Adam said while adjusting his sunglasses. "Send word ahead to double the foot patrol."

John fired up the engine and pulled back onto N Street, retracing their path back to Connecticut Avenue. The Metro PD cruisers flanked them at the front and the rear.

Josslyn harrumphed beside him. "Wouldn't it be wiser to go in quietly? The sirens will only alert everyone on the grounds to be on the lookout for someone important."

"You never practiced much stealth when you were playing activist and stirring up protests," Adam countered. "Why start now?"

She snapped her jaw closed so tightly Adam could practically hear her teeth grinding. John turned onto Connecticut Avenue heading north the ten blocks to Woodley Park and the zoo.

"When we get there," Adam instructed her. "Stay put until the foot patrol moves into place. The last thing I need today is for you to slip your leash and disappear into the crowd."

Her eyes narrowed again. "You being the expert on disappearing and all."

Christine glanced over her shoulder at him. Funny, but she looked a little squinty-eyed, too. Adam knew his partner was trying to decipher the She-Devil's cryptic remark, but he wasn't going to help her out by filling in the blanks. He shrugged at Christine who shook her head before facing front again.

They skirted around the parking lot to the area designated for employee parking. John pulled behind several yellow school buses where a golf cart with two Uniform Division officers waited on board. They would shuttle them down to the elephant house.

"Doolittle has arrived at the Serengeti," Christine announced to headquarters.

Josslyn let loose another frustrated sigh. Adam bit back a grin.

"How about Babar instead of Doolittle?" he suggested.

Slowly, she turned to face him, a pained expression on her face. "No."

Adam shrugged. "Back to the drawing board, I guess."

He climbed out of the SUV half expecting her to ignore his instructions and follow him. But, much to his relief, she stayed put. Adam scanned the surrounding lot with a trained eyed. People assumed they should look for something out of the ordinary, but in most instances, it was the ordinary that spelled trouble. Adam knew better than to trust a woman pushing a baby stroller. Or an old man with a dog. He'd honed his alertness at a young age. He'd had to.

"It's a straight shot to the elephant house," the Uniformed Division officer said. "The crowd is pretty light today. Mostly school kids running around."

At Adam's nod, Christine opened Josslyn's door. Despite their run-in with a mysterious van driven by gun-toting men, she looked as cool and composed as the Queen of England when she exited. The woman didn't rattle easily. But then, he knew that about her already. He begrudgingly admitted it was one of the things he admired about Josslyn. Not that he'd ever admit that out loud.

Christine accompanied her to the golf cart and, with a smile to the Uniformed Division officers, Josslyn climbed aboard. Adam and Christine took their positions on the back bumper, both of them keeping their eyes peeled. The cart navigated a line of school kids oblivious to anything but the bison in the field to their right. They were twenty-five yards from the elephant house when the She-Devil took off.

CHAPTER FOUR

T HE INCIDENT WITH the van rattled Josslyn. Not that she wanted to admit it to anyone, but she was actually grateful the Tower of Testosterone had her back. Especially since the guy in the passenger seat looked vaguely familiar. She needed to get in touch with Trevor and Hugh to make sure they were okay. Her brother-in-law wasn't exaggerating when he'd said she'd stepped in a few hornets' nests. But if that was what it took to out the leaders of the nasty animal trafficking ring, Josslyn was committed to doing so. According to intelligence the advocacy group received, the money fronting the ring came from within Washington, DC. She'd just have to hurry and find that connection before someone got hurt.

The trumpeting of an angry elephant startled Josslyn from her thoughts. She knew that elephant. *Dax!* At the sound of metal crunching accompanied by another frantic cry, Josslyn leaped from the golf cart and sprinted around to the back of the elephant barn.

"Be careful with him!" she shouted to the handlers attempting to unload the six-ton bull from the trailer.

The men and women surrounding the eighteen-wheeler practically turned in unison to glare at Josslyn. Once again, she'd spoken out of turn. From the looks of it, they *were* being careful.

Dax, however, was having a temper tantrum. The elephant kicked at the travel crate with his back foot while dragging his tusk against the metal bars like a prison convict. The tension in the yard didn't improve when a trio of Secret Service agents and Uniformed Division officers came storming up behind her. Making matters worse, Agent Lockett, of course, had his gun drawn.

"Must you?" Josslyn spoke softly so as not to rile up Dax further. She gestured to the gun in frustration. "He's in a cage, for crying out loud. He isn't going to hurt anyone. Except for maybe you. He's not especially fond of men who wave guns in his face."

Agent Lockett studied the crowd before replacing his gun in its holster. "I told you to stay put."

Josslyn appreciated how he kept his voice low and even. His eyes, however, were a different story. Gone were the sexy laugh lines. They'd been replaced by a stern look that clearly said he didn't appreciate her not following his orders. He looked a lot like her father did when Josslyn acted impulsively. Judging from his expression, he didn't like it any more than Daddy had. Too bad she couldn't placate Agent Lockett with a kiss on the cheek and hug. She opted for humility instead.

"I wasn't thinking," she apologized—mostly sincere. "I heard him in distress and I just wanted to get to him."

She took a step toward the animal hauler before his hand on her arm stopped her.

"Hold still for one minute," he commanded before motioning to Agent Groesch with his chin. The agent walked along one side of the perimeter while the officer from the Uniformed Division surveyed the other side. Dax let out another cry of frustration, rattling the crate with his tusk.

"Show's over," the zookeeper in charge of the elephants announced to the assembled crowd. "Dr. Benoit and I will handle it from here."

He walked over to Josslyn and Agent Lockett with his hand extended. "Glad to have you here, Dr. Benoit." He gestured toward Dax. "Your boy enjoyed his quarantine in our Front Royal facility a little bit too much. He didn't want to leave."

Josslyn shook his hand. "Just wait until he picks up the scent of the female elephants in the barn. He'll be singing a different tune."

"Let's hope so," he said. "We'd like to add to the herd as quickly as possible."

She glanced down at Agent Lockett's fingers still wrapped around her. "May I do my job now?"

"That depends," he responded. "You're not getting in there with that thing."

"That *thing* is a big spoiled baby. And, no, only a crazy person would get in a crate with a distraught elephant."

He arched an eyebrow at her as if to say she might fit in the crazy person category. "Let's hurry this up, then. I don't like you being exposed in such an open area." He slowly released her arm.

She proceeded toward the crate.

"Hey there, big guy," she cooed. "It's okay. I'm here."

At the sound of her voice, Dax trumpeted wildly, stomping his foot like an angry two-year-old. She stopped short of the crate and picked up a long-handled broom used to scrub the elephants during their bath.

"Shh, Dax," she continued in a soothing tone. "This is your new home. I promise you're gonna like it here."

The elephant let out a sorrowful wail of protest before leaning into the bristles of the broom Josslyn had inserted between the bars of the crate to scratch behind his ears.

"That's my boy," she said. "Relax and we can let you out to explore. There's an old friend of yours here. I'm sure you're going to want to say hello."

Dax sighed and flapped his ears indicating his contentment. Josslyn relaxed too. She brushed him a little more vigorously while speaking softly to the zookeeper.

"Is the barn ready for him?"

"Yes. He'll have the run of the bull area since he's our only male right now. We'll keep the cows out on the trails for the rest of the day so he has a chance to settle in."

"Okay, have the driver back the crate up to the entrance and we can let him out," Josslyn instructed.

She walked alongside the hauler, continuing to soothe Dax with the stroke of the brush and her voice. As soon as the trainers lifted the gate, Dax ambled out of the crate into the large indoor enclosure, its floor covered in sand. The skylights in the high ceiling and the wire rails made the space seem open and airy. A moat flowed between the sand and the fence adjacent to the public viewing area.

Throughout the pen, there were special showers Dax could operate with his foot allowing him to rinse off whenever he wanted. Outside was a yard filled with logs to occupy his time, a grassy knoll and deep pond for him to bathe in. The staff had constructed a huge cake made up of vegetables to welcome Dax to his new home. A large crayon banner, presumably made by school children, hung above the steel door to the enclosure.

The zookeeper explained that, even though he'd been quarantined at the zoo's other facility, Dax would be kept indoors for twenty-four hours more just to be sure he was free of any pathogens that could have come from his previous zoo.

"That will give him time to settle in before we introduce him to the rest of the herd," Josslyn agreed.

The elephant trumpeted loudly again, letting everyone within the zoo know he had arrived. An answering call came from the vicinity of the Elephant Trails exhibit where the females were spending the day. Dax halted in his exploration, his ears perked as he lifted his trunk into the air.

"Nothing like the scent of a woman to alter your mood, huh, buddy?" Josslyn teased from outside the enclosure.

Dax turned at the sound of her voice. The ground trembled as he lumbered over to the steel wire fence.

"One of those ladies will be very happy to see you," Josslyn said to the elephant. "You two have a history together."

His ears flapped when he reached the balusters separating them.

Josslyn couldn't help but grin at the elephant she'd known for nearly ten years. "I've missed you, big guy."

She reached out a hand toward him. Dax weaved his trunk between the bars and let it hover over her outstretched fingers. A gentle puff of air tickled her palm as he seemed to reassure himself it was really Josslyn. Slowly, his trunk moved up her arm to the side of her face where he gently brushed against her skin. Josslyn closed her eyes waiting for his signature slap on the head, but it never came.

"Shit," Agent Lockett breathed from beside her.

Josslyn's lids snapped open. She hadn't realized the Secret Service agent had followed her into the staff enclosure. She nearly laughed at the sight of Dax's trunk dislodging the agent's sunglasses from their perch on top of his head.

"It's not funny," he said. "Tell him to cut it out."

"He's just curious."

Dax's trunk made a beeline south trailing down along Agent Lockett's body. Josslyn did laugh at the agent's giant step back when Dax broke the plane of his belt buckle. Undeterred, the elephant stretched his trunk out farther, bringing it into contact with the gun holstered on the agent's thigh. Agent Lockett moved faster than a cobra, striking the elephant on the trunk before Dax could explore more. Dax responded with a meaty snort, spraying the man in the chest with mucus before stomping away from the fence.

The Tower of Testosterone went still. Josslyn wisely

swallowed another laugh. Agent Groesch wasn't as circumspect.

"I wish I'd videoed that," the other agent chuckled.

"Can we take this reunion inside?" he managed to grind out through his tight jaw.

They entered the barn through the staff door allowing them access to the catwalk above the indoor portion of the exhibit. Multiple individual stalls lined the perimeter, some of the stalls more closed off than others, allowing for the difference in personality of the elephants housed there. Josslyn replaced the broom in the cavernous elephant bathing room when they passed through it.

"Now what?" Agent Lockett asked.

"Now I go to the desk they've assigned me to fill out paperwork." *And check in with Hugh and Trevor.*

"Lead the way."

"Surely you're not going to watch me work all day?" Josslyn protested. She couldn't make those phone calls with him listening in.

"It will be the highlight of my career."

Josslyn locked eyes with his, willing him to back down. But it was no use. She'd just have to find another way to shake him. She turned on her heel and headed to the cubicle she was given.

"We'll take turns down here," Agent Groesch said.

"I'll take you on a tour later if you'd like," Josslyn said to her.

"That would certainly help with this assignment." The agent clearly wished to remain professional, but Josslyn could tell by the light in her eyes she was delighted to be at the zoo.

The same couldn't be said for the agent who followed her to the warren of cubicles on the second floor. Josslyn swiped a few paper towels from the break area and tried to hand them to Agent Lockett. He arched an eyebrow at her in question.

"For your shirt," she said.

"I've been doused with worse."

The man really was insufferable. Or a machine. Or a jerk. Or all three.

"Of course you have. You're a big bad special agent. There's no telling what you've immersed yourself in to do your job." She ducked behind the cubicle wall, hoping he'd stay on the other side of it.

He didn't.

"I've immersed myself in many things," he said, positioning his hard body so close to hers she could feel a flush beginning to rise beneath her clothing. The icy words coming out of his mouth quickly cooled it, though.

"Including two hours in the Pacific Ocean to save your smart little ass," he continued. "I'd do it again because it's my *job*. But I'm not going to spend the next few weeks taking sass from you about my profession."

The last word came out with a groan before he swayed into her. Josslyn braced her palms against his chest in order to keep him upright.

Because it's my job.

Just as she suspected, she'd merely been a job to him.

Their hot and steamy hanky-panky just a perk of the assignment he'd been given. Her chest ached a little at the confirmation, but she would die before letting him know how he affected her.

"Agent Lockett," she murmured. "Are you okay?"

His heart was beating steadily beneath her fingertips but his breathing was heavy against her neck.

"Yeah," he said. "I just need a minute."

Placing his hands on the desk behind her he leaned his forehead on her shoulder. Josslyn couldn't resist inhaling the woodsy scent that had captivated her earlier.

"Sure," she said softly. "As you just so kindly pointed out, I owe you a hundred and twenty of them."

She felt him smile through the cotton of her sweater. "I don't bring it up because I'm keeping score."

"Well then, your comment about my ass being little earns you something."

"Women." He groaned. "You're all alike."

Josslyn didn't realize she'd begun kneading his shoulders until he stood up abruptly and her fingers were left dangling in midair. She quickly shoved her hands behind her back as he widened the space between their bodies.

"Concussion aftershocks," he said by way of an explanation. "I'm still sensitive to light, it seems."

He pointed at the fluorescent lights overhead.

"Maybe you should sit down," she suggested.

"I'm fine."

Josslyn studied his face, taking in the tightness around his mouth and the dark smudges beneath his eyes.

"You're not fine."

"I. Am. Fine," he repeated.

She mimicked his earlier words. "You men are all alike." She pulled the desk chair out. "Sit or I'll yell for Agent Groesch."

He looked like he might argue until Josslyn opened her mouth to shout for his partner. With a huff he dropped into the chair.

"That's more like it," she said, resting a hip against the desk as she scanned an urgent text from Trevor. "I can't have you passing out on me."

"I would think you'd be happy to be rid of me."

"Actually, I've had a change of heart. I've just been invited to a party tonight and I need a date. I've decided that you'll do just fine."

◉

HOURS LATER, ADAM paced the residence floor in the White House waiting for the She-Devil to emerge. Fortunately, he'd been able to grab a few hours of rest during the afternoon. His head no longer felt like it housed a disco, but he was still embarrassed at the way he'd nearly collapsed in her cubicle. He was also angry. Because, of course, she'd found a way to use the incident against him.

"There's no way in hell we are going out on a date, sister." He'd argued when she brought up her silly proposition.

"Well, of course, if you're not up to it," she'd challenged. "I can let the director know you're lying about the status of your recovery. I'm sure he can find someone else to escort me. But either way, I'm going out tonight."

No way was Adam giving the director any more reasons to sit his ass down. Which was how he found himself wearing out the carpet in the Center Hall dressed in slacks and a stupid sports jacket when he'd rather be watching the World Series in a pair of sweats while holding a cold beer in his hand.

"It's not a date," he mumbled under his breath.

"Are you talking to yourself, Adam?"

He looked up into the inquisitive eyes of Marin Chevalier, Griffin's fiancée. She was carrying a paper plate with some sort of baked good on it. Adam's stomach growled at the delicious scent.

"Don't you look handsome tonight," she said with a saucy grin. "Big plans?"

"I'm working," he said with a little more force than was necessary. "Tell me that's for me?"

"Not if you're *working*," she mimicked his tone. "Imagine what would happen if I started feeding all the agents in the White House?"

Adam snatched the plate from her outstretched hand. The fact was, Marin had been baking goodies for the Secret Service agents long before Griffin saved her from a murderous art thief. It was one of the reasons many of the agents were despondent she was stepping down as executive pastry chef to instead fill the role of the late White House curator.

"Mmm." The flaky pastry practically melted in Adam's mouth.

"Hey!" Ben shouted through the earpiece. "What are you eating? Is Marin there? Damn it. That better not be my beignet!"

"Too late, sucker," Adam said as he licked the powdered sugar off his fingertips.

Marin's eyes widened. "Is that Ben in your ear? You really *are* working. I love when you boys play secret agent. Tell him I sent his home with Griff."

Adam chuckled. "Which means it never made it out of the Crown."

Ben swore in Adam's ear.

Marin stepped in closer to brush a speck of sugar off Adam's lapel. "Are you sure you're well enough to return to duty?"

"I'm fine," he repeated for what felt like the millionth time. "Besides, this isn't real duty. A rookie could handle this detail."

Ben tsked. "You're forgetting about the two goons who chased you down this morning."

"I thought we decided that was a coincidence?"

Marin looked at him quizzically. Adam gestured to his ear.

"You know me. I like to be thorough. I'm still checking out some leads before we put that incident to bed," Ben responded.

The back of his neck tingled. Adam didn't believe for one second that the She-Devil wasn't up to something.

When was she not? He was glad Ben would have his six tonight, keeping an eye on Josslyn electronically if they somehow were to get separated. Not that he had any intention of letting that happen.

"Fine or not," Marin was saying, "you take care, you hear me?"

A throat cleared just as Marin leaned in to press a kiss to Adam's cheek.

"Ready for our date?"

Marin's eyes were wide again when she stepped away. A mischievous grin tugged at the corners of her mouth.

"*Not* a date," he clarified before either woman said another word.

"Thank you, Marin, for making beignets for Daddy. I admit to enjoying more than my fair share." Josslyn patted her stomach which was wrapped in a soft-looking violet sweater that tied at the waist. A short suede skirt and thick-heeled booties—both black—left a generous section of her sleek legs exposed to the elements. *Not to mention the eyes of every male they came in contact with.* A vivid memory of those long legs wrapped around his waist made his jaw clench.

"With Arabelle and her parents living in San Francisco now, I have no one to bake treats for. I'm happy to spoil your father," Marin said. "You two have fun tonight."

Adam pierced her with a glare that should have had the chef retreating to the kitchen. She stood at the top of the stairs and winked at him instead.

"Coming?" Josslyn called from the landing of the center

staircase.

Adam trailed her down the steps. "Do I get to know where we are going?"

"The deal was that I agree to a Secret Service escort everywhere I go," she said. "But no advance teams to turn my social life into a tabloid story."

Adam pulled open the door of the SUV waiting for them at the bottom of the North Portico steps. "And here I thought I'd make an appearance on *TMZ*."

"So you did dress to impress."

"Yeah, just not for you," he said before slamming the door and rounding the rear to the other side.

"She just gave the driver an address in McLean," Ben relayed via the earpiece. "I'm running it now."

"Affirmative," Adam replied before opening his door and sliding into the back seat.

Little did she know, but after this morning's episode, an advance team of Uniformed Division officers would be surveilling the place the entire time she and Adam were at the party.

"At least fill me in on what type of party you're dragging me to. A birthday party? Engagement party? One of those kinky sex toy parties?"

Ben chuckled in Adam's ear. The woman seated next to him just gave him the side-eye.

"Don't you wish," was all she said.

They were quiet for several minutes as the driver navigated through Georgetown.

"The house belongs to one of those crazy rich Asians,"

Ben informed him. "New Taiwanese money made during the tech boom at the end of the century."

Adam sighed heavily. While he would have been uncomfortable watching women drink cosmos and dish about naughty lingerie, he would have preferred that to whatever Josslyn had mixed herself up in this time.

"I don't know the hosts," she said out of nowhere. "I'm meeting a friend there."

"If you're meeting someone, why make me pretend I'm your date?"

"I told you. I don't want the world knowing the Secret Service is babysitting me. Besides, my friend will be there with his fiancée. Her cousin lives in the house."

"Friends from the zoo?" Adam kept fishing for information.

"No." She glanced out the window, avoiding his eyes. "David and I work for Global Wildlife."

Adam made a rough sound at the back of his throat. "Ah, more tree-huggers."

Her head whipped around. "Have you got something against animals, Agent Lockett? Did a dog bite you when you were little or maybe your cat ran away to live with the old lady up the street? Is that why you take your big guns out and shoot them?"

"That's pretty juvenile, even for you."

"Oh, and it's not juvenile to gun down a defenseless animal that never did anything to hurt you?"

"That's a ridiculous argument, but to set the record straight, I've never been into hunting."

"Oh, that's right. You use your big gun to kill people instead."

The air went still in the back of the SUV.

"Harsh," Ben's voice spoke in Adam's ear.

"Clearly you didn't retain anything from our discussion earlier today," Adam bit out. "I use my skills for many things. Every single time I do it's in an effort to save someone else's life."

"And every time I protest I do so in an effort to save some *animal's* life," she countered.

The headlights from a passing car illuminated her face. She looked fierce yet vulnerable at the same time. Saving animals was her passion, sure, but there was something else driving her. Something Adam recognized instantly. Her need to justify her survival, her very existence, struck a familiar chord within him. That need was something Adam saw when he looked in the mirror every day.

"For tonight, let's just agree to disagree," she suggested. "If anyone asks, you're my father's nurse. No one will want to strike up a conversation about an Alzheimer's patient. Everyone's afraid they can catch it somehow."

They rode in silence the rest of the way to McLean. The house sat back behind an iron fence. Lights lined a steep driveway that wound around trees ending at a spectacular antebellum-style mansion. A valet opened Josslyn's door while Adam made his way round from the opposite side. She surprised him by looping her arm through his and sidling up next to him. But when she went to take a step, her bootie slipped on the slick flagstone drive. Josslyn lurched forward, bending at the waist in an effort to catch herself before she face-planted. Adam quickly wrapped his arms around her and pulled her toward him. Her ass was suddenly brushing up against his body. The feel of his gun in its holster obviously surprised her because her eyes were wide and panicked when he steadied her. She glanced at his crotch, before understanding dawned.

"Can you please be less obvious with the tools of your trade?"

Her breathless command had the opposite effect and Adam was glad her gaze was anywhere but on his zipper now. He didn't bother biting back his teasing grin.

"As you wish." Adam pulled her along the walkway toward the front door while Ben chuckled in his ear.

The scene that greeted them resembled a frat party Prince Harry might once have thrown. Waiters dressed in white dinner jackets circulated the vast living room, weaving between a vicious game of beer pong and people flipping plastic cups. A live band was set up on a bandstand beside the indoor pool where lanterns shined down on couples engaged in a fierce battle of chicken fighting. A woman in a tiny bikini was about to lose both her perch on a man's shoulders and her top at the same time.

Marin would be enthralled with the ornate decorations, many of which looked valuable even to Adam's untrained eye. Josslyn flitted from room to room, smiling and chatting with those who recognized her but clearly on the lookout for her friend, David. They found him in the karaoke room.

"David!" Josslyn wrapped her arms around the other man's neck. They stayed that way for longer than Adam thought was necessary. He cleared his throat.

She shot him a look when they finally pulled apart. "David, I'd like you to meet Adam Lockett, my daddy's nurse. Adam, this is my dear friend, David Chen."

Josslyn was spot-on about the nurse cover. David and his fiancée, Lin, barely gave him a second look. Adam made a mental note to remember that for future assignments.

The four of them strolled through the party once more, making their way back to the pool area where the band played. The trio of friends sipped on champagne while Adam chugged a bottle of water.

"Dance with me, David," Josslyn insisted a little too eagerly, handing her half-full glass to Adam.

"Sure." David gave his fiancée a quick peck on the cheek before leading Josslyn out to the pool deck, hand in hand.

If Lin objected, it didn't show. Adam took the opportunity to fish for more information, any clue he could uncover about what exactly she was up to tonight.

"Your cousin really knows how to throw a party."

"Yes," she said, the bit of hero worship in her voice was hard to miss. "He's been kind to introduce me to his friends while we are in Washington."

"Have you and David known Josslyn long?"

Lin shook her head. "I believe David has, but I only met her for the first time this evening."

Before he could press her any further, a group of young Asian women swallowed Lin up in a wave of giggles, carrying her off to the where the others danced, all of them singing and gyrating to an Asian tune Adam didn't recognize.

"Anything on this David dude?" Adam quietly asked Ben.

"American born. Raised by two professors who fled China in the eighties. Both teach at Cal State. Both shun anything remotely having to do with Chinese culture. David and Josslyn met in grad school where they bonded over saving the whales. He teaches public policy at UC Santa Barbara currently, although, this semester he's a guest professor at American University. He's a bit more active than his parents at taking on the policies of China. As such, he's banned from most of Asia for his various smear campaigns he's enacted against companies he claims to be whaling."

"Great."

The music died down just as Adam uttered the word. A woman next to him eyed him curiously. Josslyn arrived, her checks glowing from the dance. She fanned her face.

"I must look a mess. I'm going to find the powder room and freshen up."

Adam manacled her wrist with his fingers before she could take a step. Her eyes narrowed to slits.

"That's not how we are playing this tonight, sister," Adam reminded her.

"What? I can't go pee without an escort?"

He didn't bother responding. Instead, he laced their fingers together, pressing his palm against hers. Ignoring the warm sensation shooting up his arm, he led the way into the house. She huffed but wisely didn't protest.

"Try that way." She pointed to a long, dark hallway devoid of any guests.

"I'm sure there's something back by the bar."

Josslyn yanked his arm in the direction she'd indicated. "That one probably has a line. I'm in a hurry."

They made their way down the empty hallway. From the looks of it, this area of the mansion housed mostly guest bedrooms. Josslyn located a bathroom several doors in.

"See, no line," she said before shutting the door in his face.

Adam leaned up against the wall closing his eyes to give his aching head a break.

"She's a piece of work," Ben said.

"And she's up to something," Adam whispered. "Any ideas?"

"The host is a thirty-something millionaire who makes more money than he reports. He has ties to several tech companies here in DC, but he doesn't seem too involved with the day-to-day operations. His major accomplishment seems to be getting kicked out of Oxford for cheating. He mostly spends his days living the spoiled playboy life from what I can tell. The guy has a few arrests for cocaine possession. Mostly while traveling abroad. He keeps his nose clean here in the US." Ben laughed at his pun.

"Any ties to animal poachers?"

"Not that I can find, but that doesn't mean anything. If he's involved in trafficking he'd have multiple layers between him and the boots on the ground."

"Yeah." Adam sighed.

Despite the rave going on at the other side of the house, the hallway was blissfully quiet and Adam took a moment to clear his head while he waited for Josslyn to return.

"You got another letter today," Ben informed him.

Adam's lids snapped open. So much for clearing his head.

"I told you to pitch them."

The silence stretched for a long moment.

"You can't ignore him forever, dude," Ben said quietly. "He's getting out."

Ben's words had Adam's temple throbbing again. That explained why his friend kept tossing the letters in Adam's face. Ben had put the pieces together.

"I don't have time for this shit, Bennett. I'm working a detail." Adam glanced at the fitness tracker on his wrist. "Speaking of which, where the hell is she?" He tapped on the door. "Did you fall in?"

The back of his neck tingled again when there was no response.

"Damn it," Ben swore. "The locator on her phone puts her several rooms away."

Adam jimmied the lock into the bathroom which had an adjoining door to a bedroom. She'd slipped out past him while Adam was confronting the demons from his past in the damn hallway.

"Point me in the right direction, Ben," he growled. "And then turn off the mic because I'm going to tan her sweet little ass."

CHAPTER FIVE

J OSSLYN SLIPPED INTO the darkened study and tapped on
the flashlight in her phone. The GWC had long suspected the money behind the traffickers came from a wealthy
Asian businessman. But could she really be so lucky as to
stumble upon the man bankrolling them so easily? From
what David described to her while they were on the dance
floor, maybe so.

Earlier in the day, when he and Lin had toured the
house, David was stunned when he spied damning evidence their host was involved in animal trafficking
somehow. But Lin's cousin had been in the study with
them and David wasn't able to snap any photos of his
trophies. He'd prepared Josslyn for the sights that would
greet her, so the lunging Bengal tiger didn't startle her as
badly as it might have. Still, the animal's lifeless eyes were
eerie enough to send a shiver through her.

The room was a taxidermist's showroom with a dozen
or so rare animals mounted on the walls or posing on the
floor. An assortment of lethal-looking weapons were
juxtaposed among the stuffed menagerie, including a
samurai sword that looked as though it had been used a
time or two throughout the centuries. It broke Josslyn's

heart when she nearly tripped over a stuffed white tiger embryo.

So that she wouldn't be seen from the window, she switched the flash off her camera, hoping the light from the flashlight would be enough to capture the images she needed. Time was of the essence. Agent Lockett wasn't the type to wait outside a closed door for long. Spying the tusks in the corner of the room, she swore quietly when she saw some belonging to the rare black rhinoceros. Lin's cousin shouldn't have been in possession of one much less the four he had on display.

Carefully navigating the dark room, Josslyn moved closer. Aiming her camera to take a picture, she swallowed a scream when a large hand suddenly clapped over her mouth. She felt a moment of panic until she recognized the familiar woodsy scent.

"What are you doing?" he growled against her ear, his muscled body wrapping around her like a blanket. For such a big man, she marveled at the sniper's stealth. She hadn't heard a sound before he was on her. Another tremor ran through her body before she found her mettle.

Josslyn peeled his fingers away from her face.

"Nothing." Her harshly whispered denial made his grip on her body tighter.

"Liar."

He turned her within the circle of his arms but he didn't release his hold. Now, their mouths were within inches of one another. They remained that way for a long moment, their eyes locked in some sort of silent battle until voices in the hall startled them both out of their trance.

"Now look what you've done," she accused. "You've brought the damn cavalry."

The voices drew closer. Agent Lockett reached between their bodies for his stupid gun. Josslyn shook her head vigorously.

"My way," she whispered just as the door handle began to turn.

Sweeping at papers on the desk behind her, she pulled him closer against her body. Seeming to sense her plan, the idiot opened his mouth to protest. Josslyn covered it with her own, thrusting her tongue against his to keep him from talking. She dug her fingers into his rock-hard thighs in an attempt to bring their bodies even closer. Something ignited within her at the contact.

He returned her kiss with a punishing one of his own. Too bad it was having the opposite effect on her senses. The more he dished out, the more her body sang for more. As their tongues parried for dominance, Josslyn gripped his skull in order to fuse their mouths together. She swallowed a groan coming from the back of his throat. Heat pooled in her belly. Time and awareness faded away until all that was left was his mouth torturing hers, her hips grinding into his. They might have stayed like that forever for all she cared.

Unfortunately, they had an audience.

"Who the hell are you two and what are you doing in my office?"

It took a moment for Josslyn to rouse herself from her

sensual fog. Lin's cousin didn't sound pleased to have his inner sanctum invaded. And Agent Lockett was once again reaching beneath his sports coat, presumably for his weapon. Josslyn stepped in front of him as she slid off the desk.

"My apologies," she said, her voice hoarse and her lips tender. "We lost track of where we were."

Someone flipped the light switch. The animals appeared even more grotesque under the soft glow. Lin's cousin, on the other hand, appeared loaded. Josslyn drew in a quick breath for small favors. With luck, an hour from now, the man wouldn't even remember he'd caught her in a compromising position.

The two men accompanying him were a different story. One began speaking in rapid-fire Mandarin. Lin's cousin's eyes seemed to grow soberer as his friend likely was connecting the dots to her identity.

"There are many bedrooms in this house," he argued. "And yet I discover you in my office?"

"Because no one would think to look for us here," she improvised. She was grateful the Tower of Testosterone remained stoic behind her. No doubt it cost him to do so. Josslyn laced her fingers through his and gave them a squeeze. "As you can probably imagine, we don't get a lot of privacy. I'm sorry to intrude. We'll just be going."

Josslyn went to take a step, but one of the men with Lin's cousin held up a hand while the other closed the door. Behind her, Agent Lockett tensed in readiness for a fight.

"Not before you and your friend have introduced yourselves." Lin's cousin sat in the leather chair beneath the imposing samurai sword, almost as if he was making a statement. One of his companions slipped a tumbler full of something into his hand before his butt had time to settle in the chair.

"I am Kuan-yu Tseng," Lin's cousin said, smugly. "But then, you already know that, I'm sure."

He was openly leering at her now. Josslyn braced herself for what would come once she introduced herself. Tseng would want something. A political favor. They always did.

"Josslyn Benoit," she managed to get out around the bile that was forming in her throat. "And this is—"

"Adam," Agent Lockett interjected not bothering to elaborate further with his last name.

"I'm her father's nurse." Agent Lockett pulled her behind him. "And they're expecting us back at the White House shortly. Again, we apologize. We meant no disrespect."

He moved with authority toward the door, Josslyn in tow. Tseng's men seemed to size up Agent Lockett, but with the briefest of head shakes from their boss, they both stood down.

"You and I share mutual interests, Dr. Benoit," Tseng said just before they reached the safety of the door.

Josslyn stiffened slightly at the use of her professional moniker. Most people knew her as nothing more than the First Lady's radical little sister.

"Perhaps we should have dinner soon to discuss those interests?" Tseng continued, his dark eyes much more focused now.

Agent Lockett's grip tightened around her fingers.

She hesitated for the briefest of seconds. "That would be nice."

They were out the door and down the long hallway before Josslyn could take a breath. Agent Lockett was mumbling something about the car.

"I need to find David," she protested when he led her toward the front door.

"Oh no," he growled. "Playtime is over for tonight."

Josslyn tried to pull her hand from his, but he only tightened the grip until her fingers were numb. The chilly night air caused her to shiver when they exited the house. As if by magic, their car was waiting outside. He pulled open the back door and practically tossed her inside.

"Hey!" she cried. "You don't get to decide when we leave. I have a deal with the director. You are *not* the boss of me."

He leaned down so their noses were almost touching. She could just make out the tight lines around his mouth—a mouth that had done amazing things to hers a few minutes earlier.

"That's your problem, sister. You don't respect the rules. It's a good thing for you your father isn't in his right mind. Otherwise, he'd take you over his knee for that little stunt you just pulled back there. And I'd be right there, cheering him on."

Josslyn's lips moved, but she couldn't seem to make any words come out. *How dare he bring up her ailing father!* She tried to scramble out of the car, but he was too quick for her. He shoved her legs back inside nearly slamming the door closed on top of them. The locks clicked almost immediately. He didn't bother maintaining their cover as a couple, sliding into the front seat instead of joining her in the back.

"Doolittle is returning to the Crown," he announced over the SUV's radio.

Josslyn kicked the back of his seat.

"Buckle up back there," he said. "Or the next time we go out, we'll have to put you in a toddler seat." He turned the radio to a hard rock station and let it blare.

She fumed the entire ride back to the White House. As they drove closer, passing through the security checkpoint at the south entrance, Josslyn's throat became choked with emotion. She hated the sensation of being kept in a cage. It reminded her too much of growing up in her grandmother's home. And she hated even more that the man seated in front of her could wound her just with a simple statement about her daddy. Her mission to expose animal traffickers wasn't some sorority stunt. It was important and worthwhile. She was contributing something to society, damn it. And the Tower of Testosterone could shove it where the sun didn't shine if he didn't like it.

The car pulled up to the entryway, but her door remained locked to the marine guard who bent down to open it. Agent Lockett did the honors instead. There was no avoiding his extended arm without making a scene. William, the White House butler for the past twenty years, greeted them with a broad smile.

"Evening, Miss Josslyn."

She was ashamed when the best she could manage was a nod. Her throat was so tight, she thought she might die of asphyxiation, but she didn't dare let the man beside her know how much he'd affected her. They passed through the lovely Map Room and Josslyn attempted to extract her arm from his clutches so she could disappear upstairs with some of her dignity intact. Of course, he had other plans.

"Kill the videos in the China Room, Bennett," he said as he pulled her to the right and into the room displaying the china from nearly every president to inhabit the White House. The preservation lighting gave the space a relaxing glow. Slamming the door closed behind them he thrust her into the center of the room and released her, finally. Josslyn rubbed the tender area on her forearm in an effort not to have to meet his hard stare.

"Now kill my mic."

Josslyn did meet his eyes then. The man was talking to the air.

"I said kill it!" he shouted, startling her.

"Your brain is more scrambled than you let on if you're talking to voices in your head." She tried to slip past him. "You might want to get your crazy looked at by a professional."

Once again, she underestimated his quickness. His arms were around her like a vice before she took two paces.

"Well, as they say, crazy recognizes crazy because you are one crazy-ass woman." His arms pulled her body flush against his. "You don't seem to understand that these people you're constantly chasing don't give a damn about lives. Animal *or* human." He shook her gently. "When the shit hits the fan, they won't care who your brother-in-law is. You need to end this little caper before someone gets hurt."

Josslyn pounded her fists against his chest to no avail. "Caper?" she cried. "This isn't some *caper*. Just like what you do is . . ." She sought for an argument, but his close proximity coupled with her anger had sucked out her brain cells. "What you do."

She leaned her forehead against his chest with a bang. They stood there like that for a few heartbeats before he reached down and gently lifted her chin with his finger.

"I mean it," he murmured. "No more sneaking into places. No more ditching your detail." His mouth moved a little closer to hers. "Definitely no dinner with Tseng. And absolutely no more kissing."

"Uh-huh."

His nostrils flared when her tongue darted out to moisten her lips. And just like that, they were both doing what they'd seconds ago agreed not to. Pulling her body against his, he molded his lips over hers. He kissed her urgently, mating with her tongue as he invaded her mouth. Her fingers traveled up his neck to glide through his silky hair so she could bring them closer. A soft moan escaped the back of her throat when his fingers slid beneath her sweater to skim along her spine. She arched in closer, coming into contact with the proof of his desire. Shamelessly, Josslyn ground her hips against his, forcing a groan from deep within his chest. Their breathing became fractured as they both struggled to maintain an upright position.

"Damn it." He ripped his mouth from hers and pushed her body out an arm's length away from his.

Gasping slightly, Josslyn was grateful for his hands on her shoulders keeping her from staggering into one of the display cases filled with valuable dishes.

"Go to your room, Josslyn," he whispered. "Get some sleep and forget all about this."

She nearly raised her hand to slap him, but something stopped her. Probably the part of her that wanted him to kiss her again. And that thought made her angry.

"Like I said before, you're not the boss of me. If you have an issue with how I live my life, step down from my detail. I'll happily tell the director you're not fit to protect me."

He released her so abruptly, she wobbled on her booties.

Storming past her, he jerked open the door. "Go ahead." He left without a backward glance.

Josslyn reached up and pulled out the medallion buried beneath her sweater. She sighed heavily as she brushed it over her kiss-swollen lips. He was calling her bluff and both knew it. The man knew too much about her now. Including the way she kissed. Her cheeks flushed with desire. She told herself it was embarrassment.

"Tomorrow is another day," she said, replacing the medal and squaring her shoulders.

As she was straightening her clothing, her hand brushed against a piece of paper stuck to the back of her skirt. The sticky note was bordered with Chinese symbols, likely a stowaway from her close encounter with Agent Lockett on Tseng's desk. She started to wad it up when she noticed part of the note was in English. Josslyn's breath stilled when she recognized the name written on it.

Christian Sumner.

THE WATER LAPPED at Adam's shoulders. Dawn was beginning to break, leaving them vulnerable to snipers in the boats cruising the area searching for them. Not to mention the sharks that were starting to prowl for their breakfast. After nearly two hours of treading water, Adam could barely feel his legs. They had one life vest between them. Of course, he'd given it to the woman he'd been sent to rescue.

Josslyn's eyes were closed, but he didn't doubt for a minute that she was awake. He could feel the rapid beat of her pulse in her wrists resting against the back of his neck. Her lips were swollen from her constantly licking the salt water from them. Or maybe just from talking nonstop for the past couple of hours. Adam wasn't really sure. They looked pretty damn tempting, though.

Her body was nestled against his. The lithe legs wrapped around his waist did little for his sanity but a lot to keep him warm. The end of her ponytail sluiced through the water, her hair fanning out like a paddle. Adam should have been concentrating on keeping watch for the pick-up signal. Instead, all he could think of was plundering her mouth. Not to mention various other parts of her body.

She's the president-elect's sister-in-law, for crying out loud. *There would be absolutely no gratitude hookup coming after this rescue. Not to mention she was willful, spoiled, and a freaking tree-hugger. The worst kind of woman for him.*

But then his hand cupped her firm ass and all the noise about who she was and what he was disappeared. She was a woman and he was a man. Plain and simple. And despite his belief they would be rescued, he didn't want to take the chance that if these were, in fact, his last hours on earth, he hadn't tasted those luscious lips of hers. He leaned in to do just that.

"Tell me something about you," *she murmured before his mouth could make contact.*

"Why?"

Her eyelids lifted slowly. "Because you already know everything there is to know about me. Everyone does. At least the me that both sides of the campaign defined me as—the love child of the widowed surgeon general and the ambitious Cajun medical researcher trying desperately to find a cure for the cancer that would eventually take her life. They conveniently leave out the part that I was supposed to be a means to an end. Except my umbilical cord didn't hold the key they were hoping for. And in the end, all they had to show for their efforts was plain, old me."

Adam could practically taste the bitterness emanating from her words. He kicked the water harder as though he could kick away her misery somehow.

"*Come on, Jason Bourne,*" she teased. "*I dare you to tell me your life story. I doubt yours is anywhere near as tragic as mine.*"

He wished he could say it wasn't. But he didn't talk about the first eighteen years of his life with anyone. Not even his closest buddies. As far as anyone knew, his life story began when he walked through the gates of West Point. And that was the way Adam preferred it.

She nuzzled his neck. "*You need to keep talking so you stay awake.*"

Hell, she was probably right. And what did it matter what she thought of him anyway? Their odds for survival were getting slimmer by the minute. Thanks to her dramatics on the whaling vessel, they were miles away from the designated rendezvous point. The first op that he failed at would likely be his last, a point his superiors constantly preached during training. Adam always believed he'd be the exception. Until now.

His legs settled into a relaxed rhythm keeping them afloat as Adam let the story sputter out of him.

"*My mom died when I was a kid, too,*" he began.

"*Really?*" she interrupted, her eyes wide, presumably surprised they shared a connection. "*How old were you? How did she die?*"

"*I didn't agree to play twenty questions. I'm just reciting the events of my life. Do you want to hear it or not?*"

She eyed him warily before nodding. Women always wanted to pull out every piece of emotional baggage and examine it until everyone around them was bleeding. Adam was having none of that. Not now. Not ever.

"It was Lupus. I was eleven. My dad was in the army, so we moved around a lot. My mom was the glue that held our family together. When she was gone, things sort of fell apart." He swallowed roughly at the memory. *"Fell apart"* was an understatement. Life as Adam knew it imploded after his mother's death.

Josslyn mermaid kicked her legs between his, trying to take up the slack for keeping them above the water line. He appreciated her efforts, but rescuing them was his job, not hers.

"Save your strength," he commanded. He left unsaid the part about her likely needing that strength should something happen to him. They both understood the potential scenarios facing them.

"Siblings?" she asked.

Adam cocked an eyebrow at her. Not that her open defiance of the rules of the game surprised him. She was a radical rabble-rouser by nature.

"One. A sister. Five years older. Before you ask, she's dead."

She seemed disappointed somehow. As though having a sister would make everything better. The soon-to-be First Lady was already a young mom herself when Josslyn was born. Perhaps the two were close. Adam didn't know. He didn't need to know. Whatever the outcome of this mission, their paths would never cross again.

"Turned out, my dad was a heavy drinker. At least he turned into one after my mom died. I'm not sure if he was angry at her for dying or if he was angry to be saddled with two kids. It sure felt like the latter." Guilt seized Adam's vocal cords for a long moment. *"My sister escaped by falling in love.*

Except the guy was twenty and she was seventeen. My dad found out about it when he discovered the pregnancy test in the trash."

A forlorn sigh escaped her lips.

"My sister knew a good thing when she saw it and she de-cided to run away," Adam continued, surprised at how painful the words still were even after all this time. "I foolishly thought that maybe things would be better without her in the house. It would just be us two guys. My dad couldn't complain about that. And just maybe things would settle down and he'd act like my dad again."

Josslyn's fingers dug into the back of his shoulders as though she could sense what was coming.

"My dad had different ideas. He was going to bring my sister back whether she wanted to come home or not." Adam's chest constricted painfully as the memories of that violent evening threatened to rip him apart again. "I tried to stop him. But I was twelve and while my dad found solace in a bottle, I'd found mine in multiple bags of cookies. It wasn't a fair fight to begin with, but winning was everything for my old man. He beat me senseless and locked me in the storage unit behind our carport."

The sea seemed to still around them. Josslyn wisely kept her mouth shut, but Adam could sense the energy it was taking her to hold back.

"It took most of the night, but my father located them," he continued. "By this point, he was rip-roaring drunk. The poor kid tried to outrun my dad in a car. My dad chased him for two miles until he ran the kid's car off the road into a ravine. It wasn't until the cops showed up that my dad discovered my

sister was in the car with him. They were both killed on impact." Adam swallowed painfully. "My dad had some sort of breakdown. It was five days before anyone found me in the storage unit. I was shipped off to West Virginia to live with my hillbilly grandparents, who, at the time, could barely make ends meet. And my dad was sentenced to twenty years in a military prison for the vehicular homicide of three innocent people."

Her mouth formed an O but no words came out. Probably a first for this woman.

"And that's my story."

Josslyn pulled her hands from behind his neck, treading water now to support herself. Tracing his jaw with her fingertip, she brought her mouth close to his.

"Not all of it. I have a feeling the best is yet to come for you," she whispered. "But you definitely win tonight."

Adam couldn't help himself. He kissed her. Instead of ravishing her like he'd been contemplating moments before, he slowly explored the recesses of her mouth. Taking his time to savor the softness within. Best of all, she let him. Her lips gently welcomed the invasion, encouraging it even. He left her mouth to kiss her eyelids, her nose, her forehead before returning to her lips.

They grabbed onto one another, each one trying to keep the other from submerging beneath the ocean while their tongues tangled and their lips fused. At that point, if Adam had to choose between surviving and having this woman, he was sure he'd choose Josslyn. Time seemed to stand still until the shrill sound of the homing beacon bounced up from the water beside them.

✦

WITH A START, Adam sat upright in his bed, the chime of his alarm reverberating through his tender head. He swiped at the beads of sweat along his temple, struggling to catch his breath.

Damn it.

It had been over a year since he'd dreamt about that mission. Silencing the alarm clock, he flopped back down onto the mattress. Kissing her last night had been the mother of bad ideas. But then, she started it with her cockamamie scheme in Tseng's office. He could have backed off, but one touch of her tongue and his body was all in. Just thinking about it had him primed and ready for action.

Furious at his body's betrayal, he tossed the sheet back and jumped out of bed. A shower would fix everything—a very cold shower.

Naked, he strolled to the bathroom adjacent to his room, checking the messages on his phone. His shoulders relaxed when he saw he and Agent Groesch were assigned to take over the Doolittle's detail at the zoo this afternoon.

Adam wasn't surprised that Josslyn's threat had been an idle one. He *was* surprised at the pleasure he felt that she hadn't outed him to the director. And he didn't like the feeling at all. Turning the faucet to icy, he stepped into the shower. If five minutes under the spray didn't exorcize his lust for the She-Devil, he'd ask the cute physical therapist out to dinner and hope she was up for dessert.

Once he had his libido in check, he could focus on the detail. Josslyn had seriously misplayed her hand by not getting him kicked off her team. Now, Adam knew the game she was playing. And no way was he going to let her search out the animal traffickers. If he had to shadow her day and night, he would. He told himself it was to keep her safe.

CHAPTER SIX

J OSSLYN SPOTTED HIM among the crowd of onlookers seconds after he entered the elephant house. She watched out of the corner of her eye as he exchanged a few words with one of the other agents who'd been assigned to her detail this morning. The two men shared a laugh. A residual smug smile remained on Agent Lockett's face when his gaze finally locked with hers. The usual challenge was in his eyes. The force of it was doing strange things to her insides.

The transition of duties complete, he took his place at the corner of the viewing platform, his stare trained on the crowd. She'd need him to pose as her date again if they were to meet with Tseng. And there was no way she wasn't pursuing this if Christian was involved somehow. Convincing the Tower of Testosterone to play along would take some doing. But given how he'd kissed her the night before, she suspected she might have the upper hand.

"Did you know that elephants have fingers on their trunks?" Josslyn returned her attention to the group of squirming fourth graders she was lecturing. "Elephants living in Africa have two of them." She held up two fingers. "They use them like pinchers to pick things up off the ground so they can put them in their mouth."

The children sat forward when the trainer brought one of the female elephants up to the fence behind Josslyn.

"This is Mila," Josslyn continued. "She's an Asian elephant. Asian elephants only have one finger in their trunk."

As if on cue, Mila stretched her trunk through the cable fence and proceeded to play with Josslyn's ponytail. The children were enthralled, scooting closer while their chaperones urged them back.

"Now she's just showing off," Josslyn joked. "If Mila were back in Asia, she would use her trunk like a giant rope, wrapping it around things she wants to pick up. Did you know an elephant can lift over seven hundred and fifty pounds with their trunks?"

The chatter among the children increased several decibel levels as they debated among themselves just how much seven hundred pounds was. Like a baboon grooming its mate, Mila continued her exploration of Josslyn's hair.

"How come that elephant doesn't have any tusks?" a girl called out.

"Because it's a girl," a boy in the back quickly answered. "Girls are too stupid to have tusks."

A chorus of cries about the *S* word ensued while a teacher admonished the little bully.

Josslyn attempted to regain control. "In the species of elephants that live in Asia, only the males have long tusks, but not *all* the males." She smiled serenely at the boy who'd made the sexist comment. "The females and some males have short little stubby tusks that protrude an inch or two from their lip. They aren't made up of ivory. Therefore they are small and brittle. These are called tushes."

She waited for the obligatory snickering to die down before continuing.

"In Africa, both the male and the female elephants have tusks. They—"

Suddenly, a girl sprang up from her seat on the floor. Agent Lockett shifted slightly toward Josslyn, but the girl turned to face her classmates.

"Do you know that elephants are going extinct because people steal their tusks?" the girl exclaimed. "They gun down the elephants in the wild and rip their tusks right out of their heads. They have to touch their brains to do it!"

Some kids groaned while others seemed to be lapping up the details with a macabre appetite.

"Soon there will be no more elephants left because these mean people steal their tusks to wear round their necks or something. We have to do something about it!"

The girl turned around to face Mila. The tears streaming down her young face startled Josslyn. A burst of pride ripped through her. Had she been this passionate at ten years old? Would her daughter be as passionate? Would she even have children?

Without thinking, Josslyn wrapped the girl up in her arms, quietly shushing her while giving her a gentle squeeze. Over the girl's head, Agent Lockett's gaze met hers. Apparently, he could read her thoughts because he was having trouble keeping his eyes from rolling out of their sockets.

"I'm so sorry." One of the chaperones—the girl's mom from the sound of it—pried her from Josslyn's arms. "Her father let her watch something on *Animal Planet* that he shouldn't have. Come along, Maddie."

Josslyn refrained from shouting "Go, Maddie" or "Good for Dad," but she very much wanted to. Maddie represented the future generation of animal rights' activists and Josslyn didn't want the girl's mom or anyone else—she looked over at Agent Lockett—subduing the youngster's passion. Refocusing her thoughts, she jumped back into the lecture.

"Elephants have a keen sense of smell. Better than a bloodhound. Using their trunks, they can smell water up to twelve miles away. That's farther than your school is from the zoo."

The kids giggled, some of them pointing at Mila. Josslyn glanced over her shoulder to see the elephant using her trunk like a telescope to sniff out the occupants of the room. Flirt that she was, Mila had her trunk aimed at Agent Lockett who was doing his best to keep out of sight. Mila brought her trunk back and buried it in Josslyn's neck.

"Elephants like to touch frequently," she went on. "They use their trunks as a form of tactile communications."

Mila's trunk swung back to Agent Lockett. The children's heads pivoted to follow. He took another step back. Mila trumpeted.

"Look at his gun!" one of the boys whispered loudly.

"Is he here to protect the elephants from poachers?" a girl asked, her eyes wide and her voice shrill.

"I'll bet he has a knife, too."

"Hey, mister, can we see your gun?"

The kids called out questions as the teachers tried to quiet them. Mila dragged her trunk along Josslyn's neck seeming to urge her to move closer to Agent Lockett. The children scooted closer to him, as well.

"His shirt says Secret Service," one boy commented. "Are these the president's elephants?"

"These are everyone's elephants," Josslyn said, trying to regain control. "They belong to you and me and the president."

"They shouldn't have guns around kids," a girl announced to the teacher. "My mom didn't sign me up for that."

Her words brought Josslyn up short. She didn't have to think if she ever acted like Little-Miss-Panties-in-a-Wad. Josslyn had sounded just like that last night in the car with Agent Lockett. Childish and entitled. He'd said he didn't hunt, yet she'd treated him like those idiots whose idea of a great vacation was shooting a defenseless animal and mounting it on their wall.

A silent exchange seemed to occur between him and Agent Groesch. Suddenly the teachers and chaperones were rounding up their charges. Amid a chorus of thank you, the children were led out the door of the elephant house.

Mila flapped her ears at Agent Lockett. Being the Tower of Testosterone, he ignored the animal. The elephant dipped her trunk into the moat lining the interior of the fence.

"No, Mila," Josslyn commanded.

Agent Lockett turned at the sharp tone in her voice.

Mila flapped her ears again.

"She's flirting with you," Josslyn tried to explain to him.

"You've got to be kidding me."

"Would it kill you to come over here and give her a pat?"

From across the room, Agent Groesch choked on what might have been a laugh.

"That's not in my job description." Ignoring the forlorn elephant, he braced his feet and clasped his hands behind his back.

"I tried, Mila. I guess he's just not that into you." Josslyn was bending down to retrieve her iPad when a spray of water doused the cement floor behind her.

"Mila, I said no!" She reprimanded the elephant. But it was too late; Mila was already ambling back out into the yard, her tail swishing with delight.

Agent Lockett, however, was not so delighted.

Mila's aim was dead-on, drenching his upper body. He shook his head slightly, the move sending droplets of water flying. Biting her bottom lip to keep from laughing, Josslyn offered him her sweatshirt to towel off. One look at the water sluicing down his stony face and she couldn't contain the laughter any longer.

"I'm glad one of us is amused."

"Hey, at least you and she have something in common," she chuckled. "You can both shoot straight."

Scowling, he snatched the sweatshirt from her hand.

His expression made her giggle even harder. Burying her face against his damp chest, she laughed until her side ached. For his part, Agent Lockett didn't move a muscle, annoyance and water dripping off his chin.

"Are you done yet?"

Taking a step back, Josslyn wiped her eyes. "You have to admit—"

Her voice froze. It was almost as though she'd conjured up the image of him from that long-ago night. Wet and disheveled like he was, he looked almost vulnerable. The complete antithesis from the stoic, calculating sniper's demeanor he wore like a shield. She reached up her finger to catch a droplet of water curving down his throat. But as usual, he was faster. His fingers snared her wrist midway.

"Don't."

◉

DAMN IT, WHY did this woman have to keep touching him? Technically, he was the one doing the touching right now, but, as usual, she started it. And why did she have to have such a captivating laugh? The very sound of it made the muscles at the back of his neck loose and edgy at the same time. And now she was looking at him as though she wanted to discuss her emotions. That was not happening. Her lips began to wobble.

"Don't," he repeated with a little more edge this time.

He released her wrist.

"I—"

"Woman, don't you ever listen?" he growled. "I said *don't*. Now, if you'll go with Agent Groesch, I'm going to change. At least I came prepared today. I don't make the same mistake twice."

He let the veiled warning float between them. She crossed her arms over her glorious chest, covered up today by a Smithsonian-issue chambray button-down shirt.

"Except that you did make the same mistake today." She gestured to his wet body.

The back of his neck became a vice again. She was beyond infuriating.

"I just wanted to say thank you," she murmured.

"For playing the buffoon and letting your elephants humiliate me?"

Her chin rose up a notch. "No, you arrogant ass. For before. For saving my life. For treading water all those hours. For keeping the sharks and the whales at bay."

She'd gone there anyway even after he'd told her not to. Well, he wasn't interested in a walk down memory lane. Adam never looked back. Only forward. And right now, he needed a dry shirt.

"And making me feel safe and—"

"I was just doing my job," he interrupted. "Nothing more."

He shoved the sweatshirt back at her, but she just stared at it.

"I never saw you after they pulled us from the water," she said quietly.

Adam scrubbed a hand down his face. "That's the way it works," he lied.

It wasn't the way it worked, but after the SEAL team plucked them from the sea, he'd instantly regretted telling her his secrets. Knowing his past gave her power over him. And Adam had vowed never to give another individual the kind of power his father had wielded over him. No matter how amazing her kisses were.

He draped the sweatshirt over her shoulder and edged past before she could get in another word.

"You're on point, Christine. I'm going to change."

If Christine sensed anything between him and Josslyn, she wisely kept it to herself. Adam made his way out of the elephant house.

"Dude, did you go swimming?" one of the Uniformed Division officers joked when Adam approached him for the keys to the SUV.

"Something like that. Agent Groesch has Doolittle. Keep an eye on the entrances."

His phone rang as he headed toward the parking lot.

"What do you have for me, Ben?"

"For starters, I have a few questions about what went on in the China Room last night."

"Hanging up now," Adam snapped.

"Okay, moving on," Ben said. "Metro PD still hasn't located the Mercedes from yesterday, but they're still going with the wrong place, wrong time theory."

"And you?"

"I'd like a better image for the facial recognition software. But I was able to make out a tattoo on the passenger's neck."

"And?"

"It doesn't fit the profile of any of the gangs in or around DC, much less the East Coast," Ben answered. "In fact, it matches ones worn by members of the Nimba tribe in Zimbabwe."

Shit.

"I sifted through custom's data," Ben continued. "And wouldn't you know it, seven people entered the US from Zimbabwe the day after Doolittle was dragged back here kicking and screaming. Four women, one child and two men. One of those men sports the very same tattoo as our guy in the Mercedes."

"That's a hell of a coincidence." Adam wound his way through the crowd milling around the exhibit of American bison.

"That must have been some sort of fact-finding trip for the Smithsonian she was on."

Adam huffed. "The only facts she was interested in are those about an animal trafficking ring she's trying to expose. The Smithsonian documentary was her cover."

His gut clenched at the chaos created when civilians attempted to play spy. Given Josslyn's track record as an activist, it was a wonder she'd made it out of Africa at all. Still, she'd held her own the night before at Tseng's house. She was better at subterfuge than most. Not that he was going to tell her that.

"Any connection between her friend Tseng and the Zimbabwe tribe?" he asked Ben.

"None that I've found yet, but I'm still running down leads. Aside from his fondness for cocaine, Tseng's led a pretty boring, if not entitled, life."

"Except for the illegal zoo he keeps on display in his study." Adam didn't bother hiding his disgust. While he wasn't against hunting for sport, he drew the line at killing a wild animal for its tusk or its foot.

Unlocking the lift gate of the SUV, he pulled his gym bag from the back where he'd placed it before the shift change.

"I don't care how clean Tseng appears," Adam said as he juggled both his cell phone and his comm unit while he shrugged out of his damp shirt.

Ben chuckled. "You sure you just don't like the way Tseng was coming on to your date last night? I mean the guy tried to poach her right under your damn nose."

Adam swore when he got tangled in the wet fabric.

"Funny," Ben continued. "You tend toward women who are more nurturing and settled. But I think wild might be more your thing."

"There's nothing *funny* here," Adam argued once he'd pulled his new shirt on. "And there's definitely no *thing*."

"Whatever you say."

Adam was tucking his shirt into his pants when his senses prickled. Scanning the quiet parking lot, he spied a lone man standing thirty yards from where he was. A man with a lot of ink around his neck.

"Ben," Adam said quietly. "Can you describe that tattoo?"

His friend was suddenly all business. "Three-dimensional. Black rhino horns juxtaposed to form a necklace."

Shit.

The guy was on the run before Adam could reattach his comm unit.

"Lock down Doolittle," Adam shouted into the microphone as he took off after the man.

He chased the African back into the zoo, his earpiece dangling at his neck. Fortunately, the guy bypassed the elephant house, sprinting instead toward the valley section. Adam wove his way through preschoolers trying to close the gap, but the other guy had too much of a lead. They passed the ape house where a crowd gathered to watch the orangutan goof around on a tightrope overhead.

Adam swore silently when he thought he'd lost his mark, but just then, a woman yelled at someone to watch out. He caught sight of the tribesman ducking down the path leading to the anteater house. This area of the zoo wasn't as congested as other areas and Adam had a sudden, terrifying thought. *What if this guy is the decoy?* He didn't dare take his hand off his gun in the holster to reinsert his comm into his ear, but he hoped like hell Christine had heard his plea and gotten Josslyn to safety.

The guy made the mistake of looking back over his shoulder. Adam gained a few yards before the African jumped over a fence leading into a dark cave-like structure. Drawing his gun, Adam followed him in.

The sound of rapid clicking stopped him in his tracks. Wherever they were, it was dimly lit. A sweat broke out at the base of Adam's neck at the sound of flapping behind the mesh cages.

"They can't get you," he admonished himself. "Move your damn feet."

Too bad his feet weren't listening. Suddenly he was back in that storage area, cold, hungry, and tormented by the damn bats whose habitat he'd unwillingly invaded.

"Agent Lockett!"

The Uniformed Division driver bounded into the exhibit, snapping Adam out of his funk.

"Come on," Adam commanded as they made their way through the dark passage.

They ran out into the bright afternoon sunshine, but the African was long gone. Adam grabbed his phone and dialed up Ben.

"Tell me you have eyes on him," Adam panted.

"The sea lions are just starting their show," Ben said. "Cameras lost him among the crowd. We've got video rolling along every inch of Connecticut Avenue, though. We'll get him."

Adam swore violently. He reinserted the earpiece of his comm unit.

"Where's Doolittle?" he demanded.

"Secure in the Serengeti," Christine quickly responded. "You okay?"

No. He'd gone wussy and lost the freaking suspect.

"Yeah," he said. "The suspect is still at large. Prepare Doolittle to return to the Crown immediately."

CHAPTER SEVEN

AGENT LOCKETT DIDN'T accompany them back to the White House. According to Agent Groesch, he'd stayed behind to track down leads.

"And he's sure it's the same guy who was in the van yesterday?" Josslyn asked. "I thought that was just a mistaken identity thing?"

Although that niggling feeling that she recognized the passenger in the van continued to haunt her.

"We're just covering all the bases right now." Agent Groesch had clearly mastered the doublespeak class during her Secret Service training.

William was waiting for her again at the front door.

"Good afternoon, Miss Josslyn," the butler said. "You're home just in time to have tea with your father. Chef Chevalier made apple tarts. And let me tell you, they smell delicious."

"Everything Marin makes is delicious," Josslyn replied with a smile. "I'm going to gain ten pounds the first week I'm staying here."

She took the stairs up to the residence floor, surprised that her father was seated in the West Hall chatting amiably with the mansion's head housekeeper, Terrie.

"There's my girl."

Her father's words stole her breath.

"What have you been up to today, Josslyn?" he asked.

Terrie rose from the sofa.

"He's having a good day," she whispered as she gave Josslyn's shoulder a gentle pat. "Take advantage of it while it lasts."

It was true that some Alzheimer's patients experienced days where their memory was functioning, but Daddy hadn't had one of those in nearly a year.

"Oh, Daddy." Josslyn leaned down and wrapped her arms around his neck. "I've missed you."

The smell of his cologne mingling with ever-present butterscotch candy he munched on wrapped around her like a blanket, comforting her in its familiarity.

He patted her on the shoulder. "I'm here now," he said.

The physician in him was always cognizant of how fleeting moments like these were. The thought made her eyes burn.

"You've been with your pachyderm friends today, I see. Or, rather, I smell."

The sound of his laugh made her smile.

"Only the elephants." She slid to the floor, resting her cheek against his legs just like she'd done as a child. "I brought Dax here from San Francisco. We're hoping he'll mate with one of the females and help populate the herd."

He ran his palm over her head. "That's my daughter, the elephant matchmaker."

"Hey, I prefer to think of myself as a sophisticated genetic engineer, thank you very much."

"Well, whatever it is that you call yourself, I know you do your best at it." He kissed the top of her head.

They sat there in a comfortable silence. Her father enjoyed one of the apple tarts while Josslyn tried to soak up of every minute of his lucidity. Storing up the memory of his laugh, his touch, and his smile so she could pull them out and savor them in the future when his recollection of her was locked up tight in his mind again.

Footsteps on the plush carpet behind them shattered the moment. She looked up as Director Worcester and a wary looking Agent Lockett purposely strode into the room.

"Please excuse us," the director said. "Dr. Benoit, would you mind if we borrow your daughter for a few moments?"

"I mind," Josslyn snapped. She had no idea how long this time with her daddy would last and she deeply resented the interruption. "Isn't it enough that you threw my whole schedule into a frenzy with your wild-goose chase today, Agent Lockett?"

The director sighed resolutely. "We're still trying to determine if it *was* a wild-goose chase, as you call it. This will only take a moment."

Agent Lockett remained stoic beside his boss, but she couldn't help noticing how his eyes softened when he looked at her father.

"Josslyn," Daddy said. "Don't be so fresh. I'll be right here when you get back."

The juvenile part of her wanted to make him promise, but Daddy had little to no control over his mind. Rising to her feet, she kissed him on the cheek. "Save one of those tarts for me."

"I make no promises," he said as if he'd read her thought from a second ago.

She followed the director and Agent Lockett into the Yellow Oval Room. The adjacent Truman Balcony offered a spectacular view of the afternoon sun sliding behind the Washington Monument.

"I'll get right to the point," the director began. "It seems that whatever you got mixed up in while you were in Zimbabwe might have followed you here."

"*Whatever I was mixed up in?*" she practically shouted as her agitation grew. "We were filming a documentary. We ran into some poachers. They discovered us filming. Trevor got shot. The marines came in and rescued me. Again. End of story."

The silent communication the men exchanged infuriated her even more.

"Are you going to tell me what this is all about?" she demanded.

The director nodded to Agent Lockett. He opened up the tablet he was carrying and powered it up. "Do you recognize this man?"

Josslyn sucked in a breath, willing her knees not to buckle. "Is this the man you were chasing today?"

When neither man answered, she took the tablet from Agent Lockett's hands. Her mind hadn't been playing tricks on her. It *was* him.

"You know him." Agent Lockett edged closer.

She deflected. "Was this picture taken today?"

"Damn it, Josslyn, stop playing games," he ordered. "How does this guy fit into the puzzle?"

"You tell me," she countered. "You're the one with his picture."

She was glad for the director's presence because Agent Lockett looked as if he might strangle her.

"He's one of seven people to come from Zimbabwe since you arrived here two days ago," the director explained.

"Seven?" Josslyn whipped around to face the director. "Do you know anything about the others?"

She swallowed a frustrated scream as the two men exchanged another one of those looks.

"Four women, two men, and one child," the director answered.

Hope fluttered in her chest. "A child? How old?"

Agent Lockett pressed a button on his phone. "Ben, can you give me intel on the others from Zimbabwe?"

Josslyn's heart beat furiously while they waited. Finally, the tablet beeped. Not waiting for Agent Lockett, she swiped at the message. She released a breath she wasn't aware she'd been holding in when she caught sight of the photo of Ngoni looking back at her.

"He's safe," she murmured.

A wave of relief washed over her. They hadn't gotten the young informant killed. She'd need to let Trevor and

Hugh know as soon as possible. And then she needed to figure out why Ngoni's older brother was chasing after her. Before she did any of that, however, she was spending time with her father.

"Who's safe?" both men demanded.

"Can this wait until later this evening? My father could be sundowning as we speak."

The director looked as if he was going to deny her request, but Agent Lockett interceded on her behalf.

"Fine. But only if you agree to tell us *everything* that you know," he insisted.

She was tempted to lie, but the softness was there in his eyes again. And he'd taken her side against the director. That had to count for something. She suspected he'd guessed a good portion of her story anyway.

"Fine," she agreed, mimicking him.

He studied her for a long moment. "Enjoy your time with your father," he said quietly, gesturing for the director to precede him out of the room.

"Agent Lockett," she called after him. "Thank you."

"I'll be downstairs waiting," he replied, the softness completely evaporated from his eyes. "Don't make me wait all night."

✦

"FIND THE KID," Adam commanded into the phone. "Doolittle was worried about him for some reason. He's the key to whatever this is. If we find him, we find the guy with the rhino tattoos."

Clicking off the phone, he rested his forehead in his palms and sighed.

"That sounds like a book," a familiar voice said. "*The Guy with the Rhino Tattoos.*"

His friend, Griffin Keller, sat down in the chair opposite Adam. They were the only ones occupying the Secret Service director's office on the ground floor.

"What are you doing here?" Adam asked. "Last time I checked you were a G-man now."

Griffin left the Secret Service a few months back to take a job at Treasury, one with more predictable hours. Apparently, that was what settling down did to a man. Ben and Adam teased their roommate mercilessly, but Griffin just kept flashing his trademark dimples. It was hard to deny being engaged made the guy happy, but Adam would just as soon keep his independence. *Thank you very much.*

"Marin and I are going out on a date," Griffin said. "You remember what those are, don't you?"

Shit!

Adam glanced at his phone. Seven eighteen. He was supposed to pick up Kathy—Katy, whatever the physical therapist's name was, forty-eight minutes ago. He quickly scrolled through his contacts. *Kasey. That was her name.* She picked up on the first ring.

"I'm terribly sorry. Something came up here at the White House and I couldn't get to a phone."

Griffin smirked at the lie. Adam flipped him off. He offered the obligatory rain check and, to his relief, she agreed.

"Two dates in two nights," Griffin teased when Adam finished his call. "You're definitely feeling better."

Adam scowled at him. "Last night wasn't a date."

His friend's grin grew. "That's not how Ben described it. In fact, he said there was some tonsil hockey being played."

"Ben has a big mouth."

Griffin sobered up. "Look, you get a free pass here because you've never actually worked a detail before," he said. "But rule number one—never get romantically involved with a protectee."

"Seriously? This from a guy who's marrying the woman he was protecting?"

"Technically, I wasn't protecting Marin," Griffin pointed out. "I was *investigating* her. There's a difference."

Adam bristled. "First of all, the only one who categorized last night as a date was Doolittle. And secondly, I *am* investigating her."

That got his friend's attention. "You think she really is up to something?"

"When is that woman *not* up to something?" Adam ran his fingers through his hair. "She doesn't seem to realize that when you start throwing flames, there's a good chance you'll get burned in the process."

"Does the president know?"

"The director briefed his chief of staff an hour ago," Adam replied. "Short of physical restraint, there's not much we can do except have eyes on her twenty-four seven."

"And which part did you volunteer for?" Griffin asked. "The physical restraints or the twenty-four seven surveillance?"

Adam didn't bother responding. As much as he liked the idea of tying Josslyn up to keep her out of trouble, the erotic image caused beads of sweat to form at the back of his neck. He sighed in frustration. Griffin laughed out loud.

"What I'm going to do is my job," Adam announced. "Which is to keep her from putting herself in harm's way while the professionals get to the bottom of this."

He swore beneath his breath, still angry for missing a good opportunity to resolve the situation when he'd lost the guy in the zoo. Disgust burned deep in Adam's belly at the way he'd frozen up. That hadn't happened in years. He blamed his dream last night. And he blamed the recurrence of that damn dream on the She-Devil.

They'd move a lot more quickly toward solving the situation if she'd only cooperate and share what she knew. And Adam was sure she knew quite a lot. He could have insisted she talk earlier, but that would have meant tearing her away from her father who was shockingly lucid for the first time since he arrived months ago. He'd seen the way her eyes kept darting back to the sofa where the older man was sitting. As frustrated as the woman made him, that hint of vulnerability shadowing her face got to him. He made a mental note to keep his guard up to that in the future.

The sound of high heels tapping on the marble floor drew both men's attention to the doorway. Marin strolled into the office, looking like she'd just stepped out of the pages of *Maxim*. The dress she wore fit her like a second skin. Its clingy blue fabric made the blue of her eyes even bolder and her hips more provocative. No doubt about it, his friend was a lucky man.

Both men stood to greet her. Griffin draped an arm around Marin's shoulders before flashing Adam a proprietary grin that very clearly said, "She's all mine." Little did Griff know, he was actually the one enslaved. His buddy would find that out soon enough, Adam thought with a chuckle.

"Have they finished dinner?" Adam asked her.

Marin nodded. "A little while ago. It was just Josslyn and her dad tonight, so the meal was very casual."

"Is Dr. Benoit still . . . himself?"

She smiled warmly. "He is. The First Lady had hoped this might happen. Josslyn hasn't taken her father's Alzheimer's well."

That might explain some of her increased rash behavior, but it didn't excuse it.

"Is he still up?"

"His nurse was on the way in when I came downstairs."

Adam grabbed his tablet and headed for the residence floor. The director was still at dinner in the Navy Mess. Technically, he should wait for his boss before interrogating her. But Adam had a few persuasive tools in his arsenal that might just make Josslyn open up. And he'd rather the director not witness them.

"Enjoy your date," he called over his shoulder.

Taking the stairs two at a time, he quickly rounded the corner into the dimly lit Center Hall, stopping short at the sound of music. Josslyn and her father were sitting side by side on the bench in front of the Baldwin grand piano President Truman had brought to the White House. She played a tune unknown to Adam while Dr. Benoit hummed along. Once again, this tender side of Josslyn baffled him. *Among other things.*

The piano music ended and a restful quiet settled over the long, narrow room. Adam hesitated to intrude on the precious moments between parent and child, but it was only a matter of time before the director arrived. He needed to get Josslyn alone quickly.

"Excuse me," Adam said.

"Ah, just in time." Dr. Benoit turned to his daughter. "My medicine is beginning to tire me out. But here is a handsome young man to keep you company in my absence."

He kissed her on the cheek. Josslyn wrapped her arms around her father's neck tightly. A murmured exchange followed. Her father tapped her chest. The smile he gave didn't quite match the sorrow in his eyes. Apparently, she saw it too because she looked away quickly.

The nurse escorted the doctor to the stairs. Dr. Benoit stopped short of Adam.

"Look after her," he instructed quietly.

"I'll do my best," Adam assured him without hesitation.

The doctor nodded with a wry grin. He was likely

aware of the force of nature his daughter was. With a last tender look back at her, Dr. Benoit left the hall. Josslyn stayed where she was, plunking at the keys of the piano.

Adam decided to get right to the point. "Who is he?"

"The guy who outran you today?" She played a few bars of "The Monkey Chases the Weasel." The woman had to be the most maddening female on the planet.

"Yeah," Adam bit out. "That guy."

She sighed as her fingers danced over the keys of the grand piano playing the opening strains of Toto's "Africa."

"Joss," Adam urged.

The use of her shortened name seemed to startle her. She mashed the keys down making the piano sound otherworldly before spinning around on the bench in a huff. But she didn't meet his eyes. He wondered if she too was suddenly consumed with memories of what they'd shared that night in the Pacific. At some point during their escapade, she'd stopped being the sister-in-law of the then president-elect and had simply become Joss, a vulnerable, passionate, woman. A woman, he was beginning to realize, he still very much craved.

Adam physically shook the thoughts from his head. His first priority was to do what he'd just promised her father and keep her safe. In order to do that, he needed answers and he needed them now. "You said you'd come clean."

"I'm getting really tired of being made the culprit here."

He crossed his arms over his chest and cocked an eyebrow at her. She jumped from the bench and began pacing the hall.

She heaved a weary-sounding sigh. "He's a member of a tribe in Zimbabwe that we believe works for one of the largest animal poaching rings on the African continent."

"We?"

"For the hundredth time, members of Global Wildlife Conservation," she snapped. "Contrary to what you believe, I'm not just running some solo vigilante mission against anyone I believe is harming animals. The GWC has spent years acquiring evidence."

"And this guy somehow figured out you were on to him when you were out on the plains filming a documentary for the Smithsonian? I'm not buying it."

She wandered over to the octagonal partners' desk that stood as the dividing point between the Center Hall's two receiving areas. "We were working with an informant. He was supposed to meet us that day."

"The kid."

Josslyn nodded. "Ngoni has dreams of playing basketball one day." She smiled. "He hasn't figured out that his height puts him at a distinct disadvantage. He just wants a better life for himself and his family."

"And your friend from the van and the zoo?"

"Ngoni's older brother, Mandla. Definitely *not* my friend." Her response was laced with disgust. "He enjoys the money that poaching brings in a little too much."

"And he doesn't want you or his little brother messing that up." Adam blew out a breath. "Would Ngoni's own brother hurt him?"

Josslyn gnawed at her lower lip. "I don't know," she whispered. "I hate to think that we put him in this position. It has to mean something that Mandla brought Ngoni with him, right?"

That look was back in her eyes. Adam suspected she tried very hard not to let anyone get a glimpse of her vulnerability. Especially not him.

"Unless Ngoni is being used as a pawn," Adam responded. "And Mandla can only save him by eliminating you."

Adam was being deliberately cruel for even saying the words out loud in front of her. But she needed to know her willy-nilly actions had consequences.

So why did he suddenly feel like such an ass?

Reaching a hand down to steady herself against the mahogany desk, Josslyn drew in a shaky breath. Adam was across the room in four long strides. He gathered her up in his arms before she lost her balance.

"Shh," he soothed. "We're going to figure this out."

She leaned into him, holding on as though they were still treading water in the dark ocean. Adam brushed his lips over her silky hair. Why was it that he only had two settings with this woman—throttle her or kiss her?

"I know you think I'm impetuous," she murmured against his chest. "But someone has to speak for the animals. At the rate the poachers are killing them, the African elephant will be extinct in a decade."

Impetuous didn't even begin to describe her. Still, deep down, he admired her for her convictions. She wasn't one of those women whose beliefs shifted like a tree branch in the wind. Adam liked that about her. Hell, he liked a lot of things about her, especially the parts of her pressed up against him. He stroked a hand up and down her spine. They stood there for a long moment, locked in another inappropriate embrace. Except each time Adam touched Josslyn, it felt less and less inappropriate.

The sound of footsteps coming up the stairs forced Adam to reluctantly release her.

"Agent Lockett." Josslyn was seated back on the piano bench when Director Worcester strode into the hall. "Our friends at the FBI may have something for us."

"They've found Ngoni?" she asked.

The director looked at Adam questioningly.

"The boy," Adam explained. "It seems his brother, Mandla, is the one following her. He's involved with a crew of tribesmen that Miss Benoit and her friends at the GWC suspect are poachers. The little brother was going to rat them out."

"Not *suspect*!" She jumped to her feet. "We have *evidence*. And this animal trafficking ring is one of, if not, *the* largest poaching organizations in the world. For your information, animal trafficking is nearly a twenty-billion-dollar-a-year business. Ivory brings in more money than gold, oil, or cocaine. These syndicates are very sophisticated. Many of them are the same gangs who deal in guns and narcotics. They have to be stopped."

Her impassioned speech left her cheeks flushed and her breasts heaving. She was sexy as hell standing there defending her cause. Too bad the director didn't see it that way.

"All the more reason you'll be confined here at the White House until these men are apprehended," he announced.

"What?" Her hands went to her hips as she glared at the director. "That's not what I agreed to. Kindly allow me to remind you that I can decline Secret Service protection at any time."

Never one to back down, the director kept his voice and his emotions even when he responded. "Allow me to remind you that I take my orders from the president of the United States and until such time as he instructs me to release you from your protective detail, I call the shots around here."

Josslyn mumbled something that didn't appear to be ladylike. "Fine. Then double my detail. Triple it. But I need to be at the zoo this week. Zara has already begun doing her estrous walk. Dax will be pawing at the barn door tomorrow to get to her."

Say what?

Adam didn't realize he'd said it out loud until Josslyn rolled her eyes at him.

"To put it in terms you might understand, she's in heat. Dax was brought in to mate with her."

"Surely that's something the two elephants can accomplish without you present?" The normally unflappable director tugged at his shirt collar.

"It's common protocol for one of the zoologists to be in attendance."

"Jesus." Adam pinched the bridge of his nose.

What would this woman get into next? He had a hunch she was playing the director to get out of being under lock and key at the White House. But it didn't matter; the director wouldn't budge.

Except he did.

"Fine," Director Worcester acquiesced. "We'll close off the elephant house for the next few days. I'll speak with the FBI. They're trying to find a way to flush the Africans out. This could be it."

"Like hell!" Adam's voice echoed throughout the hall. *Had the man gone crazy?* "We have no idea what these guys want from her. That's an asinine suggestion."

Adam's chest grew tight. He told himself it was because the director was cavalier with Josslyn's safety and security. But he suspected it was because he was beginning to think of her as more than just a protectee. And he was suddenly very uncomfortable at the idea of her exposed to any form of danger.

"I don't believe you're in a position to argue, Agent Lockett," the director said. "Besides, I thought you'd jump at the chance to handle the tactical aspects of this assignment."

"I'm fine with that plan," Josslyn agreed with the director.

"Of course you are!" Adam fired back.

She huffed a sigh before crossing her arms beneath those attractive breasts of hers. "It's the only scenario that allows me to continue on with my work and helps us find Ngoni."

Adam swore viciously beneath his breath. The woman was too damn defiant for her own good. And the rest of the world let her get away with it. Well not him. But for now, he'd do whatever he could to keep her safe. He'd save the part about taming her for later.

"I'll set up a conference call with the zoo security and the FBI." The director made his way to the stairs. "You'll want to sit in, I'm sure, Agent Lockett."

"Yes, sir," Adam said, but his feet seemed to be rooted to the carpet.

The sound of the director's footsteps on the stairs faded. A slow, triumphant grin formed on Josslyn's lips.

"Delilah," he muttered.

"Excuse me?"

"That's going to be your new code name."

She laughed at him then, the husky sound of it making his head spin.

"I like it better when you call me Joss."

Adam shoved his fingers through his hair. "Yeah, well, I need you to be Doolittle. Or PITA. Or Babar if I'm going to be able to keep you safe."

Her grin became even more glorious. *Damn it.* Spinning on his heel, he followed in the director's footsteps.

"Adam," she called after him.

It wasn't lost on him that she used his first name. Once again she was changing the rules of the game to suit her purpose. He paused at the top of stairs unable to resist a glance back at her.

"Good night," she whispered.

CHAPTER EIGHT

"STAY AWAY FROM the open areas of the exhibit," Agent Lockett—*Adam*—instructed.

Josslyn did as she was told, keeping herself concealed behind the large protective screen the Secret Service had erected on the viewing deck. She marveled at how quickly Adam and his colleagues were able to secure the elephant barn so she could come into work. Guilt tightened her stomach, however. Her stupid pride ran away with her the night before. She could have just as easily observed the elephants from the closed-circuit video link on her computer. But, as was her nature, she'd balked stubbornly at the idea of being confined and told what to do. In doing so, she'd made Adam and his team work through the night. Not to mention ruining several field trips for area school children when the exhibit was closed to the public. The least she could do was to follow instructions and be congenial in return.

Truth be told, her insides were clamoring to be more than just congenial with Adam. If the previous two days were any indication, the connection they'd forged that night on the sea hadn't faded despite his abrupt disappearance and nearly two years of no contact. The knowledge was both arousing and disarming to Josslyn. While the Secret Service agent made her feel safe and protected with just his presence, she feared parts of her were definitely *not* safe from Adam Lockett the man. He made her want things, things out of her control. And that feeling unsettled her more than whatever it was Mandla wanted from her.

Dax trumpeted from his side of the barn. Zara answered with a low hum of her own. The three other females paraded around the compound.

"So what happens now?" Adam asked.

"Don't tell me no one ever explained the birds and the bees to you?" she teased.

"Funny." He waved a hand toward the cows in the yard. "There are four females out there. Does your boyfriend Dax play stud with each of them?"

"Don't be ridiculous," she scoffed. "He's an elephant, not a sailor on shore leave. He'll mate with Zara." She pointed to the younger female standing apart from the others.

"What makes you so certain he'll pick her?"

"Zara and Dax have a history."

Josslyn gave the signal to one of the trainers to open the door to Dax's enclosure. The females chorused when the big bull rumbled into the yard. He took several moments to sniff at the other cows before making a beeline toward Zara. For her part, Zara played hard to get for all of two minutes before she allowed Dax to brush up against her.

Josslyn sighed happily, resting her forearms on the metal fence to observe. "I told you. Those two are meant to be."

Beside her, Adam mumbled something under his breath.

"What was that?" she asked. "Please, Special Agent Lockett, if you have something to say, share it with the rest of the class."

He peered over his ever-present aviator sunglasses at her. "I said, it's just like a woman to turn a basic natural act into something that's all"—he waved a hand in the air— "rainbows and glitter."

"*Rainbows and glitter?*" She didn't know whether to laugh with him or at him.

"Yeah, all that crap that makes women happy."

"Trust me. It takes more than rainbows and glitter to make a woman happy. Unless she's twelve." It was her turn to eye the Secret Service agent from head to toe. "I would have thought a man like you would know better," she challenged, totally ignoring her resolve to be amicable.

She was playing with fire and judging by the way his jaw tensed up, both knew it. He was saved from responding when Dax trumpeted loudly to the rest of the herd that he'd made his choice. Zara hummed again, intertwining her trunk with the big bull's.

"See what I mean?" Josslyn grinned. "An elephant never forgets."

Adam groaned. "You're asking me to believe his desire to mate with Zara is based on something more than just natural physiological chemistry?"

Resting her chin on her forearms, she watched Zara

jauntily parade over to the far side of the yard. Dax followed closely behind her. "Believe what you want. But humans aren't the only animals capable of love."

"What a bunch of drivel. I would have thought a scientist like you would know better," he said, mocking her earlier words.

Josslyn refused to concede the point. "Spoken like a typical man. Several animal species mate for life, you know. Swans. Wolves. Penguins." She ticked them off on her fingers. "Others, like elephants, tend to seek out the same partner time after time. Zara and Dax already mated successfully once. Unfortunately, their baby didn't live. We're hoping for a better result this time."

"All the more reason he should pick the horny one." He gestured to Mila.

Josslyn rounded on him, not bothering to contain her pique despite her vow to be congenial. "This may seem like a big joke to you, but this isn't the middle school locker room. I assure you, there is actual, unrefuted scientific evidence to back up the assertion that animals do experience feelings, not the least of which is love. I know because I spent the better part of my PhD studying it."

She balled her fingers into fists. He was just like everyone else in her family, dismissing her research as fluff and egocentricity—an indulgent princess playing scientist. But unlike everyone else's, Adam's respect mattered to her. She'd have to examine why later, but for now, it was maddening enough to know it was important to her.

Mila blasted a call through her trunk as if to punctuate

Josslyn's frustration. Adam cocked his head slightly to the side.

Josslyn threw up her hands. *What was the use?* The man thought rainbows and glitter could satisfy a woman, for crying out loud.

"Mila is past breeding age," she enlightened him. "She's not even in estrous. For that matter, neither are the other two cows."

The corners of his mouth curved up in a satisfied smile. "I rest my case. Dax made his selection based purely on chemistry. There's nothing romantic about his decision at all."

She sighed in exasperation. "I should have known a big alpha male like you would have something against romance."

"Romance is overrated."

"And love?" The question slipped out before she could stop it.

With a suddenly dry mouth, she wrapped her arms around her midsection, waiting impatiently for him to answer. His expression was hard to decipher behind those damn sunglasses. Given how much coordination needed to be done to make the zoo safe for her to come to work today, those lenses likely hid the dark smudges caused by a sleepless night. Guilt niggled at her for being so demanding. He'd nearly passed out on herthe other day, yet he muscled on as if it were nothing.

Her chest ached for the young boy he'd once been— alone, scared, and defenseless. She knew very little of his life apart from what he'd shared with her that night in the ocean. But she was in awe of the man who had risen above his traumatic childhood. He wouldn't be on her detail if he wasn't well respected by the director, or the president, for that matter. Surely, he'd known love in his life. She tried to ignore the parts of her that were suddenly jealous of whomever he did love.

"It's possible to have chemistry—very passionate chemistry—without love." He uttered the words quietly.

Josslyn struggled not to react to their intensity. Or their challenge.

Jealousy knotted her stomach even more, which was ridiculous. She barely knew the guy—the years of fantasizing about him didn't count. Still, she was curious. And more than mildly aroused, damn it. She attributed her sudden lusty desires to all the pheromones floating up from the elephant yard below.

"Spoken from experience, I presume?" She tried to appear nonchalant as she asked the question, but the hairs were standing up at the back of her neck.

A muscle ticked in his cheek. "I haven't had any complaints."

Oh my. Try as she might, she couldn't contain the flush burning her cheeks.

"Well, good for you," was all she could think of to say.

This time the smile he gave her was downright cocky. "Actually, based on the feedback I've been given"—he lowered his voice an octave—"I'm better than good."

Josslyn spun on her heel and turned around to avoid

melting into a puddle at his feet. Ignoring his satisfied chuckle, she blew out a slow, calming breath, trying to refocus her attention on the reason they were at the zoo in the first place. She needed to concentrate on the mating habits of elephants, not those of domineering, dark, and brooding snipers.

Dax and Zara had completed their coupling. If the zoo was lucky, the two would mate again several more times during the next few days, increasing the odds of a pregnancy. For now, it was satisfying for Josslyn to see the elephants relaxed in one another's company. Zara basked in the afterglow, humming contentedly while Dax flapped his ears and kept the other females away from her.

"Don't even try to tell me what they're doing now is some sort of pillow talk because I'm not buying it," he said as if reading her mind.

Josslyn wheeled around to put the smart aleck in his place. But the words froze on her tongue when she spotted the man approaching Adam from behind. Before she could catch her breath, Adam's big body was shielding hers, his gun drawn and pointed at the would-be intruder.

"Freeze!" Adam snarled.

Trevor's good hand—along with his eyebrows—shot to the sky. "Whoa, there, mate. I come in peace."

"For heaven's sake, don't shoot him again!" Josslyn scrambled out from behind Adam's tense frame. "Trevor, what are you doing here?"

"Careful, sweetheart." Trevor groaned when she hugged him. "I'm still on the disabled list."

She glanced at his bandaged shoulder, held immobile by the sling he wore. It wasn't like Trevor to miss any opportunity for sympathy and coddling at home or in a hospital. Something must be seriously wrong if he'd made the sixteen-hour trip to the United States so quickly after being shot.

"I Skyped with Hugh last night to tell him Ngoni is alive," Josslyn informed him. "He said you were recovering at the Australian consulate."

"Yeah. I know." Trevor glanced over at Adam before lowering his voice. "You have a detail now?"

Adam had sheathed his gun and assumed the posture of unobtrusive bodyguard. She didn't have to see behind his sunglasses to know where his eyes were, however. She could feel them boring into her skin as he tracked her movements.

"For the time being. Harriett and Conrad insisted," she explained.

Trevor was constantly going on about individual freedoms and the overbearing power of those in power. He'd always supported her right to go without Secret Service protection. His response, therefore, caught her off guard.

"Good." He nodded at Adam before clutching Josslyn's forearm and gently dragging her to the other side of the viewing pavilion.

Unease tickled her spine. "What's really going on, Trevor? Why aren't you back in Zimbabwe recuperating?"

"The Australian ambassador kicked me out." Trevor wrapped his good hand around the back of his neck. "He said he couldn't guarantee my safety if I stayed in the country."

His words astounded her. "The tribesmen wouldn't dare come after you on embassy grounds."

"Sweetheart," Trevor drawled. "It's just as we suspected. This ring of barbarians has its tentacles everywhere, including inside the embassies."

She thought of the Post-it note from Tseng's office. Christian Sumner's name was the only thing she could decipher. As much as she despised the little despot, Christian was a bootlicker, not a risk taker. Sucking up was his superpower. Josslyn had difficulty imagining him coloring outside the lines much less involving himself in something illegal and abhorrent. Still, there had to be a connection somewhere for Tseng to have his name. She'd just have to get the rest of the note translated. Discreetly. Too bad David didn't read or write Mandarin. She'd reach out to a friend at the University of Maryland tomorrow.

"Alyssa?" she asked, belatedly remembering the graduate student.

"I had to break her heart and send her back to Atlanta. Safety first."

Josslyn pressed her fingers to her temples. "We have to find Ngoni. Once he's safe, he can help us unravel just who is behind this."

"I agree. In the meantime, we need to figure out what was on that video that was so damning."

"Did Hugh come with you?"

Trevor shook his head. "He's hiding out in Iceland, but

we can download the video if we need to."

"It might be a good idea to have someone at Fish and Wildlife look at it. They have jurisdiction over animal trafficking matters."

Josslyn jumped at the sound of Adam's voice behind her.

"Aren't Secret Service agents supposed to be strong, silent types?" Trevor joked.

"Yes, they are," Josslyn agreed, turning to glare at Adam. "This is a private conversation, Agent Lockett."

He had the nerve to look impish. "Yes, well, Nancy Drew, we've been ordered back to the Crown. It seems there are some leads on the African boy you're looking for."

◈

WHY DON'T YOU get someone at Fish and Wildlife to look at it? Adam had seriously lost his ever-loving mind. And it hadn't taken a lead pipe to the head to accomplish it—just a whirling dervish of a woman with no sense of self-preservation. Now it seemed that instead of reining the She-Devil in, he was encouraging her in her shenanigans.

"Do we have a contact at Fish and Wildlife?" he asked the director as they made their way to the Map Room to meet with the FBI agents helping to flush out Mandla and his little brother. "They might be more tuned in to whatever Doolittle and her friends stirred up in Zimbabwe. Illegal animal trafficking is within their scope of authority."

"Way ahead of you." The director indicated a tall black

man admiring the ornate Chinese tea box just inside the room. "Allow me to introduce you to Terence Shaw, director of Fish and Wildlife's International Affairs Division. Agent Shaw heads up our government's investigations into animal trafficking. Agent Shaw, this is Agent Lockett. He's been coordinating Miss Benoit's security detail."

Agent Shaw extended his hand. "You don't look too battle weary," he joked. "But give her time. I've been tracking Miss Benoit's activities for the past couple of years. That girl is like Joan of Arc, singularly focused on saving animals from extinction no matter what the consequences."

Two days ago—hell, two years ago—Adam might have described Josslyn the same way. But watching her interact with the school children, the elephants, and the staff at the zoo, he was beginning to develop a new-found respect for her as a scientist whose extreme activism was rooted in something more than just a bleeding heart.

"If you've been following her for years, why the hell weren't those Africans stopped before they left Zimbabwe? And why were tribesmen shooting at her while she was filming a damn documentary?"

Adam's angry outburst had the Fish and Wildlife agent eyeing him speculatively. "Interesting."

His response did nothing to cool Adam's anger. "It would be nice if we knew what we were dealing with here. It makes it kind of hard to protect her if we don't know all the facts."

"Stand down, Agent Lockett," the director ordered. "Agent Shaw was invited here to do just that—give us the facts."

The director gestured for the Fish and Wildlife agent to take a seat in one of the chairs spread about the room. The two FBI agents were already seated, their faces giving nothing away. Adam slumped onto the sofa across from them.

Before they could get started, Josslyn waltzed into the room, the Aussie surfer trailing behind her. She'd changed out of her zoo uniform to form-fitting brown denim jeans and a long cable-knit sweater that showcased her curves. The men all shot to their feet. Agent Groesch wore a bemused look as she took her position at the door. Josslyn had likely railroaded right through Christine to get to the meeting.

"Please, don't let me interrupt," Josslyn drawled. "But since this affects me, I believe I'll sit in."

With all the poise and decorum of royalty, she perched her fine ass on the edge of a spindly antique chair. Her partner in crime stood behind her, resting an elbow on the chair back. The director looked as though he might object, but he was a man who picked his battles wisely. Instead, he introduced the other men in the room to Josslyn and her friend.

"With all due respect, what does the US Fish and Wildlife Service have to do with poaching?" Trevor asked.

To his credit, Shaw didn't even flinch. "Poaching has many implications beyond just the threatened extinction of animals. Selling ivory can be a lucrative cash influx for terrorists. While you and your counterparts are working to protect the elephants, many of the tribes are fighting among themselves to protect their livelihood. The effects of which are felt internationally. Therefore, the US has multiple agencies dedicated to monitoring and eradicating poaching. I happen to chair a task force coordinating those investigations throughout the world."

"Got it," Trevor responded.

"I understand you have some leads on the men we suspect of trying to confront the car carrying Miss Benoit and her detail yesterday," the director began.

"*Doctor* Benoit," Adam interjected.

He was just as surprised as everyone else in the room at his interruption. But given her passionate defense of her work earlier—not to mention the respect from her colleagues he'd witnessed over the past several days—Adam figured someone needed to speak up for her.

Director Worcester cleared his throat. Agent Groesch's eyelids fluttered briefly before she regained her composure. For her part, Josslyn rewarded his outburst with a soft smile, its warmth making Adam shift uncomfortably in his seat. He didn't need any more of the woman's hero worship. Hell, all he'd done was point out the obvious.

"The passenger, whom you chased through the zoo, Agent Lockett, is part of a gang of international animal traffickers," Agent Shaw explained.

Josslyn heaved a sigh. "Really? You're going to lead with that? We'd already established who they are and who they work for. If this is the level of investigating the government is doing, I'll take my chances finding Ngoni on my own." She started to rise from her seat.

Adam was inclined to agree with her. So much for the Fish and Wildlife Service. But no way was she running off to find her informant unchaperoned.

"If you'll indulge me." Agent Shaw waved her back into her chair. "I'm leading up to your friend Ngoni, who is fine by the way."

Josslyn gasped. "You've seen him?"

One of the FBI agents chimed in. "The task force has been tracking him and his brother since they left Zimbabwe. Mandla left Ngoni with relatives at a home in Bailey's Crossroads, Virginia."

"Again, that would have been nice to know before now," Adam snapped. "How about the brother? Do you have eyes on him? Or is he going to jump out of the shadows at her again?"

Agent Shaw relaxed into his chair, leveling Adam with a chilly look over his steepled fingers. "That's highly unlikely."

"I'm afraid that isn't a satisfactory answer to those of us in charge of Miss—*Doctor* Benoit's protection," the director said.

Adam dug his fingers into the sofa to keep from decking the arrogant Fish and Wildlife agent.

"Mandla is no longer a threat to the First Lady's sister," Agent Shaw announced. "He was found earlier today with his throat slit."

The color drained from Josslyn's face. Adam itched to comfort her, but her surfer friend was already doing a good job of it. Trevor's hands massaged her shoulders with a too-familiar intimacy.

"Any leads?" the director asked.

"None so far, but we'll let you know if and when we do."

"How? Why?" Trevor demanded.

"You tell me, Mr. Kearn," Agent Shaw replied. "What were you filming out in the bush that day?"

"Elephants," Josslyn answered for him, her tone biting. "It wasn't supposed to be anything more until the poachers showed up."

"But you intended to meet Ngoni?" Shaw asked.

"He was going to give us information on the ringleaders," Trevor said.

Agent Shaw leaned forward, resting his elbows on his knees. "Give you? Or *show* you?"

A taut silence settled over the room.

Trevor swore quietly.

"It's doubtful Ngoni could give you names because this ring is careful not to use them. If they weren't, our operatives would already know who to arrest," Shaw explained.

"We need that film," Adam said.

"Hugh and I looked at it for days. We couldn't identify anything or anyone out of the ordinary." Trevor pulled out his phone. "I can get it from him, though."

Shaw looked over at the FBI agents. "Can your lab run it through artificial intelligence databases?"

"We'll do it," Adam interjected before the other agents could speak up.

"Agent Lockett is correct," the director added. "Our cybercrimes lab doesn't have the backlog of cases that the FBI's does. And Ben Segar is a master at finding a needle in a haystack using AI. Since these individuals pose a threat to a member of the First Family, it falls within our purview."

The FBI agents nodded.

"Do we know who we're looking for?" the director prodded.

Agent Shaw sighed theatrically. "Our intel reports that someone high up in the organization was in Zimbabwe that day. We have conflicting accounts as to exactly where in the country he or she was, with some saying that this person was hunting big game at the time of your encounter."

"Any names to get us started?" the director asked.

"Just theories." Agent Shaw evaded answering. "But I understand you've already made the acquaintance of Kuan-yu Tseng, Doctor Benoit?"

Josslyn exchanged a look with Adam before responding. "Yes. Is he the one financing this operation?"

"All roads point to his involvement, but we've been having trouble making anything stick. He was supposedly in the air on his private plane on route from Asia to DC when you shot the video, but we have no way to confirm that." Shaw was back to hiding behind the steeple of his fingers. "We can't seem to get anyone close enough to eke out any evidence against him."

Adam didn't like the way Agent Shaw was eyeing Josslyn. For her part, Josslyn sat up a little taller.

"He offered to buy me dinner," she stated.

"Not happening," Adam said at the same time.

"I agree," the director added. "It's one thing to allow her to perform her work duties, but thrusting her into a covert role in your operation is totally out of the question."

"You're forgetting that I can decline protection at any time," she argued.

"Josslyn." Trevor placed a restraining hand on her shoulder. "Don't be ridiculous."

Shrugging off her friend's palm, she jumped to her feet. "We are so close to blowing this ring out of existence, Trevor. Think about how many more elephants will be lost if I *don't* help out. It's just dinner."

Adam shot from his chair. "Until it isn't!" He stalked over to her. "You said yourself these guys all used to deal in drugs and guns. It's too dangerous. Someone has already had his throat slit. And don't argue that he was a bad guy. We can't ensure your protection. No way, no how. You'll have to send one of your other Mouseketeers in to get the evidence because it's *not* going to be you."

They ended up facing one another like a pair of duelists, each one waiting for the other to make their move. Impatience radiated off of her. It crackled around them in the tense silence. Josslyn blinked slowly. Once. Then twice. She opened her mouth to speak, but surfer dude beat her to it.

"I agree," Trevor said, earning him a gold star in Adam's book. "It's too dangerous to meet with this guy. We'll have to find another way."

With a slap to his thighs, Agent Shaw rose from his chair. "Well, it was just an idea, anyway. We'll continue digging on our end. If anything comes up on that video, please contact me immediately, Director Worcester. Day or night. I'm usually in the office until seven each evening."

He headed for the exit.

"What about Ngoni?" Josslyn asked, her concern etched on her face.

Agent Shaw turned to address her. "We have someone on the inside keeping him safe. Don't worry. He's quite enjoying his time in the US."

"I want to see him," she insisted.

"I don't recommend it," Shaw replied. "A visit from you would attract too much attention. We don't know if whoever killed Mandla could be after the boy, as well. I'd rather keep his presence here in the US a secret for the time being. As I said, Ngoni is safe where he is."

"And what of Dr. Benoit's safety?" Adam added. "Mandla may be dead but how do we know the threat to her is over?"

"The poachers' fears of you finding something on the video recede with each passing day you don't announce it to the world," Agent Shaw said. "And so does the threat to Dr. Benoit's safety. If there ever was any real danger. I suspect this has more to do with a dispute among the poachers." He gestured to the FBI agents. "Between our informants here and in Africa, along with these gentlemen, we have them closely monitored now. If anything changes, we will, of course, alert you immediately."

With that, the three men left the room.

"Well that was reassuring," Trevor mumbled sarcastically. "Does anyone else feel like he was leaving out a chunk of the story?"

"That wasn't the best example of interagency coordination," the director agreed. "Let's get that video to Agent Segar right away. The sooner we find the missing clue, the sooner we'll be able to bargain for the rest of the story."

He and Trevor headed for the Cross Hall. Josslyn was still remarkably quiet, a fact that should have had the rest of them scared shitless, because a contemplative She-Devil was a dangerous She-Devil.

Adam couldn't stand her silence any longer. "Out with it."

She tilted her head at him.

He sighed. "Whatever scheme you're hashing out in that overactive brain of yours."

Shaking her head, she took a step closer. "Actually, I was thinking of us."

What the hell? Feeling almost as blindsided as he did when he'd been cracked in the head, Adam glanced around the room to make sure the others were gone. "There is no *us*."

She took another step closer so only inches separated them. "You stuck up for me. You called me by my honorific."

"Of course I did," he argued. "It's my job."

Josslyn shook her head. The warm smile was back on her lips—the one that made his chest tight. The gray eyes studying him so intently were full of wonder. "No. That's not part of your job. And neither was it part of your job to disappear immediately after we were rescued in Asia."

Adam's head had begun to pound. Just like a woman, she was reading too much into things.

"Since I know a little bit more about what my job entails, I'm going to have to disagree. Now if you'll excuse me, I need to help Ben figure out what's on that damn video."

Her hand on his arm stilled him. "Adam."

"Don't," he urged her. "You're making this more than what it is."

"Am I?"

He squeezed his eyelids shut hoping to lessen the throbbing that had begun behind his pupils. Her fingers slid up his arm to his shoulder.

"You're going to deny there's something between us?" she whispered.

"No." His eyes snapped open. "But it's just chemistry. And we're not ever acting on it because women like you *always* confuse it with something more."

Pulling his arm free, Adam turned on his heel and marched out of the room.

CHAPTER NINE

*E*XHALE BEFORE YOU *pull the trigger. Focus on the sights, not the target.*

The familiar refrain of his grandfather's gruff instructions echoed inside Adam's head whenever he aimed his rifle. It was good to hear the old man's voice again. It meant Adam was finally regaining that part of his mojo the pipe-wielding terrorist had knocked out of him. He blew out a slow, relaxing breath, willing his grandfather's pack-a-day timbre to drown out the other damn voice in his head.

You're going to deny there's something between us?

Closing one eye, Adam squeezed the trigger on the SR-16 rifle. The target at the edge of the range kicked back when the bullet sliced through the kill zone. He repeated the action nine more times until the target was a tattered shell waving frantically in the late October breeze.

Adam might have lost his mind, but he could still shoot, damn it. Next, he'd calibrate his scope. That ought to relax him enough that he could concentrate on solving the mystery of why Mandla and his cohorts would be stupid enough to go after someone as high profile as the sister-in-law of the president of the United States. Ben had been toying with the video all night, but still, no leads. The five tribesmen had nothing distinguishing about them.

Fortunately, Josslyn wasn't due at the zoo until later today. She was meeting a fellow zoologist at the University of Maryland for coffee. Using the excuse that he had physical therapy this morning, Adam sent Christine and another agent to chaperone.

Following PT—which was conveniently not with Kasey because he wasn't sure how he'd handle that situation right now—Adam hurried off to the Secret Service's Rowley Training Center in Laurel, Maryland. He needed time to blow off some steam at the rifle range. He'd meant what he'd said to Josslyn the day before. They could never act on the chemistry between them. Too bad his body was pissed off at his brain's decision.

As he left the range, he yanked off the noise-canceling earmuffs and shoved them in his jacket pocket.

"Nice shooting there, boss," one of his CAT teammates called. "I'm curious though, was the elephant porn you witnessed yesterday more of a turn-on than those ten perfect kill shots you just fired?"

The rest of the wiseasses on the range broke out in a chorus of laughter.

Adam dipped his sunglasses down on his nose to level a glare at their ringleader. "I suggest you forget the stand-up routine and work on your marksmanship," he warned. "Or you'll find yourself telling jokes while on foot patrol outside the Crown. We'll see who's laughing then."

The threat had the desired effect. The agents scrambled in multiple directions, most of them heading back to the range to shoot. Shoving his glasses back into place, he stalked toward the locker room, only to halt in his tracks when he came face-to-face with the woman he'd been trying to get out of his mind all morning. Adam whipped off his sunglasses, but it was no use, she was still there.

Dressed in houndstooth trousers, a tailored white blouse with a leather biker jacket over top and kickass high-heeled boots, Josslyn looked every bit as out of place at the shooting range as she was. She eyed the rifle in his hand with disdain. "As much as it pains me to admit it, you totally are a badass with that thing."

Adam didn't appreciate the compliment any more than he appreciated her sudden appearance in his sanctuary. "What the hell are you doing here?" he growled. He glanced over Josslyn's shoulder at a smirking Agent Groesch. "Have you lost your mind, Christine?"

The other agent shrugged. "We were driving by and she wanted to see the place."

"And you should have told her no."

"It's not our job to tell a protectee where they can and cannot go," Christine replied. "Unless there's a safety issue."

Adam opened his mouth to claim just that but Josslyn cut him off.

"Don't make a fool of yourself arguing that I'm not safe here surrounded by dozens of highly-skilled Secret Service agents."

She had him by the balls and damn it if both women didn't know it. Still, he'd take it up with Christine later.

He shot the other agent a look that said just that, but she only smiled smugly in response. The sound of dogs growling and barking immediately caught Josslyn's attention.

"Oh, the K-9s are trained here, too." She was already headed in the direction of the kennels. "I've always wanted to see how they do that."

A saner man would have let her trounce off toward the K-9 center, her BFF, Agent Groesch, tagging along behind her. But Adam clearly wasn't sane. At least not where this woman was concerned.

"You can't just waltz in there while they are teaching dogs to take down an intruder," he said as he charged after her.

"Surely they are behind a fence or something." But her voice trailed off as her attention veered in yet another direction. "What is *that*?"

Adam groaned as he followed her wide-eyed gaze to the shell of the airplane resting on a makeshift airstrip in the middle of a field. "Air Force One and a Half."

"No way!" She changed direction heading toward the hollowed-out replica of the presidential aircraft the Secret Service used for training exercises. "Can we go inside?"

Adam wrapped his fingers around her arm pulling her to a stop. "No."

"It's not like I haven't seen the real thing," she argued.

"Then you're not missing much." He tugged her over to a more secluded area on the path. Christine had committed a significant breach of security by disappearing somewhere between the shooting range and their present location, but Adam was glad for the opportunity to question Josslyn privately because no way had she just dropped into the training center on a whim.

"Let's cut the bullshit and tell me exactly what you're doing here," he demanded.

Josslyn shook his hand off. "Or what? You'll shoot me with that big powerful rifle of yours?"

Damn it. Adam was still carrying his SR-16. He didn't dare hand it off to anyone else. Snipers were a bit possessive about their tools of the trade. She smiled slyly as if she knew exactly how the mind of a sharpshooter worked.

"Fine," he relented. "Have your fun. Agent Groesch can take you on the grand tour, for all I care. I've got other things to do." Like get his head examined. "I'll see you at the zoo this afternoon."

"Wait!" This time it was her hand on his arm. "I came to tell you I'm not going to the zoo today."

Her words stopped Adam in his tracks. She'd been insistent to the point of belligerence that she be allowed to continue her work in person at the zoo each day. What had happened this morning to change that?

He shifted his rifle between their bodies forcing her to take a step back. "Let me guess, your coffee with a colleague wasn't to discuss the mating habits of elephants," he said.

Annoyance flashed in her gray eyes. Evidently, she didn't appreciate the way he could read her. "Dr. Young works with us at the GWC."

Adam's temples pounded. "Then whatever it is you're

planning, let Dr. Young handle it." He turned to walk away.

"He's a fifty-two-year-old Taiwanese professor who is tone deaf and doesn't care for opera."

He took the bait. "What does opera have to do with saving animals?"

An appreciative smile played at the corners of her mouth. She enjoyed toying with him. Adam nearly scoffed at her, but he suspected her story was about to take a turn he wasn't going to like.

"The opera is at the Kennedy Center this evening and there's a very exclusive cocktail party beforehand hosted by the ambassador from Zimbabwe. And you and I are invited."

Adam's aching head constricted at the thought of spending the evening in a dark, crowded concert hall listening to men and women wail.

"Not happening. Until we find out why Mandla was targeting you, you're only allowed to mix with the general population for work purposes."

Her smile all but disappeared. "The director has already agreed. Both Agent Shaw and the FBI said I'm no longer under any threat. And I want to go to the Kennedy Center tonight. And I need you to go as my date."

"Shaw and the FBI can't guarantee anything." He maneuvered them behind a giant oak tree. "You'd be a fool to go."

Adam probably should have taken a minute to think his response through because his words were like oil to fire.

Josslyn was far from a fool. Her posture grew rigid as she jabbed a finger into his chest. "As Agent Groesch has already pointed out, you can't tell me where I can and cannot go. I've agreed to allow the director to order a sweep of the area beforehand, but I *am* going to this opera tonight. If you'd rather not pose as my date, then I'll find another agent."

The headache that had been threatening squeezed his brain like a boa constrictor. Like hell was he allowing anyone else to act as her date. She'd likely slip off to do God knew what at the first opportunity with the poor idiot none the wiser. He backed her up against the tree trunk before placing his rifle next to them. Adam needed both hands free to strangle her. Instead, his fingers gently cupped her chin.

"You need me to act as your date because Tseng will be there," he accused. "Isn't that right?"

Josslyn swallowed roughly against his thumbs, but her eyes met his in challenge. "Yes. Given how serious we played things the other night, he'll wonder why I'm with someone else."

Adam rested his aching temple against the tree trunk just above her shoulder, trying unsuccessfully to suppress the potent want this woman seemed to dredge up within him. He inhaled the scent of her coconut shampoo before a strand of her hair got tangled in the stubble of his day-old beard. Her hands found their way beneath his jacket, warming a path up his chest.

"You could have explained all this at the White House

later."

"I know," she murmured against his neck. "But you've been working long hours, pushing yourself when you're still not 100 percent. I wanted to give you time to rest before tonight."

Her intuitiveness surprised him. Her concern cut him to the quick. Adam jerked his head back to glare at her. "That's not how this works, Josslyn. My job is to keep *you* safe for however many hours it takes in a day. You, on the other hand, have no responsibilities for me. Our relationship only goes one way."

The biting response he expected never came. Instead, her face softened and her hands wrapped around his neck. "You're such a silly man," she whispered as she reeled him in closer.

And, like a lamb to slaughter, he went.

A low growl escaped the back of his throat when her lips met his. With the merest brush of a kiss, she'd completely short-circuited his brain, making Adam lose all sense of propriety. The sounds of the shooting range, the dogs barking, and the cars practicing pit maneuvers on the track a mile away receded into the background until all that was left was the pounding of their hearts and their breathy moans. Josslyn's fingers dug into his scalp while her tongue darted in and out of his mouth. He could taste her need, her want, and it was a heady feeling. Adam responded by cupping her ass, bringing her into contact with the part of him that wanted to dart in and out inside of her. She reacted by playfully nipping at his lip before smoothing over it with her tongue. His entire body ached at the wicked thoughts of where he wanted her tongue to go next.

His pulse pounding, Adam left her mouth to trace the smooth column of her neck with his lips. "Siren," he breathed. "That's going to be your code name because you make me crazy." He dragged his teeth along the tender skin along her collarbone. He'd meant to punish her but the lusty sound of her sigh was hurting him more.

Her fingers had somehow left his skull to slide into the waistband of his pants where she was tracing lazy circles against his skin. "This wouldn't be so crazy if we were somewhere private."

Reluctantly, Adam reined in his runaway libido, lifting his lips from her neck and his hands from her sweet ass. He took a step back before pulling her fingers from his body. She had the decency not to protest, but the sexy pout of her kiss-swollen lips said it all.

"I told you last night. There isn't going to be anything more between us."

"And, yet, here you are kissing me," she pointed out.

"Because you started it. Again." He grabbed his rifle and gestured with his chin for her to head back down the path in front of him. "Don't expect a repeat performance tonight."

She glanced back over her shoulder at him but wisely kept that luscious mouth of hers shut. Likely she was going through all the tricks in her arsenal to ensure there was no truth to his last statement. He'd be ready for her, though. Adam only hoped his will was stronger than the She-

Devil's.

◈

DRESSED IN A long, sequined Vera Wang gown she'd worn to one of her brother-in-law's inaugural events, Josslyn tried to appear casual as she and Adam strolled beneath the flags hanging high above the Kennedy Center's Hall of Nations. She did her best to ignore the murmurs among the guests, treating them all to the fake smile she'd perfected while on the campaign trail. One of the perks to her brother-in-law being president was that she could crash these diplomatic events on a whim. The First Lady's chief of staff didn't even bat an eyelash when Josslyn requested she secure an invite for her on such short notice. Judging by the stir within the crowd already, the other operagoers weren't as indifferent, however.

As she suspected, Dr. Young had no difficulty translating the note this morning. Unfortunately, the scribbles on the Post-it were random and didn't seem to form a cohesive missive. The date and time for the gala were included along with a shopping list of some sort. And then there was Christian Sumner's name in bold black letters. Josslyn's stomach rolled at the thought he could be using his position to aid animal traffickers. As much as she disliked the little jerk, she had difficulty picturing him abusing his power in such a way. But she couldn't know for sure without following up, which meant tonight's foray into the Washington DC social scene couldn't be helped.

Josslyn hated all things politics. Christian, on the other hand, would be in his element as the highest-ranking diplomat invited to sit in the presidential box. As a de facto member of the First Family, she was rungs above him on the social ladder, however. He wouldn't appreciate sharing the spotlight with her. And he would appreciate it less when she showed up with the Tower of Testosterone as her date. That thought was enough to make her smile genuine.

Many of the women they passed were casting covetous glances at the man on her arm. She had to agree Adam looked delicious decked out in a tuxedo. His transition from Jason Bourne to James Bond allowed him to blend in with the crowd effortlessly. Still, judging by the way the other women were checking him out, the clothes he wore did nothing to diminish his potent sex appeal. The hint of a five-o'clock shadow he'd left along his jaw added a little danger to his evening clothes. Except for the tightness around his mouth, he appeared to be oblivious to his admirers.

Josslyn nodded and smiled in greeting to those attempting to catch her attention, but she didn't stop to engage anyone in conversation. These people were her sister's contemporaries, not hers. She was only here to figure out the connection between Tseng and Christian. Josslyn was as much an imposter tonight as Adam.

"Are we in a race for our seats?" Adam's low voice rumbled next to her ear. "Because I'm pretty sure there's plenty of room in the presidential box."

He was right. Nerves had her racing like a gazelle

through the lushly carpeted Grand Foyer where the cocktail party was being held. Slowing her gait, she guided him past the eight-foot-tall bronze bust of John F. Kennedy. Josslyn snared a flute of champagne from a passing waiter, downing half its contents in one gulp.

"Did you know that this statue almost got dumped into the bottom of the ocean?" she babbled.

Adam arched an eyebrow at her.

"It's true. When the sculptor was bringing it to the Kennedy Center, the plane carrying it across the Atlantic had mechanical trouble. It was during a thunderstorm. Lightning struck the nose of the plane. But, as you can see, it made it safe and sound." The words poured out of her mouth breathlessly. Her heart was racing as though she were in that plane.

"And so will you," Adam said softly. "That's why I'm here. Now breathe."

Following his instructions, she exhaled a deep cleansing breath. "I'm not comfortable at these types of events," she admitted.

Adam shot her an amused look. "You don't say?" He led her over to a quiet spot in front of the windows overlooking the Potomac.

"I tend to say the wrong things, which leads to embarrassing my family." She guzzled the rest of the glass.

"In that case, champagne might not be such a wise idea." He took the empty flute from her hand and placed it on a table behind them.

Josslyn blew out another steadying breath. "Serving on

the president's detail, you're used to these types of events. I've only been in this building on one other occasion and that was when my dad was surgeon general. I'm sure you've been here hundreds of times."

"Only if you count the basement and the rooftop," he noted mildly. "You forget this isn't my regular gig either."

"That's right." She smiled up at him, some of the tension easing from her shoulders.

"But in those instances, it was my job to keep the bad guys away. I was successful because I knew what I was looking for ahead of time." He moved a few inches closer so no one could overhear their conversation. "It would be helpful—not mention less stressful—if you told me what you are up to tonight."

As much as she wanted to confide in someone, Josslyn deliberately hadn't mentioned the sticky note to anyone yet. She wanted to know for herself just how far up this ring had influence. She suspected her brother-in-law would not be happy to learn someone in his administration could be involved. Especially if it were Christian Sumner, one of his trusted campaign coordinators. "Would it ease your stress level if I told you I was just following a hunch?"

Adam groaned quietly. "In my experience, your *hunches* tend to lead to military rescue."

She was about to object, but they were interrupted by none other than Christian Sumner himself.

"Josslyn, what a surprise."

Christian's tone conveyed he was not surprised at all. She was correct in thinking he would be annoyed she was stealing his thunder. He leaned in to kiss her on the cheek—a show for the crowd, no doubt. Adam tensed at her back.

"I see you're no longer grounded after your little incident in Zimbabwe earlier this week. Or did you sneak out of the White House now that Conrad and Harriett are away?"

She wasn't sure which delighted Christian more, his accidentally on purpose letting it slip that she'd once again involved herself in an "incident," or his letting the crowd know he was on a first-name basis with the president and First Lady. Too bad neither delighted Josslyn.

Adam slipped his arm through hers. "Darling, aren't you going to introduce us?"

Pleasure surged through her at the look on Christian's face. Not only that, but her good parts were doing somersaults at the possessive way Adam drawled the word "darling."

"Um, of course," she stammered. "This is Christian Sumner, the Undersecretary of State for Africa. Christian this is—"

"Adam, her father's nurse," Adam interjected before extending his hand with what felt like a dare.

Christian eyed Adam carefully before finally shaking his hand. Josslyn made a mental note to call her sister and fill her in before Christian began to ask questions. As it was, the little turd was already drawing false conclusions.

"Worming your way into all aspects of the First Family's life, I see," he said to Adam, his voice laced with disgust. "Don't get too used to it though. Josslyn is quite fickle where men are concerned."

She was grateful for the arm Adam snaked around her waist, drawing her in closer because her hand was twitching to slap the Undersecretary of State for Africa. While it might not be cause for a military rescue, it would be another scandal to add to her long list of previous embarrassments.

"Since you're no longer under White House arrest"— Christian was the only one to laugh at his pun—"I will expect you at the Elephant Trails on Saturday evening for Boo at the Zoo. I've lined up several corporate representatives the State Department would like to get involved in helping with Africa's infrastructure. My wife has another commitment that evening and she won't be accompanying me. But, I'm sure my guests would enjoy a few fun facts about the elephants from the president's sister-in-law."

Josslyn opened her mouth before thinking better of it and quickly closing it again. Christian wasn't going to give her orders. But if she could do something to help the elephants and the natives, she would. Even it meant kowtowing to the little monster.

Fortunately, a passerby called out to Christian and he was off without another word.

"Asshole," Adam muttered. "Remind me not to sit too close to him or he might find himself falling off the balcony."

Josslyn relaxed into his embrace. "Not if I push him first."

They shared a knowing smile for a long moment before they were brought back to reality by the chimes announcing the show was about to begin. Adam indicated she should precede him up the stairs to the commander in chief's private entrance to the balcony.

"Doolittle to the owner's box," she heard him murmur.

She eyed him sharply. He wasn't wearing his comm device in his ear in order to maintain his role as her date.

"Talking to yourself again?"

He took her elbow and guided her down the narrow hallway. "Nope. Just keeping Ben apprised of our location."

"Ben is here?" An unsettling feeling danced up her spine as she realized he'd been talking to someone named Ben the other night when they were in the China Room at the White House.

"Nope. He's in his lab. But he's got eyes on all the entrances and exits."

"Do those eyes extend to the White House, too?"

"Of course," he responded.

"*All* the rooms?"

A slow, taunting grin spread over his face. "What do you think?"

Her cheeks burned. "Tell me this Ben guy isn't some perv watching me shower?" she managed to choke out.

"Well, he is a bit of—" Adam winced as he cupped a hand over his ear. "Okay! The guy's a freaking Boy Scout. He'd like you to know he'd never invade your privacy like that."

"Oh, I'm just supposed to take your word?"

"The cameras in your bedroom turn off when you enter. The rooms are monitored using body heat sensors to detect when an unauthorized person enters the room while you're in it." He winced again. "Stop that. I'll tell her. Ben said you're welcome to come see the CCTV center for yourself if that will make you more comfortable."

While not completely mollified, Josslyn did feel a sense of relief. Adam had never lied to her before. Nor had he taken advantage of any situation involving her, in spite of her insistence that he should. Ben sounded like he might be another one of the good guys. Still, she'd be dressing in the dark for the duration of her stay.

With a nod to the marine guard, they were admitted into the anteroom at the back of the box. Two waiters stood at the ready. Christian ushered in a group of dignitaries and lobbyists, introducing them to Josslyn almost as an afterthought. Most had ties to Africa in one way or another. She was disappointed that none of those interests were in conservation and animal preservation, however. Josslyn made a mental note to discuss this with her brother-in-law when he returned. She doubted any of the men present would take her views on the issues seriously. One of the wives of a lobbyist for a tractor company began to chat Josslyn up, gushing profusely about her dress. Josslyn was certain that, seconds after the curtain rose, the woman would be texting the Reliable Source at *The Washington Post* to rat her out for wearing the same gown more than once. If Josslyn needed an excuse to hate politics, she was living it.

The lights in the ornate Lobmeyr crystal chandelier overhead flickered and the guests in the box milled around anxiously. Adam leaned in. Her good parts did another somersault when his breath fanned her ear.

"As the only member of the First Family in attendance, you get to select your seat first."

She couldn't help the triumphant smile that formed on her lips. "Touché for me."

Settling into the center seat, she patted the chair beside her for Adam. Christian took the one on her other side.

"Won't your wife be joining us?" she taunted him. According to the little bit of Washington gossip, she'd listened to, Christian and his new bride were rarely seen together in public.

"She is stuck in a business meeting," he responded crisply. "She'll be here by the second act."

The curtain came up and the orchestra burst into a loud concerto, preventing any further conversation. Josslyn's mother had been a huge fan of music—all types, including opera. She had passed that love on to her daughter. In her frequent travels around Africa, Josslyn was always enthralled by the role music played within the various native tribes. That shared enjoyment helped her to bond with so many of the people she encountered.

Relaxing into her seat, she tried to let the music of *Aida* wash over her, hoping the power of the score would settle her nerves. It didn't work. The story of an Ethiopian princess enslaved by Egyptians didn't seem to be holding

Christian's attention, either. The glare of his cell phone screen caught her attention several times during the first act. He was texting someone fast and furiously. She suspected it might be his absent wife, but she couldn't make out the words on the screen without being obvious.

Could he be texting Tseng?

If Tseng was attending the opera, he hadn't been invited to sit in the presidential box. Josslyn wasn't sure if she was disappointed or relieved. Maybe her hunch was way off. Somehow, she didn't think so. She'd need to sit tight and wait to see how the rest of the evening played out. With luck, it wouldn't end as tragically as the opera.

She glanced over at Adam. His expressionless gaze was directed at the stage. She couldn't tell if he was enthralled or asleep with his eyes open. Almost as if he was aware of being watched, the corners of his mouth turned up in a sexy grin. He leaned over to whisper in her ear.

"Bored already?"

Josslyn snapped her attention back to the stage. She was bored. But he didn't have to know that.

When the lights came up for intermission, Christian sprang from his seat like a jack-in-the-box. "There are refreshments being served in the African Room." He indicated the exit. "Please, join me."

Josslyn rather thought the whole point of being in the presidential box was to enjoy the lavish spread provided during intermission rather than having to navigate through the crowd to get to another room within the building. Christian was very definitely up to something. She bit back a grin at the realization that she'd been right all along. Hiking up her skirt, she moved to quickly follow the other guests. The sudden sensation of Adam's warm fingers wrapped around her bare arm stopped her in her tracks. But when she whirled around to face him, the sight of his pained expression kept her angry rebuke from leaving her mouth. Guilt stabbed her in the chest. When she'd dragged him into this, she'd never considered the effects of the music and lights on his lingering concussion.

She instinctively lifted her fingers to brush them along the hollow of his cheek. "You can't be enjoying this," she whispered.

He placed his palm over hers still resting against his skin. They stood that way for several long heartbeats, his eyes searching hers. "It just got a whole lot better."

The urge to kiss him right there on the balcony of the Kennedy Center Opera House, in full view of dozens of prying eyes—not to mention cell phone cameras—was strong. But she resisted. For his sake as much as her own. Adam was only doing his job. Sure, he was posing as her date tonight, and as much as Josslyn wanted to explore more with this man, it would be unfair to force him into a relationship via the tabloids.

She lifted fingers from his cheek. Adam intertwined them with his. She told herself it was because he wanted to continue the contact and not that he feared she'd take off after Christian.

"I take it you're not a fan of the opera," she said as they made their way into the anteroom.

"My tastes run more toward country-western music. At least that's in English."

His answer made her grin foolishly. "Well, I'm sure there are those who might argue that point."

The smile he gave her made her breath hitch.

"But," she said, "if we're being honest, I prefer the Grand Old Opry to this any day."

"And yet, here we are hanging out with an obnoxious twit you don't like, surrounded by a bunch of politicos who make you feel uncomfortable, while watching singers bellow and moan in Italian. All on the off chance Tseng would be here. Except he isn't." He tugged her closer to him. "What gives, Joss?"

She hated how much her body melted every time he called her by her childhood nickname. And she hated how perceptive he was. But she loved the feel of his body against hers. She leaned closer so she could toy with the buttons on his shirt.

"We don't know Tseng isn't here. For all we know, he might be at the reception in the African Room."

Adam lifted her chin with his fingers. Bottle-green eyes peered into hers. It took some effort to keep her knees from buckling, but she managed to meet his gaze head-on without blinking. He swore beneath his breath.

"Remind me never to play chicken with you," he mumbled as he tugged her toward the stairs leading to the Grand Foyer.

She could think of any number of games she'd like to play with Special Agent Adam Lockett, but since he was going along with her plan, she decided to save that conversation for a later time. Preferably when they were in private.

They were quickly absorbed into the flow of people seeking refreshments. Adam tightened his hold on her as they made their way to the Hall of States corridor where the African Room was located. A crowd jammed the doorway but she could just make out Christian's voice rising among those guests in the room.

Despite her three-inch heels, Josslyn's view into the interior of the suite was blocked. "Is Tseng in there?" she asked Adam.

"Not that I can tell." He squeezed her hand. "But that doesn't mean anything. Cameras, Ben?"

Now why hadn't she thought of that? She looked up at Adam expectantly. A few anxious minutes later he shook his head. Disappointment weighed her shoulders down. The crowd surged around them when the chimes indicated the second act was about to begin.

Josslyn's heart wasn't into watching the second half of the opera. Nor did she want to subject Adam's tender head to any more than was necessary. She tugged him over against the wall out of the way of the wave of operagoers.

"We don't have to stay. I'd rather go home now," she announced when the crowd had thinned.

"Are you sure?" he surprised her by asking. "Just because Tseng wasn't in there doesn't mean he's not here."

"If he were here, he would have been in that room." At least that was what her gut was telling her. Too bad the Post-it note from Tseng's desk wasn't more specific.

"I just need to slip into the ladies' room before we go."

Before she'd even finished speaking, Agent Groesch materialized from out of nowhere.

"How do you do that?" Josslyn asked as both ladies entered the restroom. "And where do you hide your gun when you're wearing an evening gown?"

"In my purse." Agent Groesch lifted the hem of her evening gown to reveal a smart little pistol holstered at her ankle. "But I always have a spare here no matter what I'm wearing."

"Good to know."

"By the way, my sister's kids are very excited about the Boo at the Zoo this weekend," Agent Groesch said as they washed their hands. "Thanks so much for offering to get them tickets."

"My pleasure." Josslyn sincerely meant it.

While she didn't necessarily want Secret Service protection, she valued the service the men and women provided to their country. Their families sacrificed a lot. Anything Josslyn could do to reward that service and sacrifice, she did. "How old are her kids?"

The agent never got a chance to answer because suddenly a man wielding a lethal-looking blade was blocking the hallway leading to the Grand Foyer. As Agent Groesch shoved Josslyn behind her, another man appeared from the shadows, wrestling the knife-wielding assailant to the ground. The sound of metal scraping across the marble floor was followed by that of bone meeting bone. An instant later, the hallway was filled with a sea of security officers, led by Adam. It was over almost as quickly as it began.

"Is Doolittle secure?" Adam demanded, his gun poised at the two men being handcuffed.

"Affirmative," Agent Groesch responded as the security team led the two men away.

Josslyn gasped when she caught sight of the tattoos circling one of the men's neck. They were the insignia of the Nimba tribe. Adam must have seen it too because he swore violently.

"We're getting out of here," Adam announced as he wrapped his fingers around her arm. "Now."

Josslyn wasn't going to argue with him. His gun still drawn, he guided her toward the stairs leading to the basement garage. Out of the corner of her eye, Josslyn caught site of the man she'd been looking for slipping into the Asian Lounge directly across from the Africa Room.

"Adam," she whispered, dragging her feet to a halt. "Tseng is here."

"I don't care if Spiderman is here, we're leaving."

But Josslyn had already slipped from his hold and was headed to the door of the lounge.

"Damn it, Joss," Adam hissed, grabbing a firmer hold of her arm.

Before he could drag her off, she managed to push aside the curtain shielding the room's artifacts from view just in time to see Tseng slip into the arms of a waiting woman. The woman began kissing him passionately. Adam's breath fanned her neck as they both peered at the couple like two peeping toms. Tseng turned to press the woman up against the wall. Josslyn's stomach dropped. She had seen the woman before. Six months ago, in fact, when the Asian beauty had been exchanging wedding vows with Christian Sumner.

CHAPTER TEN

T HE CAR WAS at the stairwell doors when they stepped out into the chilly garage. Adam quickly shoved her inside, his own body following her through the same door. He spent the entire ride on his phone arguing with Agent Shaw while Josslyn wrestled with events of the previous few minutes. They arrived back at the White House ten minutes later.

"Shaw swears no one has left the house Mandla's brother is hiding out in. Not that I believe him. We need to check the ICE records to see how many members of this tribe are here in the country. And I need to see that video, Ben," Adam said into the air as he ushered her past the butler and into the Diplomatic Reception Room. "Meet us at the Crown."

Now that she had a better idea of what—or whom—to look for, Josslyn needed to look at the video, also. "I want to see it, too," she announced.

She expected Adam to dismiss her request, but he simply nodded, steering her toward the stairs.

"We'll be on the residence floor, Ben," he advised his friend.

Terrie, the head housekeeper, greeted them at the top

of the main staircase. "I'll make tea," she said after quickly sizing up their expressions. "And I'll bring the Tylenol."

Josslyn glanced over at Adam. He'd untied his bow tie and tugged open the top button of his shirt. His face was drawn and the dark circles were back beneath his eyes. She couldn't regret her doggedness to uncover the animal trafficking ring. And the men and women of the Secret Service would give their lives to protect the president of the United States. But between the concert and the scuffle in the hallway, she worried that perhaps she should be a bit more sensitive to those she dragged into her cause.

Fergus yapped at Adam from his doggie bed in the West Sitting Room. Before Josslyn could shush the animal, Adam was bending down scratching him behind the ear.

"How's your father?" he surprised her by asking.

She suspected he was trying to distract her. But she appreciated him asking nevertheless.

"Trapped back in his addled mind again," she replied softly.

As if someone had flicked a light switch, her father had morphed back into the man with no recollection of his second daughter. Rationally, Josslyn knew how the disease progressed. But that didn't make it hurt less. Not wanting Adam to see the tears threatening in her eyes, she wandered over to the half-moon window overlooking the Eisenhower Executive Office Building. "The odds of him having another good day are slim, but I can always hope."

"No matter where his mind is, he cares about you."

Stunned, she stared at his reflection in the window. His

attention was still focused on Fergus, who was flipped over on his back while Adam crouched down to rub his belly. Her heart did a little somersault at the scene. Just as she suspected all along, there was a sensitive man behind that sniper's rifle. She was sure he didn't show this side of himself to many people. Josslyn felt flattered to have a glimpse at this Adam. Knowing how he grew up, she was even more in awe of his tenderness toward others.

"What about your dad?" The words slipped out unbidden.

She suspected Adam had little contact with the man who'd been so cruel to him all those years ago. But knowing what she now did about his personality, she wondered how much it cost Adam to be estranged from his only living parent.

His fingers stilled briefly on the dog's belly. Fergus whimpered, flailing his legs to get Adam to keep worshiping him. The silence stretched between them as Adam gave in to the dog and resumed the petting. Josslyn assumed he would ignore her question until his quiet response shook her to the core.

"He's getting out."

Adam continued to pet the dog, but his flat voice and tense shoulders told her everything she needed to know. He was in more than just physical pain tonight. Her feet moved toward him, only to stop suddenly when she heard voices in the Center Hall. Trevor and another man strode toward them. Fergus yapped happily, likely assuming more belly rubbing was in his future.

"Are you okay?" Trevor asked, his good arm snaking around her shoulder and pulling her in close.

Josslyn drew in a pained breath. While she wanted to get to the bottom of the trafficking ring, she resented the interruption from her former lover. Adam's revelation suddenly seemed more important. She glanced over at him. He'd donned his usual stoic mask while he quietly spoke to the other man she assumed was Ben. The sandy-haired stranger looked as concerned about Adam as she was.

"When was the last time you rested that peewee brain of yours?" he teased.

"I've got his Tylenol right here." Terrie arrived carrying a tray laden with coffee, tea, cookies and the aforementioned pain reliever. She handed a bottle of water to Adam along with two pills from the bottle. "Take these or I'll rat you out to the director."

Adam looked as if he might argue before he tossed both pills into this mouth and chased them down with a swallow from the bottle of water.

"Oh, tell me Marin made these snickerdoodles." Ben grabbed two cookies off the tray. "Try one of these, Trevor. I guarantee they're better than anything you'll get down under."

Trevor made his way over to the cookies while Josslyn stole another glance at Adam. Fergus was circling his legs yapping for attention.

"Let's go, Fergus," Terrie said. "It's time for you to go out one last time before bed."

At the mention of the word "out," Fergus began trotting toward the stairs, Terrie following behind him.

"If you two are finished with your bedtime snack, maybe we can get a look at that video," Adam said.

Ben sheepishly took a seat on one of the sofas. He pulled a laptop out of his backpack and placed it on the coffee table in front of him and powered it up.

"Trevor and I have been in my lab poring over it since last night. Nothing jumps out." He looked up at Josslyn. His face was full of sexy boyish charm as he patted the sofa beside him. "Why don't you sit down here, Dr. Benoit. In my experience, a fresh pair of eyes always helps."

"Please, call me Josslyn," she said as she sat down beside him.

He winked at her behind the wire-frame glasses he placed on his nose. "Special Agent Bennett Segar at your service. But you just call me Ben."

"That's because there's nothing special about him," Adam grumbled before dropping down onto the sofa on Ben's other side.

"The ladies beg to differ, my friend." Ben tapped out a code on the keyboard and the screen came to life.

An unsettling chill came over Josslyn when the video popped up on the screen. She'd relived the moments in the bush numerous times in her dreams this week. Trevor had, too, she suspected. Reaching behind her to where the Australian stood peering over Ben's shoulder, she patted his hand.

"Watching this won't bother you?" she asked.

Ben chuckled beside her. "Don't worry about him.

He's had ample comfort from the ladies on my team."

Trevor gave her a cheeky grin when Josslyn snatched her hand back with a chagrined smile of her own. "I'll just bet."

"Can you zoom in?" Adam's tone was all business.

"Not without distorting the image," Ben replied. "This is as close as it gets. I'm running each individual's image through artificial intelligence databases, but so far, no hits."

Despite knowing what was coming, Josslyn jumped when the female elephant stumbled to the ground. She thought she heard a change in Adam's breathing, but other than that he gave no clue that the video affected him. He was studying the screen intently, likely looking for any of the tattooed men they'd seen over the past few days.

Josslyn was looking for someone else. She leaned in closer to the screen. Despite the warm weather that day, the tribesman wore batik scarves wrapped around their heads. Several were also sporting sunglasses. They were the same scruffy band she remembered, but, at the time, she hadn't noticed the great lengths they'd taken to avoid being identified. Following her hunch, she analyzed the heights and frames of those pictured. Three were average height, while one towered over the rest. She zeroed in on the shortest of the group.

She pointed to the screen. "Could that one be a woman?"

Trevor leaned in closer over her shoulder. Ben tapped the mouse and the video froze. He zoomed in on the individual she indicated. The image was distorted, but she could clearly make out his or her hand poised with a knife, ready to extract the female's tusk while the others were gesturing to the baby elephant. Josslyn dragged her sweaty palms along the sofa cushion. Knowing what followed in the video, she jumped to her feet and paced across the room.

Adam was beside her in less than two steps. "The woman with Tseng. You know her."

This was the tricky part. Josslyn didn't have any actual evidence to point them toward Christian's wife. But her gut was telling her not to ignore her being at the concert. Not to mention her make-out session with their chief suspect. Aside from the fact Christian was an annoying little turd, his family went way back with the president's family. Given that his wife was obviously cheating on him, what harm would it do to throw the woman under the bus?

"Not exactly. But I know her husband. In fact, you met him earlier this evening. She's married to Christian Sumner."

Adam blinked twice, seemingly to process the information.

"He was in Zimbabwe when we were there," she continued. "I never saw his wife, though. But Agent Shaw said one of the financiers of the ring was there that day. It could just as easily be her as anyone else."

Ben let out a low whistle from behind his computer screen. "According to Google, the woman is loaded. Josslyn's right, she could just as easily be financing the whole shebang herself."

"And having diplomatic immunity would give her much greater access to come and go as she pleases," Trevor added.

Adam was still staring at her intently.

"You saw for yourself she's involved with Tseng," she said softly. "It's not that farfetched a theory."

"No, it's not." He rubbed at his temple. "And if she knows you were in Africa that adds one more person to the potential pool of players who don't want you digging any deeper into this ring."

Josslyn wrapped her arms around her midsection trying to suppress a shiver.

"We need to figure out who's calling the shots here," he added. "And how the guy at the opera with the blade and other dude with the tattoos fit into all of this. Something tells me that wasn't just some random fight you stumbled upon."

"According to Christine, Metro PD took them to lock-up at the second district station." Ben pulled out his phone. "The director sent her over to follow up. Maybe she can fill in the blanks."

"You don't seriously think those guys were after *me* tonight?" Josslyn asked although, deep down, she suspected he was right.

"Until we can confirm otherwise, that's the scenario we are going with." Adam took a step closer. "I need you to promise me that you'll behave."

Josslyn bristled beneath his arrogant stare. "Be*have*?"

Trevor laughed behind her. "That's like asking the sun

to stop shining."

Josslyn didn't appreciate his words any more than Adam's. Her glare let both men know it.

"Christine may have something," Ben interjected. "I'm headed back to headquarters to see what I can flush out." He patted Trevor on the back. "I'll drop you at your hotel on the way over. Adam, I'll meet you back at home to compare notes."

✦

"BEHAVE?" JOSSLYN REPEATED.

Sensing Josslyn's impending eruption, Ben—better known as the brain of their trio—wisely executed a hasty retreat with the Australian in tow. But Adam couldn't regret his choice of words because Josslyn was a loose cannon where trouble was concerned. He did regret not taking a large step away from her, though, especially when she looked like she wanted to unman him and hand him his own nuts in a paper bag.

"Yes," he said, standing his ground. "*Behave.* As in listen to those of us in charge of keeping you safe. As in not taking any side trips into private offices or remote African watering holes or the *fucking hold of a Japanese whaling ship!*"

Josslyn's smokey eyes grew wide at his outburst. Adam's head pounded and he wondered if he'd finally lost his mind. One thing he never lost was his cool, though. *Ever.* But this woman seemed to bring out the worst in him. But it was his job to keep her safe, damn it.

Except, somehow, it had become more than that. How and when that had happened, he didn't know. But he needed to make her understand that her safety meant following the rules. His rules to be specific. Before he could finish reading her the riot act, however, she spun on the heel of her stiletto and marched away from him.

"Just where do you think you're going?"

"Apparently, the only place I can go without a security detail—to my room."

He stormed after her. "Doolittle to the Queens' Bedroom," he barked into his transmitter.

"Not that I have any real privacy in this place," she grumbled. "I'm surprised you haven't attached an ankle bracelet to me."

"Don't give me any ideas."

She charged into her suite. Before she could slam the door in his face, he stupidly followed her inside. He expected her anger—welcomed it, in fact. But it was the hurt reflected in her eyes that caused his lungs to seize up.

"Be sure and tell whoever is watching that the second body in the room is yours," she choked out. "I don't want the CAT team barging in here."

Neither did he. "Doolittle is secure for the night."

Adam kept his gaze locked with hers as he yanked the embedded transmitter from his ear. He slid the microphone from his shirt pocket and turned the unit off.

The air in the room seemed to crackle around them.

"You should go," she whispered.

"Yeah, I should."

Except he didn't.

Instead, he gently shut the door behind them, securing the lock as he did so. He shrugged out of his tuxedo jacket, draping it over a chair before carefully removing his firearm and holster. After setting them on top of his jacket, he prowled over to where Josslyn stood. His body had been tense since first catching sight of her in the clingy dress slit up to her thigh and the damn "do-me" heels she wore. She sucked in a ragged breath, but she kept her chin up. Her boldness turned him on as much as her sexy body.

Adam closed the distance between them, reaching up to cradle her face with his fingers. "I need you to understand why it's so important for me to keep you safe."

"Because it's your job?" she whispered.

His lips hovered above hers. "Something like that."

He teased the corner of her mouth with his lips. Josslyn's hands trailed up along his chest as her hips inched closer to his. Adam touched his lips to the other side of her mouth.

"I don't want to be a job to you, Adam," she murmured against his jaw.

That's all you ever can be. He ought to say the words out loud. He was damaged goods with a black hole where his heart should be. The beautiful, brash woman in his arms deserved so much more. But the part of his body that seemed to be doing all the thinking right now ignored his conscience, instead fusing his mouth with hers.

As it was, every time their lips touched, something ignited inside of Adam. *Need.* Potent and demanding. If he wasn't careful, it would consume him. *She* would consume him. And once she discovered he was really a shell of a man, she would walk away. Leaving him alone. Just like everyone else did.

For now, he'd just savor these stolen moments with her. Taking his time with the kiss, he kept it slow and sensual. His tongue parried with hers while his hands roamed her body. A sigh escaped the back of her throat when his hands skimmed along the soft skin of her back as he lowered the zipper of her dress. Seconds later, the sequins pooled at her feet leaving her standing before him adorned only in a pair of skimpy lace panties and, *hell, yeah*, a bra that tied up in a damn bow. He might have growled at the sight.

Josslyn chuckled softly while her hands fisted in his shirt, yanking it from the waistband of his pants. Her mouth fused with his at the same time as her fingers slid beneath the fabric of his briefs. He growled again trying to regain his control. Minutes later, Adam tore his lips from hers to blaze a path along her jaw.

"Joss," he breathed against her ear.

It came out more as a plea. A plea for one of them to regain their sanity. For one of them to tear their hands and mouth off the other and walk away. But this was the She-Devil. It went without saying she was reckless. And Adam . . . well, he was just a fool. His body was on a collision course and his mind was not going to talk him out of it.

As if sensing his inner turmoil, Josslyn captured his

mouth again in another searing kiss. Her nails scored the skin along his back, igniting waves of painful pleasure. Suddenly, they were flat on the bed, his body pressing hers into the mattress. She nipped at his lips, demanding he take their kiss deeper. But his mouth had other ideas.

He scraped his teeth along the sleek column of her neck while his hands became familiar with her body. She bucked beneath him when he dragged his fingers over the lace covering her pebbled nipples. Adam tugged at the tantalizing bow between her breasts, lingering a moment to carefully adjust the chain and medallion she wore so it was out of the way. Executing a move rivaling a circus contortionist, she squirmed out of her bra. He grinned when she tossed it aside.

"You're gonna need help with these," he murmured against the soft swell of her belly before rubbing his jaw along the edge of her panties. "Lift that smart little ass of yours."

She did as she was told and Adam dragged the lace down her legs. The musky scent of her made his balls draw up tight. He traced the muscles of her thighs, bypassing the spot he most wanted to delve his tongue into, settling for her belly button instead.

"Adam." She dug her fingers into his scalp. "You're overdressed."

He was. And parts of him were protesting fiercely. But he needed to maintain control. To let her know who was calling the shots here. Adam crawled up her body, seizing her wrists with his fingers and pinning her to the bed. She leveled a challenging stare at him. Ignoring it, he brushed his lips along the slope of her nose before capturing her mouth in a hot, demanding kiss. As he expected, she gave as good as she got, thrusting her tongue and her hips wildly beneath his onslaught. He continued to kiss her senseless until she was pliant and panting beneath him. Releasing her wrists, he slid back down to her breasts. The silver medal she wore was rakishly draped over one. Adam nudged it out of the way before flicking his tongue against her nipple.

Josslyn's lusty gasp shot to his groin. Ignoring his own wants, he slipped a finger inside of her. She was wet and oh, so tight. He swallowed roughly in an effort to retain control. Her hips pressed against his hand. Adam stroked her once, twice until she was panting again. He inserted another finger matching the rhythm of her rocking hips. Her fingers dug into his scalp again as the tension built within her body. Adam blew on her nipple before taking the nub firmly into his mouth. Seconds later, she shattered around his fingers, moaning his name like a prayer.

Adam's own body was strung so tightly, he could barely move. But he needed to get out of there before he did something stupid. Mustering up every bit of sheer will he possessed, he managed to untangle himself from her gorgeous body. Her gray eyes snapped open.

"Where are you going?"

To hell, probably. He swung his legs off the bed and stood. She tried to follow but her sated body was still sluggish.

"We're not done," she protested.

His body wanted to agree with her, but his brain was back in the driver's seat. Adam put some distance between them, stopping at the chair where he'd left his sidearm.

"What just happened here?" she demanded. "Was this some sort of tease?"

Adam could feel as well as hear the hurt in her voice. He strapped his holster to his shoulder.

"This was me worshiping you." Not that she'd understand.

"No," she argued. "This was you trying to manipulate me. Again."

He added her ability to quickly size up a situation to the growing list of things about her that he found sexy. "I gave you what you wanted."

She pounded a fist on the bed. "That's not what I wanted."

Adam met her smoldering gaze with a steely one of his own. "I warned you the other night about wanting more than I can give."

His words stunned her into silence. With a nod, he turned to escape the room while he could. Just as he reached the door, one of her damn stilettos slammed into the wall next to his head. He glanced back at her.

"I'm going to the zoo tomorrow at nine," she announced. "With or without a detail."

He would have smiled at her, but given how good her aim was, he figured it was best to concede the point and get out while he could. "I'll see you at eight fifty, then."

Slipping back out into the East Sitting Room, he glanced around to ensure that no other agents were wandering about. The last thing he wanted was Josslyn's reputation being smeared because he'd been an idiot. He'd meant what he'd told her about worshiping her, though. Despite what she thought, pleasuring her had brought him satisfaction. She was a woman who deserved to be worshiped all the time. Too bad he couldn't be the one doing it.

"Oh good, you're still here."

Adam spun around to find Terrie, the head housekeeper, crossing the Center Hall.

"Did you lose something?" She held out a cell phone. "I found it by Fergus's bed. It must have fallen out of your pocket while you were petting him."

He patted the pockets of his jacket, but his phone wasn't there. "That would have been a problem later." He took the phone from the housekeeper's outstretched hand.

"Yes," she replied, eyeing him critically. "And you don't need any more problems right now."

Ignoring her cryptic remark, he nodded and headed for the main staircase.

"Agent Lockett," Terrie called after him.

This time it was his grandmother's voice playing out in his head. Her lessons on respect were ingrained. Adam halted and turned to face the housekeeper.

She inclined her head ever so slightly toward the Queens' Bedroom. "You take care, you hear?"

Message received. He nodded again before finally making his escape. Trotting down the stairs, he punched in the code to unlock his phone. Adam was surprised to see several messages from both Ben and Griffin. Not to mention four missed calls from an unknown number. He was just getting ready to call Ben back when his phone rang with the unidentified number again.

"Agent Lockett," he snapped.

There was a pause before he heard the words he'd been dreading for nearly two decades.

"Hello, Son."

CHAPTER ELEVEN

*E*IGHT FIFTY-ONE.

Adam was late. Josslyn tapped a finger against the granite countertop in exasperation. Her eyes were still gritty from lying awake all night thinking of ways to torture the loathsome man.

This was me worshiping you.

What an arrogant line. She wondered how many other women he'd shoveled that bull crap to. Josslyn didn't want to be worshiped. She was an independent woman who didn't need a man to complete her. The worst part was, the damn arrogant jerk thought he'd been doing her a favor.

"Are you okay?" Marin asked from across the small kitchen on the residence floor used by the First Family.

"Yeah, sure," Josslyn lied. The fact of the matter was, Adam hadn't done her any favors. All he'd accomplished last night was to stoke her desire for more.

More with him.

I can't give you what you need.

What in the heck did he think she needed? A flashy engagement ring like the one blinding her every time Marin flicked her wrist? No way! But another toe-curling orgasm wouldn't be out of order. Particularly if Adam was fully involved in the process. She must have sighed again because Marin was now scrutinizing her carefully.

"You haven't heard a word I've said," the chef complained.

If Marin was still talking about the merits of pumpkin spice, Josslyn hadn't missed much. "I'm sorry. I'm just a little distracted."

Marin went back to rinsing a mixing bowl in the sink. "It's okay. I remember how aggravating it was when I couldn't move without a pair of Secret Service agents following me. I'd like to say you get used to it, but I doubt you ever do."

Director Worcester informed her earlier that last night's tattooed man was undocumented and would be deported. The man with the blade was being held on a weapons charge. Agent Shaw and his team were investigating further, but the consensus was she could venture out to the zoo today. Nevertheless, an additional layer of security had been added for her safety, not to mention her annoyance.

"I don't plan on getting used to it," Josslyn replied. "This is only temporary."

Marin's face broke out in a nauseatingly dreamy smile. "Of course, there's something to be said about having an alpha man keeping you safe."

I need you to understand why it's so important for me to keep you safe.

Adam's softly murmured words reverberated throughout her body. Josslyn didn't want to be kept safe. Or worshipped. She just wanted Adam—who was now five minutes late.

"Have you and Griffin set a date?" Josslyn decided a subject change was in order.

"New Year's Eve," Marin replied. "At my family's flagship hotel in New Orleans. We'd love to have you join us."

Josslyn toyed with the medallion she wore as she paced the small kitchen. Her sister, the First Lady, and Marin's mother were sorority sisters. Despite always being included in the two families' celebrations, Josslyn often felt she was on the outside looking in. As kind as Marin was, Josslyn knew a pity invite when she heard one.

"I'm sure it will be lovely," she told the chef. "But I have no idea where I'll be at New Year's."

She glanced over at the clock on the oven. Adam had two minutes or she was leaving without him. That would certainly show him that his little lesson from the night before was wasted on her.

Agent Groesch appeared at the doorway. "Are you ready, Dr. Benoit?"

Josslyn looked past the other woman, but there was no sign of Adam. "Where is he?" she demanded.

Marin and the agent exchanged a look.

"Agent Lockett is taking a personal day," Agent Groesch explained.

"He's *what?*"

Josslyn had spent a sleepless night, formulating arguments in her head. She had a laundry list of reasons his logic was faulty. He couldn't protect her from everything. And he couldn't hurt her if her heart wasn't engaged. They could have an adult relationship based on sex alone. She wasn't one of those clingy, demanding women looking for an MRS in front of her name. Far from it. The last thing she'd expected was him to chicken out and not make this a fair fight. But then another thought hit her. Maybe he didn't want a fight. Maybe he thought she wasn't worth the fight.

"I guess he isn't cut out for the rigors of a protective detail. He probably should just stick to shooting a gun," she choked out around the painful lump in her throat.

"Adam had a family issue come up suddenly." Marin's tone had grown decidedly chilly.

He's getting out.

She recalled the pain etched on Adam's face the evening before. Could his absence have something to do with his father? Her heart lurched in her chest. He was so obsessed with keeping her safe, but who was keeping Adam safe? Safe from the pain of coming face-to-face with a man he was supposed to love, but likely despised.

"You know, I think Agent Lockett has the right idea," she told Agent Groesch as a plan began to percolate in her head. "I think I'll take a personal day, myself. I've been meaning to catch up on some journal articles and I can do it here just as easily as I can at the zoo without having to tie up multiple teams of Secret Service agents."

Marin looked a bit suspicious while Agent Groesch looked disappointed.

"Don't worry." Josslyn patted the agent's arm. "I made sure you have tickets for your niece and nephews for Boo at the Zoo this weekend. We can send someone over to get them. Or you could go yourself. They're in the top drawer of my desk."

"I'll tell the director you're staying in for the day," Agent Groesch said, her sunny demeanor restored. "Once I dismiss the team, I can swing over and pick up the tickets and anything else you need."

Trying not to grin like a loon at how easily the agent took the bait, Josslyn replied, "Just the tickets. I've got everything else I need on my laptop."

When Agent Groesch left the kitchen, Josslyn turned to Marin. The pastry chef's fiancé was one of Adam's best friends. Surely, she knew where to find Adam.

"No," Marin proclaimed before Josslyn could open her mouth.

Josslyn's opinion of the other woman shot up several notches. Obviously, she was more intuitive than Agent Groesch. Her opinion would go up even higher if Marin would just give her the information she needed. "I haven't even asked you anything."

Marin made a very unladylike noise in the back of her throat. "The look on your face says it all. Ben already told us there was something going on between you and Adam."

"We're friends," Josslyn argued. "He's gotten me out of more than one tough situation."

The pastry chef scoffed again.

Josslyn persisted. "I know about his father."

Marin's mouth dropped open in surprise. "*We* didn't even know about his father until recently."

"Like I said, we're friends."

The other woman wrung a dish towel between her hands. "I don't know," Marin whispered. "Griff and Ben are really worried about him, though. And Adam hates to be in close spaces so I imagine he's miserable on the sailboat."

"He's on a sailboat?"

"It belongs to Ben." Marin sighed heavily. "Adam's father was able to track down the address to the townhouse and he's been camped out there since yesterday."

Adam had to be desperate to avoid the man if he was willing to confine himself to a night spent in the cabin of a sailboat.

"Please, Marin," she pleaded. "Take me to him."

"Adam would kill me if you showed up with half the Secret Service in tow," Marin argued. "Clearly there's a reason he's kept this part of his life private."

"I had planned to show up alone."

"Ditch your detail?" Marin glanced past Josslyn into the West Sitting Room before lowering her voice even more. "Are you crazy? What about the guys with tattoos and the knives who are after you?"

Josslyn rolled her eyes. "If they actually meant me any harm, they've had plenty of opportunities to do me in. I'm sure all of this can be explained away as one big coincidence."

"Yeah, well Griffin and his friends don't believe in coincidences," Marin argued. "It's one of the reasons the three of them are such good agents."

"If you don't take me, I'll sneak out on my own and search every marina in Washington until I find him," Josslyn declared.

Marin blinked several times rapidly. "Coming from you, that's probably not an idle threat." She pinched the bridge of her nose. "The fact that Adam told you about his father has to mean something."

Josslyn held her breath.

The other woman heaved a resigned sigh. "Griffin will be very angry with me."

"Something tells me you might have a way to smooth things over with him."

A blush broke out on Marin's cheeks. "As a matter of fact, I do."

"Then you'll take me?"

"Can you get to the chocolate shop in the basement without being noticed?"

Josslyn nodded.

"Meet me there in ten minutes," Marin instructed. "And, Josslyn, leave your phone in your room."

The meaning of her words dawned on Josslyn. "Damn. No wonder he didn't take me up on it when I suggested an ankle monitor."

◈

THE AUTUMN WEATHER was a bit brisker at the marina. But Adam preferred the chill of the breeze over the close confines of the *Seize the Day*. Even though Ben's boat was luxuriously equipped with enough gadgets to survive a sail around the world, Adam always went a little stir-crazy after an hour or so belowdecks. Had the temperature not dipped into the thirties last night, he might have slept outside. But Adam wouldn't give his father the satisfaction of freezing to death. He was made of sterner stuff. Ironically, that was the only thing he could credit his old man for passing on to him.

Adam's phone buzzed in his pocket. "Tell me he took the check and left," he demanded of Ben.

"If only it were that easy. Dude, I think he has some twelve-step forgiveness thing he needs to get off his chest."

Swearing violently, Adam carefully picked his way toward the bow of the boat. Maybe he'd just jump in and swim to freaking Bermuda.

"I just gave him a hundred thousand reasons that he doesn't need my forgiveness," he roared.

"Do you think it was wise to just give away your inheritance like that?" Ben asked. "I'm pretty sure your grandparents didn't want the money from their natural gas well going to him."

"If it keeps him way out of my life, it's worth every damn penny."

"Well, at least he's out of our place. Griffin got him a room at The Chevalier. One of the perks of marrying into a family of hoteliers."

"Still too close. I'm staying put here until he leaves town. That money will be burning a hole in his pocket by nightfall. He'll forget all about needing my forgiveness once he cashes that check."

Ben blew out a breath. "Something tells me he isn't going to give up that easily."

"Then Griff should have gotten me the damn suite at the hotel!"

"Okay, okay. Let's talk about something else. According to the arrest records, last night's guy with the tattoo lists an address in Bailey's Crossroads. His visa is expired, so ICE is holding him. But here's the kicker. The FBI already has that home staked out."

"Which means that's likely where the boy is." Adam took a swallow from his coffee as he tucked away that piece of information.

"Not only that," Ben went on. "But the guy works at the Zimbabwe embassy, which would give him access to a certain Mercedes van that tried to gun Doolittle down the other day."

"Yet another piece of intel Shaw didn't think to share with us."

"The guy with the blade isn't talking. He's also in the country illegally, which means someone with money and connections hired him." He could hear Ben furiously tapping on his keyboard. "Josslyn's friend Tseng would have the money. But the wife of the undersecretary for Africa has both the means and the influence. I want to spend some time digging into her background this morning."

"Do that. But keep whatever you find under your hat for now. I don't want Shaw or his team in on this yet. I certainly don't want Josslyn thinking she can do any more amateur detective work." He gazed at the Jefferson Memorial in the distance. "I want her kept safe and sound at the zoo."

"She's not at the zoo."

Adam froze in the middle of taking another sip of coffee. "What?"

"She stayed at the Crown today. Christine said she wanted to catch up on some journals or something. Josslyn didn't feel the need to dispatch a detail to the zoo to do something she could do at home."

Since when did the She-Devil do anything so mundane as reading journal articles? The muscles at the back of his neck began to constrict.

"And we know she's actually there?" he demanded.

More clicks of the keyboard. "The locator on her phone has her in her bedroom. She's on her computer as we speak."

He relaxed and finally took that swallow of his coffee.

"That's weird."

Only to nearly spit it back out. "What's weird?"

"Her phone and her computer are in her room, but according to the sensors, she's not."

Adam fired off a string of obscenities as he scrambled back to the stern of the sailboat. "Alert Christine. I'm on my way."

"Dude, she could just be visiting her father or walking the dog."

Except she wasn't.

Instead, she was standing on the dock getting ready to climb aboard Ben's boat.

His best friend's fiancée shot him a pitying look from behind Josslyn. "She was sneaking out either way." Marin shrugged. "I figured this was safer. But if you want her to leave, say the word. I'm pretty sure I can take her."

"Hey!" Josslyn quickly jumped on board, just out of Marin's reach.

Adam shook his head at Marin before locking gazes with Josslyn's smoky eyes.

"Call off Christine, Ben. Doolittle is safe and sound."

"She's there? Um, should I send reinforcements?"

"No. I've got this," he lied and clicked off his phone.

The fact of the matter was, he didn't "get" anything anymore. One knock to the head and it seemed his entire routine had been upset. Hell, his entire *life*. And at the heart of his disrupted existence was this woman.

"Well, I'll just leave you two alone." Marin's voice trailed off with the breeze.

It was a long moment before either one of them spoke.

"What are you doing here, Josslyn?"

The corners of her sassy mouth kicked up and she sashayed over to where he stood like a damn deer in the headlights. Inhaling a deep breath, she gripped the lapels of his jacket with her fingers and tugged his body against hers.

"I'm here to worship you." She breathed against the stubble lining his jaw.

Adam's breath stilled in his lungs at her declaration. All the blood rushed from his brain to his crotch when she nuzzled his chin. He needed to tell her to stop. That he wasn't worth anyone's worship, much less hers. He needed to tell her to go. That he wasn't one of her precious wild animals to be saved. He needed to tell her what scared him the most. That she of all people had the power to destroy him.

Instead, his hands fisted in her long silky hair and he tipped her face up. "You shouldn't be out here with me. It's too dangerous."

"Then, by all means, let's go inside," she murmured against his lips.

It was as if his body was moving in slow motion because she slipped out of his arms and into the cabin before he could manage to stop her.

"Joss," he uttered in vain. She was already stripping out of her coat by the time he reached the galley.

"You know, my mother was the only other person to call me that. I could never abide anyone else using that name for me." A soft bemused smile formed on her lips. "Except for you."

There was another one of those sucker punches to his lungs, robbing him of his breath.

"You shouldn't have come," he managed to choke out.

"You shouldn't be alone," she countered, slipping out of her shoes. "And you're overdressed. Again."

He hated the way his heart skipped a beat at her defiance. And her understanding. He couldn't shake the trance she held him in because he was shrugging out of his jacket instead of insisting she return to the Crown.

"I don't want to talk about my father or my damn feelings."

Josslyn snaked her hands up his chest. "Good. Because talking is the furthest thing from my mind right now."

She pressed her hips against his and whatever sanity he had left quickly evaporated. Adam crushed his mouth to hers and took what she was offering. Within an instant, they were a tangle of tongues and limbs with Josslyn trying to assert herself every chance she got. But Adam wasn't having any of that. She might have started it, but he was taking them to the finish line.

Without breaking contact, he eased her back to the wide berth at the bow of the boat. The triangularly shaped cabin was mostly bed surrounded by a sleek wooden shelf filled with photos and knickknacks from Ben's adventures. Two narrow transom windows lined the bow, giving the cabin an airy feel.

Guilt niggled at his conscience when he pushed her back onto the mattress. "Last chance to make a clean getaway." His body pinned her to the bed. "Because I told you before I can't give you what you want. I'll only be using you."

She wrapped her legs around his waist, arching her pelvis against his in challenge. "What makes you think I'm not using you, too, Bourne?"

The last of his control snapped at her words. His mouth and hands made short work of her clothing. Josslyn did her part by yanking his sweatshirt over his head. She let loose an excited hiss when her fingers came in contact with his bare skin. Adam was nearly done in when she unsnapped the fly of his jeans. He bent down to kiss the wicked smile off her face when she reached inside to stroke his length.

She struggled to get his jeans past his ass. Adam nearly chuckled at her frustration.

"The fact that I want you naked is no joking matter," she complained.

He moved to the edge of the bed to unlace his boots. She took advantage of the situation, kissing her way up his back.

"Those boots are ridiculous," she murmured against his ear. "Are they even from this century?"

"A soldier's boots are the most important part of his uniform." Adam paused with his hands on the well-worn heel.

Where had that bullshit come from?

His father used to say that to his mother every night as he polished his boots. Adam shook his head in an effort to clear the memories. He had a very willing, very naked woman in bed. There was no room on this boat—or in his life—for his father.

"Are you still with me?" Josslyn's arms circled his waist.

He let the boot drop to the ground and shucked off his jeans. Turning in her arms, he flipped Josslyn back down onto the bed. "I'm about to be with you in multiple ways," he promised as he crawled his way up her body.

She bit her lip at his words. Adam soothed it with his tongue.

"I'll try to make it good for you," he whispered against her mouth.

Josslyn dug her nails into his ass. "For someone who didn't want to talk, you're sure doing a lot of it."

He silenced her with another demanding kiss. Not surprisingly, she responded with equal intensity, wrestling for control until their bodies became slick from the exertion. His limbs hummed with tension in response to her feverish pants. He let her have her way, rolling on his back so she could straddle him. She bent down to touch his nose with hers. That ever-present medallion she wore slapping into his chin.

"Now I've got you where I want you," she teased as the cascade of her silky hair brushed along his shoulders.

The sight of her glorious breasts dangling above him was almost too much to endure, but Adam managed to keep his wits. No way was he relinquishing control. Wrapping his fingers around her waist, he shifted her ass back until his erection nudged against her. Her eyes went wide before she slid her lashes closed with a low moan.

"What were you saying?" he teased.

He swallowed his own moan when she slid back further so her heat closed in around his length. Adam was playing with fire and he knew it. Sitting up he bent her back over his arm.

"Adam," she pleaded when his mouth found her breast. "Please."

"Please, what?" He teased the nub with his tongue.

"Please don't make me beg," she cried.

He chuckled against her warm skin. "It might be too late for that."

She moved again so that he was poised at her entrance. "Condom," she panted.

Trailing his fingers along the shelf, Adam pulled protection out of the Rubik's cube container Ben kept them in. Josslyn snatched it from his hands and was already ripping the package open. The look of pure bliss on her face when she rolled the condom over him nearly had him coming right there.

"Damn it, woman," he growled before reaching for her hips.

With her fingers splayed against his chest, she pushed him back onto the mattress. Adam guided her down until he was poised at her slick entrance. Their gazes locked as she slowly took him in. Her breathing hitched when he began to trace little circles along the skin at her sides. And then she began to move. Her eyelids drifted closed and her shoulders rolled back as she rode him, slowly at first and then with a vigor that had him chanting wicked words of encouragement to her.

Tearing his hands from her skin, he skimmed a finger against the sensitive nub at her core. Her breathing became more frantic. She teased his nipples with her fingernails. Adam returned the favor by increasing the pressure with his finger. They each increased their rhythm, Josslyn riding him nearly to oblivion until she suddenly shattered around him. She let out a yell that sounded like it belonged in the jungle before slumping against him. Her muscles contracted around him nearly taking him over the edge with her. But he had other ideas.

Gripping her taut ass, he rolled them over and came up on his elbows to gaze down at her. She was gasping in lungsful of air through her kiss-swollen lips. Her hair was scattered across the pillows in a riotous mess. But, She-Devil that she was, she still went for the upper hand, clenching her muscles together around his erection.

"Told ya I was going to use you," she taunted.

Slowly, he pulled himself halfway out before thrusting home again. "My turn."

Josslyn arched into him, meeting his cadence with her hips. The breath sawed through her lungs once more when he increased the tempo. Adam could feel the release building within her again. She wrapped her arms and legs around him so they were skin to skin. Sweat beaded on his forehead. Adam was holding on by a thread, but he wanted to see the ecstasy on her face one more time. He wanted her to know he was still calling the shots. Josslyn cried out and bucked beneath him when he shifted his hips slightly. She came in a rush so incredibly erotic that with a single thrust of his own, Adam followed her over the edge.

Long moments passed with only the sounds of their uneven breathing and the slap of the water against the hull filling the berth. The mattress rocked in time with the tide. Josslyn's fingers gently stroked Adam's back. He could feel her heart beating against his. The intimacy was suddenly so profound, Adam's heart stuttered.

"You're welcome to use me anytime, Special Agent

Lockett," she whispered against his neck.

Which was exactly what he was afraid of. She'd want more. *Why not?* His subconscious argued. Sex with her was like a balm to his tattered soul, bringing the pieces of his messed-up life back together, even if only briefly. But that road led only to trouble. Josslyn would eventually want even more of him. And it was better to return to their proper roles before she figured out that there was nothing more of him to give.

His body protested when he rolled off her. "There won't be any more using. Today or any day after," he declared. "Get dressed. I'm taking you back to the Crown."

Josslyn eyed him solemnly for a long, charged moment before swinging her legs off the bed. "I never figured you to be a coward," she tossed the words over her shoulder, as she made her way to the lavatory, the dimples in her ass mocking him all the way.

CHAPTER TWELVE

"A DOZEN ELEPHANTS were found slaughtered along the border of the Zimbabwe National Animal Preserve last night," David solemnly reported later that day. "All of them had their tusks extracted."

"Isn't the point of an animal preserve to *preserve* the damn animals living there?" Trevor stomped around the East Sitting Room of the White House in disgust. "When did they become breeding grounds for freaking poachers?"

Josslyn stirred honey into her tea with a little more force than was necessary, half listening to her friend's rant. From the sofa beneath the room's landmark majestic fan window, she glanced over to where Agent Groesch stood just outside the door, her back ramrod straight and her gaze focused off in the distance. The agent had been circumspect since retrieving Josslyn from the marina earlier. But she hadn't let Josslyn out of her sight.

Adam, on the other hand, had no problem letting her out of his sight. In fact, he'd been in a hurry to do so. He'd handed her off to Agent Groesch with a terse warning that losing a protectee was grounds for dismissal. Without so much as a nod in Josslyn's direction, he'd disappeared back into the marina. She rationalized the unease she currently felt was guilt for putting Agent Groesch's career at risk.

Reminding herself she'd been using Adam as much as he had used her, she tamped down on the sharp twinge in her chest. His detachment couldn't hurt if she didn't let it. She'd only sought out Adam to comfort him. To distract him from the demons he was battling. The out-of-this-world sex they'd shared was simply her reward for being a compassionate person. If they were going to return to being friends without benefits, then that was his loss—the idiot. The unsettled feeling in the vicinity of her heart was simply indigestion from eating too many of Marin's cookies.

Nothing more.

The snapping of Trever's fingers refocused her runaway thoughts.

"I'm sorry." She turned to face the two men. "What were we talking about?"

Trevor studied her quizzically while David spoke.

"We were saying that we are no further along than we were two weeks ago when you first went to Africa. We have no idea who the suppliers are—"

"Except for their images on a video," Josslyn pointed out.

"Yeah, a video that tells us exactly nothing." Trevor dragged the fingers of his good hand through his hair. "Without Ngoni identifying who's who, all we have are theories. And all of those are circumstantial. Meanwhile, herds of elephants are being slaughtered while we sit here and sip tea."

"He's right," David agreed. "We need to connect the

dots. And quickly. There are rumors this ring is facilitating a major sale of tiger pelts and bones in Taiwan later this month."

"Then I guess that leaves us with only one option." Josslyn clasped her hands in front of her to keep them from trembling. "Dinner with Tseng."

Trevor froze in the center of the room. "You can't be serious?"

Josslyn strolled over to the door and quietly closed it. "We're running out of options to solve this. You heard what Agent Shaw said the other day. They can't seem to make anything stick to Tseng. I have the perfect opportunity. The man asked me out."

"The man is a freaking crime lord!"

She put her finger to her lips hoping to calm Trevor down before the entire White House discovered her plans. "We don't know that yet. But if it will make you happy, David and Lin will come with me. We can make it a double date."

"The Secret Service won't allow it." Trevor was beginning to sound like the tattletale from third grade.

Josslyn bristled. "The Secret Service doesn't make decisions for me. As far as they'll know, I'm going to dinner with friends."

Adam would be furious. But he'd apparently relinquished control over her detail to Agent Groesch for the time being. Besides, she didn't care what he thought. Her goal was to out the leaders of this animal trafficking ring, not to make the Tower of Testosterone happy. He'd made it very clear earlier that their relationship was of little concern to him. Josslyn pressed her medallion to her breastbone trying to subdue the persistent ache there.

"Set it up, David. The sooner, the better."

The words "before I change my mind" hung back in her throat. Not only that but the familiar adrenaline rush she always experienced when she was about to take on those who harmed animals wasn't as strong this time. She chalked it up to exhaustion. Josslyn hadn't been sleeping well since arriving back in Washington. She'd rest once she exposed this ring of monsters for what they were. And she'd do it without hiding behind the shield of a sexy special agent within the Secret Service.

"I'm going on the record as not agreeing with this plan," Trevor continued while David texted Tseng.

Josslyn stretched up on her toes to kiss him on the cheek. "Duly noted. If it makes you happy, I'll take Agent Groesch with me."

"It would make me happy if I went instead."

"You're an adorable dinner companion," Josslyn reassured him with a pat to the chest. "But from the way Tseng was leering at me the other night, I think he's more of a breast man."

"As long as all the man does is look."

"He can look all he wants," she said. "As long as he talks while he's ogling. Besides, based on what I observed last night, he's infatuated with another."

She wasn't sure why Christian's wife's betrayal disappointed her so, but it did.

"We're on," David announced, his eyes a bit owlish behind his wire frames.

"That was quick." Trevor looked as surprised as David. "When?"

"Tonight. Seven o'clock at La Plume."

The knot in Josslyn's chest shifted to her stomach. She told herself it was because she wasn't comfortable with deception, but in this situation, the ends justified the means.

"In that case, I'll go and inform Agent Groesch of my dinner plans."

She didn't bother mentioning to Trevor she planned to conveniently leave out the part about Tseng joining them. No doubt the director wouldn't allow her to go if he knew that. For the first time that day, Josslyn was relieved about Adam's absence. The stinger in her chest be damned.

◈

ADAM CHECKED HIS phone for what felt like the hundredth time. According to the bank, his father had yet to cash the check. He'd been so sure his old man would simply take the money and run. But then, when did his father ever do what was expected?

"Are you even listening to a word I've said?" Ben interrupted.

Griffin chuckled as he tossed the bone from a chicken wing into the basket at the center of the table. "I told him not to get involved with a protectee, but does he listen?

Hell, no."

"I wouldn't rib him too hard given the role your fiancée played in today's great escape." Ben grabbed a chicken wing for himself.

"Marin has already apologized profusely." Griffin's dimples formed quotation marks around his wicked smile. "If it helps, I plan on having a serious discussion with her this evening about the error of her ways."

"Great." Ben tossed the empty bone into the basket. "Everyone here is having sex except me. Probably because I'm working *my ass off* trying to figure out who is after Doolittle."

The three men were squeezed around the galley table aboard the *Seize the Day*. In spite of the beer and food, Adam was still feeling a little stir-crazy. Part of that was likely due to the image of Josslyn riding him like a warrior princess earlier. The fantasy-come-to-life kept playing on a loop behind his eyelids, fueling his body's strong desire to do it again. And again. With herculean effort, he yanked his thoughts back into the conversation at hand.

"Have you found anything connecting Sumner's wife to Tseng?"

Ben groaned. "Yet another guy who's getting lucky."

"Yeah, with another man's wife," Griffin added, his voice laced with disgust.

"There is no obvious connection," Ben continued. "Aside from them both being Taiwanese, I've got nothing. They don't even travel in the same circles. Her money is old and established. His money is a result of the recent technological explosion of the last twenty-five years, although there is evidence that the finances may be stretching a bit thin among the vast network of family members. She's a well-known socialite. Tseng, on the other hand, mostly keeps to himself."

"What about her and Sumner?" Adam was curious how the obnoxious undersecretary managed to snare any woman much less a wealthy socialite. "How did they end up together?"

"That one's easier to answer." Ben pulled up a gossip site on his computer. "They met last year when he was an attaché to the US Embassy in Taiwan. It was somewhat of a whirlwind relationship that caught everyone by surprise. They had wedding ceremonies both in Taiwan and here in Washington. It was quite the political and social statement."

"Any evidence that she travels with him?" Josslyn suspected Sumner's wife for some reason. Adam still hadn't figured out why. "Could she have been in Africa last week?"

Ben brought up another article. "According to this, she was in London attending the opening of the new Andrew Lloyd Weber show."

Adam studied the photo of Sumner's wife draped in diamonds and fur as she smiled for the camera. She was accompanied by a tall Asian man who was gazing at her adoringly. "Who's the guy with her?"

"A cousin, apparently. He's the CEO of the family's pharmaceutical company. The guy has a twin brother. The two of them are known within Singapore society as the

'Twin Towers,' a reference to their six-foot-seven height. She's rarely photographed without one of her family by her side."

Griffin sighed with disgust. "With the exception of her husband."

Both men turned to stare at him.

"What?" Griffin shrugged. "Marin hears things in the White House. Sumner's father is a big Hollywood producer. The rumor is she was only after Sumner so that her family could gain access to the entertainment industry."

Adam shook his head. "Wow, if Sumner wasn't such an asshat, I might feel sorry about his wife's extramarital activity."

Griffin toyed with his bottle of beer. "Kind of ballsy of her to hook up with the guy in such a public place. If Tseng doesn't run in those circles, why pick the Kennedy Center on the night of an opera?"

"The bigger question here is how Joss was so sure Tseng would be at the Kennedy Center last night," Adam wondered.

Griffin laughed out loud. "You probably should have asked her that while you were rocking the boat this morning."

Adam gave both his friends the one finger salute before checking his phone again.

"Maybe I should stare at your phone and you can stare at this video because after three days, I've got nothing." Ben blew out an exasperated sigh. "Whoever these tribesmen are—if, in fact, they are tribesmen—they went to a lot of trouble to conceal their identities. And since we debunked Doolittle's theory that one of the people on this video is Sumner's wife that only leaves more questions. The two who came after Doolittle needn't have bothered. There's nothing here to incriminate them."

"Maybe it's not the people in the video, but something else that's incriminating," Griffin said before munching on a piece of celery.

Ben slowly looked up from his laptop. "What did you say?"

"I said maybe you're looking at the wrong thing," Griffin repeated. "It might not be something they filmed at all. The video may be irrelevant."

"But Shaw was convinced it was the video that had Mandla and his tribesmen after Joss," Adam insisted.

Griffin snorted. "The guy works at Fish and Wildlife. Is that even a real investigative arm of the government?"

Ben began mumbling to himself as he pounded on the computer keyboard. "Or maybe that particular video is irrelevant. Which means we missed it."

As usual, Ben's brain was twenty steps ahead. Adam's chest began to squeeze. "What did we miss?"

"Doolittle said they were supposed to meet someone at the elephant's watering hole, right?" Ben asked.

"The kid. Ngoni." Adam edged closer to Ben so he had a better view of the computer screen. "He was going to tip them off on the members of his tribe who are suppliers to the trafficking ring."

"But what if the people Doolittle and her team encountered weren't the guys Ngoni was going to finger?"

The sailboat seemed to still in the water. An offhand remark Agent Shaw made replayed in Adam's head.

While you are working to protect the elephants, many of these tribes are fighting among themselves to protect their livelihood.

"You don't think those were Mandla's tribesmen in the bush that day?" Adam asked. "Maybe it was another gang poaching from the poachers? And Mandla's tribesman are after them now?"

Ben nodded his head. He was already scanning through the rearview camera video from when the Mercedes was chasing them earlier that week.

"Here!" He froze the video. "Look at that motorcycle. It was advancing on you, too."

Ben clicked through to several other angles he'd likely downloaded from private surveillance cameras in the area. He zoomed in on the intersection where the Mercedes initially tried to ram them.

"It's over there," Griffin pointed to a fuzzy black image of a motorcycle just inside the frame. "Coming at them from the other direction."

Adam's heart thundered. "We didn't even see it because we were fixated on the Mercedes. Were they working together?"

"I don't think so." Ben clicked on another image, this one from N Street. "See how the Mercedes veers in front of the motorcycle here? It's almost as if they're running interference."

"Are you suggesting that Mandla was trying to protect Joss?" Adam was having trouble making sense of Ben's theory. "Not harm her?"

Video from another angle documented the moment when the motorcycle abandoned whatever it was doing and skirted down Twenty-Second Street. The Mercedes suddenly veered off seconds later.

"This video isn't conclusive either way," Ben conceded. "But, correct me if I'm wrong, it was one of Mandla's tribesmen who stepped in to stop last night's attack."

Adam's head was beginning to throb.

Ben tapped the keys again. "You saw Mandla at the zoo. I never checked the video from that area for any motorcycles fitting this one's description."

The three men sat in a charged silence for several moments while Ben loaded videos from surveillance cameras within and around the zoo. They all jumped when a similar motorcycle zoomed onto the screen.

"Check the plates," Adam and Griffin ordered Ben at the same time.

Ben brought up a split screen showing the tags from the motorcycle on N Street and the one at the zoo. They were identical.

"Who owns that freaking bike?" Adam demanded.

"Holy shit." Ben's fingers stilled on the keyboard. "You are not going to believe this. It's registered to Sumner. It was purchased by his wife the week after they were married."

The three fell silent, all of them breathing heavily as if

they'd just run a foot race until Ben's fingers began pounding the keyboard again.

"What are the odds that bike was at the Kennedy Center last night?" he asked as he scanned through videotape.

Adam scrubbed a hand down his face. "None of this makes sense. Tseng wasn't the one who tried to jump Josslyn in the hallway."

Except he'd been close by.

"But you said the guy with the blade was wearing all black like this dude on the motorcycle?" Griffin pointed out.

"Yeah. And Shaw said Mandla's throat was slit. The guy with the blade looked to be proficient." Adam slid out of the banquette seat. "And I, for one, want answers. Shaw questioned both men last night. He claimed the fight had nothing to do with Josslyn, but it didn't look that way to me. And the fact that one of Mandla's tribesman was there makes me even more suspicious. My gut is telling me he knows more than he's saying."

"It's after six," Ben said.

"The other day, he made a point to mention he worked until seven most nights."

Griffin stood, too. "I'll drive. I have priority parking within three blocks of the White House."

"I'm headed back to my lab." Ben gathered up his computer. "I can search videos faster there. If our guy on the motorcycle shows up at the Kennedy Center, I'll let you know."

"I'll tell you one thing," Griffin said once they got to

his car. "The president won't be happy if Sumner is somehow involved in this. I served on Manning's detail while he was running for office. Sumner was one of his key advisors during the campaign. There was talk the guy was angling for more than just a political appointment. He wanted to officially become one of the family." Griffin glanced at Adam from the corner of his eye.

"The president's granddaughter is a little young," Adam said before the full meaning of what his friend was saying dawned on him. It was followed quickly by a chaser of white-hot jealousy. "You're shitting me? He wanted to marry Josslyn?"

"Yep. Followed her around like a sick puppy." Griffin headed for the Fourteenth Street Bridge.

Adam rubbed his aching temple. "No wonder things were tense between them last night." Then another thought hit him. "You don't think Josslyn is zeroing in on Sumner's wife because she's jealous, do you?"

Griffin laughed. "This is Doolittle we're talking about. I'm pretty sure she's happy he managed to get hitched to someone else. Although it would have been entertaining to watch her eat the man alive."

"She's not what the media makes her out to be."

Tourists and workers streamed out of the Smithsonian as Griffin drove across the Mall toward Pennsylvania Avenue. "Oh? Then she's not really headstrong and rash? Or a prima donna the press has made her out to be? How about a rebel?"

Adam leaned his head back against the seat back and

closed his eyes. He let out a beleaguered sigh. "She is all that." *And fearless and sensitive, not to mention smart as a whip. She cares about those in her orbit, both humans and animals. Hell, she earned a PhD studying love. And she'll stop at nothing to help others.* "But most of what you see portrayed in the media is an act. It's all part of the protective shell she wears around herself to keep from getting hurt."

Griffin made the left onto Constitution Avenue in silence. They stopped at a traffic light in front of the Ellipse. "You seem to know her well. Am I to conclude this isn't just a fling?"

Adam didn't bother voicing a denial. Griffin would know he was lying. The trouble was, as much as Adam wanted to quantify what was between him and Josslyn as a fling, it was more. At least, it could be more if he let it. Except if he allowed her to see all of him—really see him— she'd run to the farthest whaling outpost, never to return. She was right to call him a coward. But what she didn't understand was he was doing it for her own good.

"Marin said Josslyn knew about your dad," Griffin said quietly. The pain in his friend's voice made Adam's head ache even more. "She knew something so private you couldn't even tell your two closest friends. *Your brothers.* How does that happen?"

"It's complicated."

Griffin stepped on the gas as they pulled onto Virginia Avenue. "Damn it. This case is complicated. But your life doesn't have to be. Not when you have friends who can help sort things out. Do you think Ben and I are so shallow that we wouldn't like and respect you if we knew about your father? Or where he was?"

"No," Adam replied vehemently. He'd trusted his buddies with his life on more than one occasion. As to why he couldn't trust them with his deepest secret, well, as he said, it was complicated.

A trio of Metro Police cruisers, their lights flashing, took up most of the VIP parking in front of the Department of Interior. Griffin managed to squeeze into a spot next to one.

"Just so you know," Griffin said as he put the car in park. "I wanted to beat it out of you, but Ben suggested we wait you out. So that's what we'll do. If it takes until we're ninety and in diapers, we'll always be around to 'uncomplicate' your life."

With a lump the size of Rhode Island in his throat, Adam followed him out of the car. They wound their way around the medical examiner's van blocking the sidewalk.

"I wonder what this is all about," Griffin mused as they headed for the entrance to the building.

"Well, if it isn't my old friend Special Agent Keller." A white-haired gentleman called out as he was coming down the marble steps. "Why is it you always show up when I have an unusual murder to solve?"

Adam's senses went on alert. Clearly this wasn't a case of some ancient civil servant dying at his desk.

"Detective Gerkens." Griffin extended his hand to the police detective. "I'd say it's nice to see you again, but . . ."

The detective pumped Griffin's hand. "I saw in the paper you're marrying that chef of yours. I always liked her—even when you didn't. Never could make her for a murderer."

Griffin broke out in one those ridiculous grins he always wore when someone mentioned Marin. "Best case I ever got wrong."

"What's this about a murder?" Adam interjected before the two men started discussing china patterns. He needed to get inside to talk to Shaw.

The detective quickly assessed Adam.

"This is Special Agent Adam Lockett," Griffin offered. "He commands the counter assault team for the Secret Service." The detective whistled as Griffin continued. "Adam, this is Bill Gerkens, one of Metro's finest."

"If I'm the finest, why do I always get the complicated cases? One of the big mucky-mucks at Fish and Wildlife was returning to the building. He never made it through the front door. Poor guy was felled by a poison dart." The detective held up a plastic baggie with a handmade dart adorned with feathers. "Now that's not something we see every day here in the District of Columbia, much less the United States."

"Who?" Adam choked out. But his gut already knew what his brain had yet to confirm. "Who was murdered?"

Detective Gerkens consulted his notepad. "None other than the Director of Fish and Wildlife's International Affairs Division."

"Shaw!"

Adam was sprinting past Constitution Hall toward Seventeenth Street when Griffin caught up with him.

"Get in, you idiot," he yelled from his car window. "The Uniformed Division will sic the dogs on you if you go charging the gates to the Crown."

"I have to get to her," Adam panted as he jumped into the car. "Whatever this is, it's getting serious."

"I'll say," Griffin mumbled as he pulled into the West Wing parking lot.

The car had barely slowed before Adam jumped out and dashed through the security checkpoint at the West Wing. He climbed the stairs, two at a time, and jogged along the West Colonnade to the Palm Room adjoining the West Wing to the residence portion of the White House. Passing the kitchen, he climbed two flights of stairs to the residence floor. He sprinted toward the Queens' Bedroom where he nearly blindsided Terrie, the head housekeeper.

"Agent Lockett," she gasped. "Whatever is the matter?"

"Josslyn. Where is she?"

Terrie tried but failed to hide a conspiring look.

"Where. Is. She?"

The housekeeper huffed. "Josslyn went to dinner with friends."

The breath seized in Adam's lungs. "Which friends?"

"Her friend David and his fiancée, Lin."

Adam might have growled at the housekeeper.

She jerked her chin up. "I overheard them mention something about the other woman's cousin, I believe."

"Oh, hell, nah!" he shouted.

CHAPTER THIRTEEN

I F TSENG WANTED to be discreet about their dinner, he'd picked the wrong restaurant. Located in the historic Jefferson Hotel, La Plume was the destination spot for those who wanted to "see and be seen." In other words, the dining room was filled with the gossiping socialites and politicos Josslyn tried to avoid at all costs. Unfortunately, in the name of preserving the African elephant, she'd be forced to spend a second night in their company.

Heads turned like a bow wave as the maitre d' led them through the elegant gray and white dining room with its walls adorned with wallpaper depicting the estate and surrounding landscape of Thomas Jefferson's Monticello. Once they'd reached the back of the restaurant, he pushed aside heavy velvet drapes to reveal a round table with four chairs arranged snugly around it, all situated within a small enclosed patio. A beautiful sculpture fountain adorned one wall while the others featured three windows shuttered to the night. Tseng lounged in one of the French provincial chairs, his eyes already glassy.

Josslyn couldn't entirely revise her earlier thoughts. While their dinner would be private, the other guests had an unobstructed view of who was coming and going into the alcove. They'd have enough information to fuel a social media storm about her. She suppressed a shudder at the thought and soldiered on.

Before slipping behind the curtain, Josslyn noticed Agent Groesch was seated at a table nearby. The agent was clearly unhappy with the partition separating them. For that matter, so was Josslyn. Once again, she'd acted without thinking things through. She was grateful to have David and his fiancée with her. But, as much as she hated to admit it, she'd feel much better with Adam by her side. Not that she needed a loaded gun to protect her. It was just that Adam's presence would allow her to relax and concentrate on finding out exactly how Tseng fit into this puzzle.

Tseng didn't bother standing at their arrival. She wasn't sure if he was just arrogant or drunk. He indicated the chair to his left. As the maître d' pulled it out for her, she noticed Tseng had put her in the one spot at the table that was hemmed in by the others. Josslyn discreetly tried to come up with an exit strategy while she shrugged out of her cashmere wrap and draped it over the back of the chair. David seated Lin and then himself.

"Champagne," Tseng announced. "We are celebrating tonight."

"Very well," the maître d' replied. "I'll send the sommelier over right away."

Josslyn arched an eyebrow at their host. "What exactly are we celebrating?"

Tseng reached over and squeezed Lin's fingers. "The engagement of my beautiful cousin and your friend David."

While Lin smiled demurely at her cousin, David looked a bit sheepish. For the sake of their upcoming marriage, he hadn't mentioned his suspicions about Lin's cousin to his soon-to-be-wife. Once again, Josslyn was reminded how her efforts to expose the animal traffickers had a ripple effect to those around her.

"You've been celebrating our engagement for the past two months." Lin blushed. "Surely there is something else we can celebrate this evening?"

"Perhaps there will be." Tseng released Lin's hand to pick up his cocktail. He peered over the rim of the glass at Josslyn, a slow grin forming on his lips. "What do you think, Dr. Benoit?"

Josslyn was saved from responding to Tseng's cryptic remarks by the arrival of the sommelier. He presented a list of wines and champagnes to Tseng who promptly waved it off.

"You must go and see the wine cellar for yourself," Tseng told Lin. "It is spectacular. They have a table in there that seats sixteen. Perhaps, if you like it, we'll have Christmas there. You go, too, David. Take your time to pick out several bottles of champagne."

The sommelier's eyes lit up at the mention of multiple bottles of champagne. Lin jumped from her seat, an elated expression on her face. David glanced warily at Josslyn. She nodded slightly indicating he should go even though she didn't relish the idea of being left alone with Tseng. But she was here for answers. The sooner she got them, the better. Besides, Agent Groesch was within shouting distance.

The drapes fluttered closed at their departure. An awkward silence settled over the little room. Josslyn took a sip of her water before diving in, head first.

"The other night, you said we have mutual interests. I can't imagine what those could be aside from David."

"Aw, David. He isn't good enough for my cousin."

Josslyn's chin jerked up at his unexpected comment. "David adores her. And he is very successful in his career."

"What's not to adore about Lin? She's a very wealthy young woman." He waved his hand when Josslyn opened her mouth to defend her friend again. "But she claims to adore him, too. She will marry him because she always does what she wants. Lin is willful." He paused before taking another drink from his cocktail. "Much like you."

The only thing Josslyn was trying to will was the waiter to return. Or even better, David and Lin.

"Why were you in my office the other night?" Tseng uttered the question quietly, but his tone meant business.

"I told you—"

"You lied." Tseng's smile turned to a sneer. "The man with you that night is not your father's nurse. He is a Secret Service agent."

Josslyn leaned back against her chair quickly trying to come up with a viable story. "I don't like people to know I have a detail. It can be intimidating."

"Do you kiss all the members of your detail that way?"

Her cheeks burned. "They would reassign him if his

boss knew about what we were doing in your office," she improvised.

Tseng's eyes narrowed. Josslyn tried to appear as if she had nothing to hide.

"The media would love that information."

As threats went, Tseng's was a good one. But two could play at this game. And, as Adam pointed out, Josslyn was very good at the game of chicken.

"Then I guess I'll tell the authorities about the collection of illegal and endangered artifacts in your office," she countered.

"Finally, we get to our mutual interests."

She tamped down on the bile that rose in her throat. "My interest is to preserve those animals you so cavalierly display in your office," she snapped.

Tseng didn't flinch. "How badly do you want to preserve those animals?"

Her heart beat faster. *Finally!* She didn't dare reach for her water because she was pretty sure her hands would betray her by shaking. "If you've read anything about me, you know that I do whatever it takes."

"That's what I am counting on."

He wanted something from her. No surprise there. Most people did when they found out who her brother-in-law was. Well, Josslyn wanted something, too. She wanted names of suppliers. And she wasn't leaving without them.

"What's it going to cost me?" she asked.

Tseng's face relaxed into a smug smile. "I stand corrected. Lin is just spoiled. You are something else altogether."

"I'm passionate about what I believe in. And I don't believe innocent animals should be slaughtered simply for their tusks or pelts."

He waved a hand at her while he took another swig from his drink. "Relax, Dr. Benoit. I am not the bad guy here."

Josslyn balled her fingers into fists. *Was he kidding?*

"Everything in my office belonged to my late uncle," he continued. "I have no interest in collecting dead animals."

The air left her lungs in an audible whoosh. Was Tseng just toying with her in hopes of a political favor? If so, he was about to find out she didn't appreciate being used.

"If it's a contribution you'd like to make, I can give you the website for the GWC. You don't need a favor from me to do so. Make it a wedding gift for David and Lin." She rose from her seat. "If you'll excuse me, I don't think we have any additional 'mutual interests' to discuss."

"Sit down," he ordered.

She contemplated her options, including calling out to Agent Groesch. But in the end, she sat. Perhaps Tseng's late uncle had left notes.

"I trade in information, Dr. Benoit. You give me what I want and I'll give you the name and address of the person who's funding the animal traffickers."

Josslyn felt like she was on a roller coaster. "You haven't said what it is you want."

He rested his elbows on the table and leaned closer to her. "Five days from now, the animal trafficking ring will sell fourteen rare tigers to a broker in Taipei, Taiwan. Two of the tigers are pregnant. You can only guess what their future is."

The bile was back in Josslyn's throat.

"In four days, your brother-in-law is going to impose sanctions against several makers of microchips. This will hurt my family financially. Make sure that doesn't happen and I'll give you the information to stop the sale of the tigers."

Her mouth dropped open. "I have no influence with the president." Why did everyone assume the president listened to her? "It doesn't work that way. You have to ask me something that *I* can do." Josslyn reached for her wrap. She'd find another way to stop the sale of the tigers. At least they had a date and a location now.

Tseng manacled her wrist with his fingers. "It works the way I say it works," he snarled. "I told you I trade in information. And now, you have too much information about me. Make this happen or I'll share the list of names of all the advocates within the GWC to the animal traffickers. I'm sure they have an easy way of dealing with your activists. Secret Service protection or no."

She tried not to react to his second threat of the evening. But this one had the potential to put her colleagues in peril. It wasn't so easy playing chicken with her friends' lives.

Josslyn snatched her hand back. "If you want help with your sanctions so badly, why not ask your girlfriend's husband. It would be more believable coming from him."

The man in front of her grew eerily still.

"Don't look so shocked. I trade in information, also. And, so far, no one knows I saw you two together at the Kennedy Center last night," she lied.

Tseng shot to his feet and headed for the exit. "I would suggest you don't go down that path, Doctor Benoit. She is a formidable opponent. She isn't likely to let your friend Ngoni live."

Stunned by his parting words, Josslyn stared at the velvet curtain trying to gather her scattered wits.

Agent Groesch charged into the room, heaving a sigh of relief, presumably that Josslyn was still alive.

"You might have mentioned you were meeting that guy," the agent admonished her.

"Would you have let me come?"

"Of course not!"

"Then you know why I didn't mention it. But let's keep this between us girls," Josslyn insisted. "No need to let Agent Lockett know about my little dinner party."

"Oh, I think it might be too late for that."

A commotion in the dining room drew both women's attention. Josslyn's stomach flip-flopped at the sound of a familiar voice. *A very sexy familiar voice.* Only it didn't sound sexy at the moment. It sounded peeved.

The curtain was nearly yanked from the rings anchoring it to the ceiling when Adam stormed into the alcove. The maître d' was doing his best to stop him. Josslyn could only imagine the image he cut making his way, wild-eyed, through a room full of influential people, all of them dressed to impress, while Adam wore faded jeans, a weathered bomber jacket that concealed his weapon but did nothing to hide his broad shoulders, and those damn battered combat boots. The intense expression on his face softened for a brief moment when his eyes landed on Josslyn. But just as quickly his nostrils flared and he was gearing up for a serious tirade.

Josslyn held up a hand to stop him. "Don't say a word."

His hands went to his hips, but he thankfully kept quiet.

"And I'm going on the record right here and now to say Agent Groesch was unaware who I was meeting with until he exited the room a few moments ago. She is not at fault. So if you're going to be furious with anyone, be furious with me."

It was several tense moments before Adam spoke.

"Finished?"

She bit her lip. "Yes, it would seem that I am."

"Christine, could you wait outside with Griffin, please?"

Agent Groesch shot her a questioning look. Josslyn shrugged and nodded at the same time.

The curtain had barely closed before Adam advanced on her.

"Can we table this until we get back to the White House?" Josslyn backed up until she was against the wall. "There are too many ears and cell phones in the other room."

Adam's hands came up around her neck. "I plan on

doing this very quietly."

And then, much to her relief, he kissed her.

◈

HE COULDN'T SEEM to get enough of her. During the fifteen agonizing minutes between when he discovered her not at the Crown and when he arrived at The Jefferson, Adam swore he was going to strangle the infuriating woman at first sight. He ended up kissing her instead. Adam was so relieved to see her alive and behaving like her frustratingly annoying self he couldn't not kiss her. Best of all, she kissed him back.

"Pita," she breathed when he left her mouth to trail his lips along the elegant column of her neck. "You should probably just go with that code name because I am a pain in the ass."

"Mmm," he murmured against her skin. "Right now, I'm just happy that creep didn't touch you."

"Well . . ."

Adam's entire body tensed up. He held Josslyn at arm's length. "Tell me that bastard didn't lay a finger on you," he growled.

Josslyn's eyes grew wide. "He did grab my wrist," she whispered.

"Which one?"

She held up her right hand.

Releasing her shoulders, Adam gently caressed her wrist between his fingers, inspecting it for bruises. If Tseng had left a mark on her, he was a dead man.

"Does it hurt?"

She shook her head.

He lifted her hand to his mouth, skimming his lips over her wrist. Josslyn's sigh was full of lust.

"You shouldn't have been alone with him," Adam told her. "He's a dangerous guy."

"Yes, but he's not the one financing the animal trafficking ring." Josslyn suddenly became more agitated. "But he gave me some information we need to act on immediately. I need to talk to Shaw."

"Shaw is dead."

Josslyn swayed toward him, her hands landing on his chest. Adam covered them with his.

"When? How?"

"Earlier today." Adam drew in a deep breath knowing what he was about to reveal would alarm her even more. "He was killed with a poison dart. One with markings from the Nambi tribe."

"Ngoni!" she cried. "We have to get him to a safe place. She could hurt him next."

"She? Who is this she?" he demanded, but Josslyn was already trying to skirt around him out of the alcove.

"I'll fill you in on the way. We don't have time now."

Adam blocked her path. "Joss, you haven't told me everything you know. I can't help you or Ngoni or the damn elephants if you don't come clean. We have to work together."

Josslyn nodded. "I will. I promise." She smiled serenely

as she cupped his cheek with her palm. "We'll be a team. But first, we need to get Ngoni."

Grabbing his hand, she led Adam out of the alcove. He wasn't sure how he felt about the whole "team" notion, but if it got Josslyn to stop keeping secrets, he'd roll with it.

For now.

Griffin and Christine were waiting to escort them out. Of course, the dining room was packed with guests, all of them taking in their exit as if it were some sort of floor show that went with dinner. With her chin high, Josslyn strolled through the restaurant, her fingers laced firmly through Adam's. For the life of him, Adam didn't know why he wasn't more concerned about breaching protocol in such a public way. At the moment, his only care was she was safe. If he had to hold her hand to keep her that way, then he'd do that, too.

"Back to the Crown?" Griffin asked.

Adam sighed. Tactically, the plan should be to enclose Josslyn within the White House as quickly as possible. But she'd never go for it. Besides, the boy would be more likely to come with him if Josslyn was the one to do the asking. "We have someone to pick up first."

John was waiting at the curb with the SUV.

"Marin's in New Orleans tonight doing wedding stuff," Griffin said after Josslyn climbed into the back seat. "Why don't I circle back over to Interior to see what Detective Gerkens can tell me? I can fill Ben in as well."

"That would be great." Adam made his way to the other side. "For every piece we try to put into this puzzle, there seems to be two more that show up."

Griffin clapped him on the shoulder. "Be safe."

"We've got twenty minutes," Adam said once the car was in motion. "Start talking, Joss."

By the time they reached the working-class neighborhood in Bailey's Crossroads, Adam knew about the rogue Post-it note, Tseng's threats, and the man's warning about Sumner's wife.

"Tseng implied she would hurt Ngoni. It's all my fault he's involved in this. I have to make sure he's safe."

Somehow during the car ride, Josslyn's hand had found his again. Adam gave her fingers a quick squeeze. "We won't let anything happen to him." He didn't dare tell her Ben's theory that Mandla was somehow protecting her. She didn't need any more additional guilt weighing her down.

"Thank you," she whispered.

"This is it," Christine said from up front.

John stopped at the end of the block of small row houses, parking behind a silver sedan. Inside was one of the FBI agents who'd accompanied Shaw to the White House the other day. He stepped out of the car and met Adam beneath one of the two working streetlights on the block illuminating the worn sidewalk.

"How many people are in the house?"

"Hard to tell," the agent replied. "We've seen mostly women and children going in and out this evening. It looks pretty domestic. We sent word to our informant you're coming. She'll do her best to smooth things along."

"How do you want to play this?" Christine asked from

the front seat.

Adam leaned in through the car window. "I don't suppose Ngoni would just come with me, no questions asked?"

Josslyn shook her head. "Let me go get him. Agent Groesch can come with me."

His concussion had scrambled his brains because he was opening the car door for her. She shivered briefly in the night air before pulling her cashmere wrap over her shoulders.

"Our contact inside is Yolanda," the FBI agent explained to Josslyn. "She's a cousin of Mandla and Ngoni. From the sound of it, the women holding down the fort for this crew will be all too happy to have one less mouth to feed."

"Agent Groesch has her comm," Adam added. "She can alert us if necessary. Just go in and get the boy and come right back out."

"Got it."

With the ease of an operative going into an enemy encampment, Josslyn paraded along the dark street to the end of the block. She turned up the sidewalk to the door the agents indicated. Christine followed closely behind her. It took everything Adam had to keep his feet rooted to the ground. Especially when the door was opened and Josslyn and Christine disappeared inside.

"She'll be fine," the FBI agent beside him said. "According to our informant, the women are unarmed."

"I don't care. We give them five minutes and then I'm going in."

CHAPTER FOURTEEN

A WOMAN IN scrubs opened the door. Judging by the look she exchanged with Agent Groesch, they had found Yolanda. Josslyn's heart rate settled a little bit.

"I'm sorry to bother you so late in the evening," she explained for the benefit of anyone behind the door listening. "But I'm a friend of Ngoni's. I just wanted to stop by and check on him."

"It's almost his bath time." Yolanda was playing her role to the hilt.

"Please. It will only take a minute."

Yolanda relented, pulling the door open wide to admit them into the crowded townhouse. From the looks of it, several families were living there at once. Given what the agent said earlier, she was hopeful the tight living arrangements would play into her favor.

"Miss Josslyn!"

Ngoni charged down the stairs and wrapped his hands around her waist. Josslyn held him to her, saying a silent prayer the boy hadn't suffered from his involvement with the GWC. His chocolate eyes were shining when he looked up at her.

"You found me."

"I'm so glad I did." Josslyn ran her hand over his head. An audience of children ranging in age from toddler to teen was staring at them from the stairwell.

"Mandla was looking for you. Did he find you?"

Josslyn swallowed roughly. Mandla had found her alright. Fortunately, Adam had been around to prevent anything from happening. Still, her heart ached that Ngoni didn't know his brother was dead.

"No." Josslyn figured it was best to avoid the topic of Mandla right now. "My friends helped me find you. Do you remember I told you my sister lives here in Washington? And when you came to the United States, you were invited to visit her house? Would you like that?"

Ngoni anxiously glanced toward the kitchen where a trio of elderly women were sizing her up. "What if Mandla comes back?" he said.

"I'll leave my number," Josslyn reassured him. "He can call us." She clucked his chin. "My sister has a basketball hoop."

The boy whooped. "I'm definitely coming!" He raced up the stairs, presumably to grab his things.

The women in the kitchen remained silent. Josslyn pulled a business card from her purse and handed it to Yolanda. "He'll be fine," she said to the women in the kitchen. They didn't respond.

Ngoni flew back down the stairs, a Golden State Warriors backpack on his shoulder. Josslyn remembered the day Trevor gave it to the boy. It was part of their efforts to buy his trust. But that trust had come at a cruel price. His brother was dead. The family Ngoni thought he'd find in the United States was handing him off to strangers without a second thought.

Without even as so much as a glance to anyone else in the house, Ngoni slipped his hand into hers and headed to the door. "Do you think it's too late to play basketball tonight?"

"If so, the hoop will still be there when you wake up tomorrow," Josslyn chuckled.

"That was easy," she said to Agent Groesch once they'd made it outside.

"Too easy," the other woman murmured in disgust. "I mean what if we were sex traffickers?"

Josslyn tightened her grip on Ngoni's hand. He was safe now. She and Adam would protect him. They were a team. She smiled in relief as they stepped off the curb.

Seconds later, all hell broke loose.

The motorcycle came from nowhere, it's engine revving loudly in the night. Agent Groesch reached for her gun as she stepped in front of Josslyn and Ngoni. The driver—dressed in all black and wearing a black helmet—turned the motorcycle sharply taking Agent Groesch out at the legs. She cried out as she went down, the sound of her head hitting the pavement reverberating through the quiet neighborhood. A gunshot echoed and Josslyn realized there was a second motorcycle with a passenger on the back who was holding Adam and the FBI agents at bay. The gunmen stood between her and Adam.

"Give me the boy," the driver of the first motorcycle

ordered.

Josslyn pulled Ngoni behind her. "No!"

Adam swore loudly enough for them all to hear. The second driver fired another round toward the agents pinned at the end of the block. Agent Groesch groaned. The passenger on the second bike jumped off and kicked Agent Groesch's gun beneath a car.

"Give me the boy," the driver repeated.

Whoever they were, they wanted Ngoni alive. But they'd have to go through her to get him.

A shot pinged off the fender of one of the motorcycles. The distraction offered her enough opportunity to pull Ngoni behind a minivan parked at the curb. Another bullet ricocheted off the pavement as she yanked Agent Groesch to safety. With them out of the way, a volley of gunfire was exchanged. Josslyn was relieved to hear sirens close by. She motioned for Ngoni to slide beneath the van. She was just about to follow him when one of the motorcyclists rounded the corner and dragged Ngoni out by the leg.

"Leave him alone!" she shouted over the boy's shrieks.

The man clasped a hand over Ngoni's mouth and turned toward his accomplices. She heard Adam yell to the agents to hold their fire. The motorcycles revved their engines as the sirens drew closer. Agent Groesch groaned again. Josslyn glanced down at the woman sprawled out next to her.

I always have a spare here no matter what I'm wearing.

Josslyn reached beneath the other woman's pant leg and pulled out her revolver. The sound of the police sirens nearly drowned out the motorcycles. Ngoni shrieked again as the man dragged him toward one of the bikes. Cocking the gun, Josslyn stood up and aimed. A second later the man holding Ngoni went down in a heap on top of the boy. A line of police cruisers swerved into view. The motorcycles took off in different directions, both of them going airborne over curbs to escape.

"Don't move, Joss!" Adam yelled.

"Federal agents!" another voice shouted at the same time.

"Ngoni, stay down!" Josslyn called out. She could hear the boy's sobs against the pavement.

Agent Groesch was struggling to sit up just as Adam arrived. He glanced from Josslyn to his partner and back to Josslyn again, confusion in his eyes.

"Wait, you took that shot?"

Josslyn huffed as she handed him the gun and raced over to where the FBI agent was helping Ngoni off the ground.

"Nice shot," the agent remarked.

She quickly turned away from the shattered motorcycle helmet and the dead man wearing it and pulled a shaken Ngoni into her embrace. Adam was by her side in an instant.

"He's right. That was a remarkable shot. Especially for someone who considers all guns to be evil."

"They are evil." She rubbed Ngoni's back. "That doesn't mean I don't know how to use one. I grew up in Texas, for crying out loud. Daddy took me to the shooting range when I was nine."

Chaos reigned around them as the different sets of law enforcement tried to sort things out. But Adam simply stared at her, dumbfounded.

"What?"

"Do you have any idea how incredible you are?" he asked.

"Oh, please. Next, you'll be telling me that my being able to shoot turns you on."

The corners of his mouth turned up in a wolfish smile. "Actually, it does, kind of."

She should be appalled. Really. Instead, she was happy to be alive. Happy that Ngoni was safe and in her arms. And a little giddy to have Adam looking at her the way he was.

Agent Groesch chose that moment to wobble over to them. "What the hell just happened?"

◈

THE SECRETARY OF Homeland Security pinched the bridge of his nose. "Let me see if I can get this straight. Two Secret Service agents allowed the president's sister-in-law to walk into the middle of a damn shootout tonight. And during that time, a man was killed? Shot by Miss Benoit, no less!"

"Doctor," Adam mumbled from his seat in the corner of the West Wing's Roosevelt Room.

Director Worcester leveled a pointed look in Adam's direction. He'd told Adam that he was to speak only when spoken to, but it was no use. Adam's ass was already cooked. He'd thrown protocol to the wind more times than he could count on this detail. But at least he'd demand some respect for Josslyn who, reckless as she was, acted with the best intentions.

"I didn't catch that, Agent Lockett. What did you say?" the secretary asked tersely.

Adam sat up straight in the leather chair. "It's Doctor Benoit. She's not just the president's sister-in-law. She's a well-respected scientist who feels very strongly about her convictions. Tonight was no exception."

Director Worcester squirmed in his seat.

The secretary stood at the head of the conference table with his hands on his hips. Over his shoulder, the famous portrait of Teddy Roosevelt as a Rough Rider hung on the wall seemingly mocking him. "And am I to understand that tonight's fiasco was because *Doctor Benoit* wanted to babysit a young African boy who comes from a village known to harbor an international animal trafficking ring? The same boy who is currently enjoying milk and cookies upstairs?"

"That's correct, sir," Adam replied.

Although he doubted things were quite so rosy in the residence. Ngoni was a bit shaken up by the entire incident. Arriving at the White House hadn't eased his nerves any. The poor boy envisioned he'd be staying in a suburban home with a basketball hoop over the garage door, not a damn castle with a bowling alley, a movie theater, and helicopter pad along with an actual basketball court. It was a lot to take in for a boy who'd come from a small village in Zimbabwe.

We're not in Africa anymore, Toto.

"Any chance we can keep the details of this incident under wraps?" The president's chief of staff looked up from the pad he was doodling furiously on. "Particularly the part about Doolittle firing a kill shot?"

There was a feeling of awe bubbling up in Adam's chest again. He'd meant what he'd told Josslyn. She was incredible. Not because she could make that shot, but because she did it despite her hatred for anything gun related. Once again, she did what she had to do to make things right.

"It was dark out there." While the darkness worked to Josslyn's advantage, Adam was frustrated that he couldn't get a clear view of the license plates on the motorcycles. "We didn't even see who fired the gun. There's no way anyone else could."

The president's chief of staff nodded.

"And the boy?" the secretary asked. "What's his real significance?"

Given the violent attempt to kidnap Ngoni, Adam suspected that he was the key to whatever the hell was going on among the poachers. He kept his theories to himself, however. There were some loose ends he needed to discuss with Ben and Griff.

"We're still trying to figure that out," the director responded. "Unfortunately, Agent Shaw is no longer able to fill us in on the details."

A reverent silence settled over the windowless room for

a long moment.

"Then it's a good thing you have us," Griffin said as he and Ben hurried into the conference room. "Because we have details."

"I thought you left the service, Agent Keller?" the chief of staff groaned. The man was still trying to recover from the media fallout after a murdering art thief terrorized Marin and other members of the White House staff earlier that year.

"Just helping out a friend tonight." Griffin took a chair at the conference table, motioning for Adam to join him. "It's just as we thought. There is a second ring trying to take over the supply routes for the animal trafficking."

Ben sat down on Adam's other side and flipped open his laptop. "And from the looks of it, Shaw was using the dark web to pit the two against one another in hopes of flushing out both the suppliers and the financiers."

"Until someone figured it out and he ended up dead," Adam concluded.

"Exactly." Ben ran his finger over his mouse. "Now all we need to figure out is which one."

"That's a job for Metro PD and the FBI," the secretary stated. He glared at Adam. "Your job is to protect *Doctor* Benoit. That is all."

"With all due respect, sir, this case is very relevant to her protection. And the boy with her," Adam replied. "As you pointed out, we think he may be the link somehow."

"Not to mention that Doctor Benoit may have unintentionally gotten herself mixed up in the crossfire between these two rival factions," the director added.

"When does she *not* get herself mixed up in something dangerous?" The secretary exploded out of his chair.

"Nice to know my reputation precedes me."

The rest of the men shot from their seats, surprised to see Josslyn poised at the threshold of the room. She'd changed from her glamorous dinner outfit to gray yoga pants and a long salmon-colored sweater. Her hair was pulled back in a messy knot behind her head. Adam took a step toward her but the president's chief of staff beat him to her side.

"Josslyn, my dear, how are you?" He wrapped an arm around her shoulders.

"I'm fine, Uncle Charlie. More importantly, so is Ngoni." She flashed a charming smile at the secretary. "I'm glad I caught you, Mr. Secretary. I wasn't sure if I should speak with you or the secretary of state."

"That depends on the subject matter," the secretary replied.

"I want to arrange for political asylum for Ngoni. His brother, Mandla, brought him to the United States to escape the violence surrounding the poaching rings in Zimbabwe. Unfortunately, he was murdered this week. We can't send an eleven-year-old boy back to Africa alone and defenseless."

The secretary cleared his throat. "The process is rather complicated and tedious."

"I'm sure with the proper nudge from the White House things can be moved along." She smiled her princess grin at the chief of staff. "Isn't that right, Uncle Charlie?"

"We'll see what we can do." He patted her on the shoulder.

Adam bit back a groan. If the man thought he'd deflect Josslyn with the old "we'll see" technique, he had another think coming.

"Excellent," she said with another one of those ethereal smiles. "How is Agent Groesch, Director Worcester?"

"She's well," the director informed her. "She has a harder head than Agent Lockett because she didn't suffer a concussion."

"That's wonderful," she said softly before finally directing her gaze at Adam.

Her normally bright eyes were dim. Adam's breath hitched at the regret and sadness he saw reflected there. Those sassy lips of hers were swollen from where she'd been gnawing on them. She was suffering. No matter the circumstances, taking another life had affected her. Nothing could prepare anyone for it. There was a part of them that was never the same. Adam could relate.

"I'll be sticking to the White House for the time being." She uttered the words flatly. "No need for anyone else to get hurt on my account. Good night, gentlemen."

Amid a chorus of good nights, she turned on her heel and slipped out of the room. Adam rose to follow her before Griff's hand stopped him. His friend shook his head slightly.

"Well, that settles that," the secretary declared. He looked at Ben and Griffin. "Whatever it is you think you have, give it to Shaw's task force. If he was playing on the dark web, he had a damn good reason. And if he died as a result, that's all the more reason to let his team handle this from here on out. Our priority is to keep Doolittle safe and sound. That's it." He pulled on his jacket. "Now, if we've solved this nonsense, I'm headed home. My grandchildren are visiting this weekend for Boo at the Zoo. I need to get some sleep before my house turns into camp chaos."

With a beleaguered look at Director Worcester, the chief of staff followed the secretary out.

The director scrubbed a hand down his face. "Tell me she was serious about sticking close to home?"

"She's rattled," Adam guessed. "And likely filled with remorse."

"We'll do what we can for the boy." The director stood. "Especially if he keeps Doolittle within theCrown." He motioned to Ben's computer. "Do as the secretary says and get that over to the task force. This isn't our case."

"Director Worcester," Adam called after him.

"If you're asking for another personal day, Agent Lockett, I'm inclined to deny it given how this one turned out."

Adam swore under his breath. In the events of the past few hours, he'd completely forgotten about his father. He quashed the urge to check his phone. Right now, Josslyn needed his attention more.

"Is there someone in the administration I can talk to about sanctions on microchips?"

The director glared at Adam as if he'd sprouted a second head. "What the hell has that got to do with anything?"

"Tseng brought it up tonight. I'm just trying to figure out how it fits into all of this."

The director narrowed his eyes. "There's no need to figure any of it out. The secretary gave you three an order. I suggest you follow it."

Ben's fingers moved over his keyboard as soon as the director left the room.

"You think this is related?" Griffin asked.

Adam rubbed his aching temples. "Tseng wants Josslyn to have the president intervene on his company's behalf. In exchange, he says he'll give her the name of the person financing the ring of animal traffickers. If she doesn't help him out, he's threatened to publicize the names of all the GWC operatives."

"Does Tseng even have that information?" Griffin sounded as skeptical as Adam felt.

"He very likely does." Ben looked up from his computer. "According to Shaw's files, he was very involved with the GWC's covert operatives, using many of them to ferret out information on various traffickers."

That explained how the task forced leader knew so much about Josslyn's activities, Adam realized. "Shaw suspected Tseng. No way he'd give him that information. At least not willingly."

"Except Shaw might not have been the only one with that information. According to the locator on his cell phone, before he met up with the poison dart outside the Department Interior, Shaw was over at the State Department." Ben paused. "His calendar lists a meeting with Sumner."

Leaning back in his chair, Adam closed his eyes against the harsh glare of the lights. "All roads lead back to that guy."

"Or his wife," Griffin added. "Do you think she got hold of the list somehow and gave it to Tseng?"

"I got the impression she's ruthless. Tseng said Sumner's wife would harm Ngoni." Adam still felt guilty for not insisting Josslyn stay in the car. "Josslyn led them right to the boy."

"Ngoni is the key somehow," Griffin stated the obvious.

Adam snapped his eyes open and stood. "Then I guess it's time we find out how."

CHAPTER FIFTEEN

"THERE'S JUST SOMETHING about boys and dogs," Terrie remarked.

The housekeeper and Josslyn stood in the third floor Center Hall looking on as Fergus snuggled up against Ngoni on one of the big leather sofas in the White House solarium. SpongeBob SquarePants was arguing with Mr. Krabs on the television, the cartoon captivating the boy's attention.

"He seems to have settled in."

Terrie nodded. "One of the ushers will stay with him tonight." She patted Josslyn's shoulder. "Don't worry. Children are resilient. He'll be fine by morning."

"If not, there's always the basketball court to distract him." Josslyn stepped into the room and kissed the sleepy boy on the head. She nodded to the usher keeping watch on her way out.

"How is he?"

Adam's softly uttered question startled her. He was leaning a shoulder against one of the bookshelves lining the wall of the Center Hall. His posture looked relaxed, but he was studying her warily.

"Quiet." Definitely a word she'd never used to describe

Ngoni before.

He nodded. "How are you?"

She sighed deeply. "I don't think sleep will come as easily for me."

"Mmm." He stepped away from the wall, carefully treading his way over to her. "You have nothing to feel guilty about."

"Don't I?" Josslyn protested. "If I hadn't involved Ngoni in all of this in the first place, those men wouldn't have tried to kidnap him tonight. And I-I . . ." The words got stuck in her throat.

She didn't realize she was shivering until Adam's arms were around her.

"Hush." He gathered her against him. "You did what you had to do."

The steady rhythm of his heart beating against her cheek soothed her. "Does it ever go away? The guilt?"

"No."

His quickly voiced honest response surprised a laugh out of her. She smacked him playfully before lifting her face to his. "You might have lied and said yes."

His green eyes darkened. "The one thing I don't ever want to do is lie to you, Joss."

Josslyn shivered again, but this time it was for a very different reason. She traced a finger down his chest. "Then tell me this," she challenged. "Were you lying this morning when you said you didn't want me?"

Adam's arms tightened around her. He was silent for so long she thought he might never answer. "I've wanted you from the first moment I laid eyes on you."

It took everything she had not to bask in the triumph of his raspy admission. Biting back a grin, she took his hand in hers and wordlessly led him downstairs to the Queen's Bedroom.

"Boots," she commanded once he shut and locked the door behind them.

Chuckling softly, he plopped down on the chintz bench in front of the antique canopied bed and tugged at the laces. One by one, his boots dropped to the floor with a thud. He hiked an eyebrow at her as if to ask "What next?"

She stepped between his knees and his breathing stilled. Josslyn tugged her fingers through his hair before reaching down to carefully lift his holster over his head. Adam's eyes tracked her every move as she walked across the room to place his weapon on the secretary.

He stood abruptly, his smoldering gaze locked with hers. Josslyn's breath hitched when he reached behind his neck with one hand and yanked his T-shirt over his head.

"I don't want to be accused of being overdressed again," he said with a wry grin.

Josslyn gnawed on her lower lip watching him shuck his jeans. Wearing a pair of navy boxer briefs, he sat back down on the bench next to his neatly folded clothes.

"Come here," he urged.

She closed the gap between their bodies in two strides. Adam's hands wrapped around her bottom, pulling her toward him so his forehead pressed against her midriff. He inhaled deeply.

"I want to give you so much more than this, Joss," he whispered. "I want to give you the whole damn fairy tale. But, after tonight, you can understand the things that haunt me. Hell, you know the whole story of my tortured life." He gulped in a breath. "You called me a coward this morning and I am. But only because I don't want to hurt you. Ever. You deserve more. So much more."

Josslyn's breath froze in her chest at his words. She didn't need a fairy tale. She just needed him. Right now. Tonight.

And maybe tomorrow.

Climbing up on the bench, she straddled his waist with her thighs before touching her forehead to his. "Silly man," she whispered. "I don't need a prince. Just you. You're perfect just the way you are."

A groan escaped his chest before his lips slanted against hers. His kiss was reverent and filled with so much promise that Josslyn's insides clenched with yearning. She raked her fingers against his skull trying to urge him on, but he refused to relinquish control. His mouth left hers to explore the tender spot behind her ear while his hands slipped beneath her sweater.

"Adam." She panted when his wicked fingers brushed back and forth over her breast.

He murmured something against her skin, but he did nothing to increase his pace. Clearly his plan was to torment her slowly. At this rate, she'd be putty before they got to the good stuff. Josslyn thrust her hips against his.

Adam laughed. "I don't know what you're complaining

about. You're the one who's overdressed this time."

Josslyn scrambled off his lap to shed her clothing. Adam crossed his ankles and leaned back on his elbows to enjoy the show. Slowly, she shimmied out of her yoga pants, taking pleasure at the wicked intent shining in his eyes when she unclasped her bra and dropped it to the floor.

"Much better," he declared as he slowly got to his feet and stalked toward her.

This time when he kissed her, he invaded her mouth passionately leaving her no quarter to take charge. Not that Josslyn wanted to any longer. The sensation of being skin to skin with him lulled her into a mind-numbing sensual fog.

Her fingers traced the muscled landscape of his back before sliding beneath his boxer briefs to his ass. Adam's chest rumbled again at her touch. He deepened the kiss until it was his air that she breathed. She wasn't sure if her knees gave out, but somehow, she ended up in Adam's arms. He carried her over to the big bed. After gently depositing her on the mattress, he stepped out of his underwear and quickly covered her with his body. They were a tangle of limbs and sheets within a matter of seconds.

"You're enough for me," she whispered when he finally slipped inside of her.

Adam stilled at her words, his eyes shuttered. She squeezed around him eliciting another one of those deep groans. The sound reverberated through her body, spurring her on. She wrapped her legs around his waist.

"You can deny it all you want, but I'm not going to change my mind. You're enough for me," she repeated. "This is enough for me."

He shook his head. Josslyn answered him with a saucy grin. Swearing, he thrust within her, the movement making her sigh. Adam moved, again and again, setting a blinding pace, but she didn't dare back down. Because there was more than just ecstasy waiting for her at the end. She was sure of it. And she was determined to do all she could to make Adam sure of it, too.

He refused to acknowledge her statement. Instead, with the precision of a trained sharpshooter, Adam tortured her with his talented body. Twice he brought her to the edge only to pull back each time. When release finally slammed into her, her bones were nothing but liquid and her brain dust. Adam remained poised on his outstretched arms breathing hard as he stared down at her. That stoic expression remained fixed on his face.

He was holding back. *Still. Damn him.* She could see it in the tension gripping his body as he fought to keep his emotions in check. To not let this be about anything other than sex.

Summoning what was left of her strength, Josslyn wrapped her sated arms around his neck and pulled him down to her. He resisted only slightly.

She flicked her tongue against the salty skin of his neck. "At some point, you're going to have to pull the trigger and hope for the best, Bourne," she coaxed. "Be a little reckless and let yourself go. I'll catch you. And I promise you won't hurt me."

His breathing fractured and he mumbled something obscene before driving into her once again. Josslyn frantically tried to match his pace when another climax suddenly snuck up on her sending her over the edge with a startled cry. Just as quickly, Adam shook with his own release before finally collapsing down on top of her. Josslyn reveled in the warm weight of him pressing her into the mattress. It was several long heartbeats before they each found their breath.

"See," she whispered against his ear. "I'm still here."

She thought he might have chuckled. Or groaned. It was hard to tell. His spent body remained sprawled on top of her as she stroked her fingers along the knots of his spine. Then his lips began to trace a path along her collarbone to her neck while his hands were making little circles at her hips. Josslyn's skin began to heat again.

"Everybody always leaves me, Joss," he mumbled against her jaw.

His words cut her to the quick. She grabbed his chin with both hands.

"Look at to me," she ordered around the lump in her throat.

Adam's bottle-green eyes were cautious when they met hers. His chin was hard as if he was primed for a knockout punch.

"You can't live your life that way. Trust me. I know what it's like to be left, too." She swallowed roughly. "But

I'm not going anywhere, do you hear? Whatever this is between us, I want to see it through."

He gazed at her with eyes filled with wonder before taking her mouth in a deep, drugging kiss. Adam communicated his agreement with his mouth and his hands. Josslyn didn't bother complaining. Not when it meant they spent the next several hours worshipping each other.

◈

ADAM TRIED SEVERAL times to slip out of Josslyn's bed, but each time she had some other erotic trick up her sleeve to keep him beneath the sheets. She'd cast a spell on him; he did not doubt that because suddenly he saw nights and weeks and months in bed with this woman. Not only that but he imagined spending days with Josslyn by his side, as well. It would not be domestic bliss. Far from it with the She-Devil. But it would be a wild ride. The thought should terrify him.

Except it didn't.

And that terrified him even more.

"It's two in the morning," she complained as he sat on the bed and tugged on his boots. "What's the point of leaving now? You need to sleep."

He glanced over his shoulder to where she was sitting in the center of the mattress with a sheet wrapped around her midsection. His junk grew tight at the sight of her. She looked like a porn star with her riotous hair, kiss-swollen lips, and beard burns adorning her skin.

"If I stay, there won't be any sleeping."

She had the decency to blush. "Don't tell me you're going back to the marina? It's freezing outside."

Adam slipped his holster on. "There's a lounge for agents downstairs in the West Wing. I have a change of clothes there. There's also a sofa where I can grab some sleep."

"Good." She toyed with the medallion she wore around her neck. "At least I'll know you won't be far away."

He prowled back over to the bed. "Mmm. That way you can't get into too much trouble."

Josslyn stuck out her tongue at him. One look and Adam suddenly regretted getting dressed so quickly. He tugged at the chain in her hands instead. Her fingers slipped away allowing Adam to inspect the medallion. His thumb brushed over the worn silver.

"It's Saint Luke. The patron saint of physicians and surgeons," she said.

"Little known fact, he's also the patron saint of bachelors."

She laughed. "Figures you would know that."

Adam let the medallion drop against her flushed skin. "Which begs the question, why are you wearing it?"

"It was my father's." She threaded it through her fingers again. "Daddy gave it to me when my momma died. He said it was so I'd know he was always with me even when he couldn't be."

"Well, that sure beats the hell out of the black eye my

father gave me after my mother died."

He instantly regretted saying the words out loud when he saw the pity in her eyes.

She grabbed his hand when he went to turn away. "Adam—"

"Don't," he cut her off.

As usual, she ignored him. "You should talk to him. See if there is any peace to be made. Not for his sake, but for yours. Aren't you interested in some closure?"

No! The only thing Adam wanted was the man out of his life.

"I don't need closure," he said. "What I need is to find out why someone went to great lengths to kidnap that little boy tonight. And why someone murdered Shaw. And Mandla." He lifted her to her knees. "What I *need* is to figure this out so I can keep you safe."

The sheet covering her body slipped to the mattress when she looped her arms around his neck. One look at her luscious breasts and the blood left his brain for a one-way journey to his crotch.

"Don't think I don't realize how you changed the subject," she purred.

To save his sanity, Adam stepped out of her embrace and yanked the sheet back around her. "We need to find out what Ngoni knows. He might not even realize he knows anything. That's what happened to Marin. She unwittingly witnessed something she shouldn't have. That could be the case here."

She sank back on her heels. "I know. He was too raw

tonight to question. I haven't even told him about Mandla. Ngoni knew his brother was looking for me." She shook her head. "It seems strange that he would be excited that Mandla was after me."

Adam sat next to her on the bed. "Because we don't think Mandla was after you. We think he was protecting you."

"What?"

"Ben studied the videos. Both times Mandla showed up, there was also someone dressed in black riding a motorcycle. From the looks of it, Mandla was running interference. He was keeping whoever it was from getting near you."

"Why?" She put a hand to her throat. "Oh, my gosh, someone killed him. Was that because of me?"

He wound an arm over her shoulder and drew her in next to him. She sighed sadly before resting her cheek on his shoulder.

"Not because of you, no," he insisted. "Because of whatever is going on among the poachers more likely."

"There were motorcycles tonight. Do you think they're related?"

"Absolutely." He didn't bother mentioning who the bike belonged to.

"Tseng knows more than he is letting on."

Adam brushed a kiss over her hair. "We'll figure it out. In the meantime, I want you to stick to your promise to stay put."

"About that." She gnawed on her lower lip. "I forgot

about Christian's demand that I speak at Boo at the Zoo this weekend. As much as I hate kowtowing to him, I can get behind the idea of infrastructure support within the continent. Especially if it provides jobs that prevent the natives from having to poach to survive."

"Get someone else to do it," he commanded. The thought of letting Josslyn outside the confines of the Crown before this was all settled made his head pound.

To his amazement, she nodded. "You're right. It's too risky right now."

"Get some sleep. I have mandatory PT in the morning, but I'll be by right after that."

As she snuggled back beneath the covers, she shot him a saucy look that made him want to join her. Adam resisted though. He wanted to spare her the gossip that would ensue if he was found in her bed come morning. As it was, he'd be taking a chance with any of the staff that remained awake.

Closing the door to the Queens' Bedroom behind him, Adam tried to stealthily slip out of the residence. His progress was foiled by a little boy, however—one who didn't seem to like it one bit that Adam was sneaking out of Josslyn's bedroom.

"That's Miss Josslyn's room," Ngoni announced, a hint of a British accent tingeing his perfect English. "You shouldn't be in there."

The kid had that right. Adam glanced around to see if anyone else was within earshot, but no one else was around, not even whoever was supposed to be watching over Ngoni.

"Shouldn't you be asleep?" he asked.

"I got hungry."

Just then, one of the ushers appeared from the family kitchen, a bag of store-bought chocolate chip cookies in one hand and a glass of milk in the other.

"I asked you to stay upstairs," the usher said.

"I was looking for Miss Josslyn."

"She's asleep," Adam and the usher said at the same time.

Adam said a silent prayer of thanks that the boy hadn't come knocking on Josslyn's door a few moments earlier.

"I've got your snack." The usher gestured toward the stairs. "Let's go back up to the solarium and you can eat them up there."

Cookies were a good incentive for making a kid talk, Adam suddenly realized. If he was going to get any information out of Ngoni, now might be the perfect opportunity.

"You call those cookies? I know where they keep the good stuff. The homemade ones." He said a silent prayer Marin had done some baking before she left for New Orleans.

Ngoni eyed him shrewdly.

"She uses chunks of candy bars instead of those measly chips."

Adam knew he had him when the boy's face lit up at the promise of chocolate. "Come on." He led the way to the stairs where they went down one flight to the chief usher's office.

"I got this," Adam told the usher. "I'll bring him back here in fifteen minutes."

They cut through the family dining room to the pantry. Ngoni's eyes went wide at the number of dishes, glasses, and foodstuff stored there. While the child appeared to have been brought up in comfort by African standards, the sight of such abundance had to be overwhelming.

"This way." Adam indicated the spiral staircase leading up to the pastry kitchen located on the mezzanine level between the first and second floors of the residence.

Ngoni cocked his head to get a better view up the stairwell.

"It's safe," Adam reassured him. "I promise."

"You are Miss Josslyn's friend?"

Something like that.

"My name is Adam. I'm the agent in charge of keeping her safe."

The boy nodded in apparent approval. "Mandla is keeping her safe, too," he said as he carefully navigated the curved stairs.

They'd guessed correctly then. Now all Adam needed Ngoni to give up was the name of whomever Mandla was protecting Josslyn from. The boy hesitated on the landing when the low-ceiling pastry kitchen seemed to appear out of nowhere. He stared openmouthed at the glass display cases showcasing many of Marin's delicate sugar confections.

Adam tapped the boy on the shoulder before sliding

past him to the back of the long, narrow room. "That looks better than it tastes. The good stuff is back here." He dug into a cabinet in the corner and pulled out a plastic container. The aroma of peanut butter filled the room as soon as he unsnapped the lid.

Ngoni grinned.

"Told ya." Adam handed him two before taking two for himself. "They're not chocolate chip, but Chef Marin makes the best peanut butter cookies."

"My grandmother makes homemade peanut butter," Ngoni said around a mouthful of cookie. "I like it better than American peanut butter."

"Homemade is always better," Adam agreed. "My grandma made the best homemade apple butter."

He poured them each a glass of milk. Ngoni struggled to hold his cookie, his milk, and the backpack he carried. Adam reached over to help and the boy flinched. Ngoni shoved the backpack onto his shoulder.

"I wasn't trying to take it," Adam reassured him. "I was just trying to help."

The boy eyed him with caution as he nibbled on his cookie.

"Do you like basketball?" Adam jutted his chin toward the Golden State backpack.

Ngoni nodded.

"Me, too." Adam leaned a hip on one of the stools. "Who's your favorite player?"

"Steph Curry," the boy said without hesitation.

"Wise choice. He's a great baller and an even better

person."

"Our teacher saw him play once. He is from the American Peace Corps," Ngoni explained. "If we are quiet and get our school work done, he shows us videos on his tablet."

"That's my kind of teacher."

"I'm going to be a basketball player like Steph Curry one day." The boy lifted his shoulders to his ears presumably to appear taller.

Adam stifled a grin. "You don't say?"

"Mr. Trevor was going to help me come to America to practice if I told him the names of the men in my tribe who work for the poachers."

Leave it to Trevor to fill the kid's head with false promises in pursuit of information.

The boy's face fell. "But then Mr. Trevor got shot."

There was only one way Ngoni could know that. "You were there."

Guilt made the boy look away. "I want to go back to my room now."

Despite his frustration, Adam had no choice but to lead Ngoni back to the usher's office.

Before the boy and the usher disappeared up the stairs, however, Adam made one last-ditch effort to get more information out of him. "You said Mandla was protecting Miss Josslyn. It's my job to protect her, too. Can you tell me who he was protecting her from?"

"The tall man," Ngoni said matter-of-factly.

CHAPTER SIXTEEN

T HE SMELL OF coffee roused Adam from sleep. A scrap of paper stuck to his cheek when he lifted his head.

"Your desk is a mess," Adam complained as he swiped the offending note off his face.

Ben stood in the doorway of his domain, the cyber lab at the Secret Service headquarters building on H Street. His ever-present computer bag was slung over his shoulder and he held a super-sized coffee in his hand.

"It's not a mess to me," Ben said. "I know where everything is. At least I did until you messed it up with your big ol' Neanderthal noggin. What are you doing in my office, Adam? Tell me you didn't sleep here."

Adam glanced at the clock. Seven twenty. "Only for the last ninety minutes. I'll give you fifty bucks for that coffee."

"You don't have fifty bucks." Ben placed the coffee down on the desk. "You gave it to your dad remember?"

Shit. Adam pulled up the banking app on his phone. His father still hadn't cashed the check.

"Take it." Ben edged the cup over to Adam. "You look like you need it more than me. I repeat my earlier question. What are you doing here?"

"Looking for the tall man." Adam took a long pull

from the coffee.

One of the things Adam most appreciated about Ben was his friend's ability to comprehend something even with the slightest clue. The trait was what made Ben so incredible at his job.

"I've gone through that video a million times and I haven't been able to identify any of them with existing facial recognition software," Ben insisted, deftly picking up Adam's shift in conversation. "I even tried the program I'm developing, but I didn't get a hit on the tall guy or any of the others. Instead, I've been trying to identify them through the dark web. If I can figure out which faction Shaw was egging on to take over the Nimba tribe's poaching gig, maybe we can find the link to Tseng, Sumner's wife, and whoever killed Shaw."

"What if the tall man is right out in the open?" Adam turned the computer monitor, so it was facing Ben.

His jaw dropped when he glanced at the screen. "The Twin Towers. Damn."

"Double damn," Adam joked. The lack of sleep these past few days was making him punchy.

Ben took over the keyboard and began punching the keys. "We know where the one brother was when the video was shot. But how about the other?"

"From what I dug up, the pharmaceutical company their family owns also dabbles in a lot of homeopathic herbs and such."

"A lot of animals are poached for their medicinal properties. Definitely a reasonable connection." Ben blew out a breath. "Bingo."

"He was in Zimbabwe that day?"

"At least his passport was."

Adam scrubbed a hand down his face. "This whole case is coming together in dribs and drabs."

"This piece of the puzzle helps. It gives me a jumping-off point," Ben said. "By the way, this guy is currently in the US. He arrived five days ago."

"You wouldn't happen to know if he owns a motorcy-cle?"

Ben tapped the keyboard. "Four of them."

◈

AFTER SPENDING AN hour sending out frantic emails to GWC operatives alerting them of Tseng's threats, Josslyn tried to relax watching Ngoni shovel down another waffle. "We have to find Mandla," he said around a mouthful of food. "I promised him I wouldn't leave that house. I don't want him to be mad at me."

"He won't be mad at you," Josslyn tried to reassure him.

"Mandla doesn't want the tall man to find me. Or you."

"The tall man?"

Ngoni nodded.

Josslyn rubbed her temple. "I'm afraid I don't know who the tall man is."

"That's okay because I do." Adam walked into the family dining room looking as if he'd slept on a park bench.

Josslyn arched an eyebrow when Adam high-fived Ngoni.

"No cookies for breakfast?" Adam teased the boy.

"I didn't realize you two had formally met," Josslyn said.

Mischief shined in Adam's tired eyes when he finally looked over at her.

"We might have raided the pastry kitchen last night," he admitted as he slid into one of the dining chairs. "But don't tell Marin."

Her chest constricted at the matching sly smiles on both their faces. It was nice to finally see the playful side of the man. She loved how happy Adam looked. She loved everything about him.

She loved *him*.

The realization slammed into her like a runaway elephant, knocking the air from her lungs. Try as she might, she'd gone and fallen for the man. A man who was her polar opposite. Except he wasn't. Not really. And if last night had shown her anything, he could love her back. At least she hoped so.

"Joss?"

She refocused her attention on Adam and Ngoni, both of whom were looking at her funny.

"I thought you were going to get some sleep," she reprimanded him.

His expression softened. "Later. Right now, I want to talk to Ngoni about the tall man." He turned to the boy.

"He's trying to take over the poaching from your tribe, isn't he?"

Ngoni solemnly nodded at Adam. "He said he will give the men work."

"But there are people who don't want the tall man and his gang to take over."

Ngoni nodded again. "Mandla says the tall man will take our money."

"That day in the bush, when the tall man shot Trevor, what else did you see?"

Josslyn knotted her fingers in her lap trying not to convey her shock that Ngoni was in fact at the watering hole that day.

"He killed Adjoa." Tears welled in the boy's eyes.

"Mandla's wife?!" Josslyn sprang from her chair and rushed around the table to comfort Ngoni.

"Why?" Adam asked.

Josslyn shot him a look that indicated he should stop probing.

Adam ignored it. "Tell me," he urged.

Ngoni gulped a sob. "Mandla and some others want the poaching to stay with the man with the fuzzy eyes. He argued with the tall man. The tall man hit him with his gun. Adjoa swung her broom at the tall man. That's when he shot her."

Adam swore violently as he bowed his head.

Josslyn was concentrating on something else Ngoni had said, though. She pulled out her phone and scrolled through the photos. "The man with the fuzzy eyes, did he look like this?" She showed him a picture of Tseng.

Ngoni nodded. Josslyn exchanged a look with Adam. Tseng wasn't lying last night. He had abdicated his stake in the trafficking ring.

"Then what happened?" Adam continued to coax Ngoni's tale out of him.

"The tall man and his friends went to the bush to get some tusks."

"You were supposed to meet Trevor and me," Josslyn added.

"I wasn't going to come because I didn't want to give you and Mr. Trevor names of the men from our tribe. I knew it would be betraying Mandla," Ngoni admitted quietly.

She patted his back. "It's okay. You should always stick up for family."

"But Mr. Trevor promised he'd bring you to the United States to play basketball if you did give him the names," Adam prompted.

Josslyn's hand stilled on the boy's back. Trevor had conveniently left out that part of the story.

Ngoni glanced up at her, his eyes shining with tears. "I knew you'd be in the bush. I didn't want him to shoot you like he killed Adjoa. So I followed them. You shouldn't have yelled at the tall man. He didn't like it."

She wrapped her arms around Ngoni to comfort him. Adam shot her a look over the boy's head as if he hadn't already figured out she was the guilty party in the bush that day.

"Not now," she mouthed.

He swore under his breath before continuing his interrogation of Ngoni. "What happened after Trevor was shot?"

"I yelled, too. I was angry they shot my friend. I told them you were very important in the United States and you would make him pay for what he did to Adjoa and Mr. Trevor. The tall man got mad. He chased me, but I am a fast runner and I know my way around the bush. He does not."

"Oh, Ngoni," Josslyn said. "I never mentioned my last name to anyone. How did you know who I was?"

"Google," Ngoni explained. "Our teacher has a computer."

Adam bit back a smile. "Then what happened?"

"I was too scared to go back to my village, so I hid in the bush. Mandla taught me places to hide when I was just a boy."

Her heart melted. As mature as Ngoni believed himself to be, he was still a boy. One who was caught up in a nasty adult game.

"When the stars came out," Ngoni continued. "Mandla came and got me. He said we could never return to our village because the tall man would find me there. Mandla said he was taking me to the United States."

"I don't understand." Adam shook his head. "It's not possible to get a visa that quickly. And a last-minute plane ticket is expensive. You arrived the day after Josslyn. How did Mandla work that out?"

"Mr. Shaw."

Josslyn rocked back on her heels. Adam's eyebrows shot to his hairline.

"Shaw?" they both asked at the same time.

Ngoni bobbed his chin up and down earnestly. "Our teacher."

She exchanged a surprised look with Adam. "Wow."

"Sometimes his father comes to our village," Ngoni continued. "He gives us candy. Mandla said Mr. Shaw's father wanted to start trouble with the poachers. He wanted the names of the men Mandla and our people sell the ivory to. After the tall man shot Adjoa, Mandla said he'd give Mr. Shaw's father all the names."

"That's where the task force was getting its inside information. From their Peace Corps teacher." Adam shook his head in awe. "Pretty ingenious."

"Yes, but the other day, Shaw still believed Tseng was funding the poachers," Josslyn remarked. "If he had the information from Mandla, why did he want me to meet with Tseng?"

They both looked at the boy.

"Did Mandla talk to Shaw's father?" she asked.

Ngoni shook his head. "Mandla said he double-crossed us. When we got to the airport in the United States, the tall man was there. Mandla got very angry and yelled at him for killing Abjoa. The tall man pretended he didn't know who Mandla was. He had big men with him. One of them punched Mandla." Ngoni's breath hitched. "The taxi driver saved us. He had a gun. He drove us from the airport.

Mandla took me to our cousin's house. He told me to stay there until he came back." Ngoni grinned at Josslyn. "But you came instead."

"I'm so glad I did." She gave him another hug. "Finish your breakfast and we'll go see that basketball court."

Adam was already dialing his phone when Josslyn caught up to him in the small vestibule off the dining room. The room served as the beauty shop for the president and his family.

"Ben, I need video from the taxi stands outside Dulles the day Mandla and his brother arrived. Look for the other Twin Tower. And a taxi driver with a gun."

"The other Twin Tower?" Josslyn asked once he'd hung up with Ben.

"Yeah, the Huang brothers. Very tall Taiwanese twins."

She sighed heavily. "More players? Just exactly how do they fit into this?"

"Brace yourself. Their cousin, Ting-Wei, is Mrs. Christian Sumner."

Josslyn strolled to the small window in the room. "Everywhere we turn, she keeps popping up."

She stared out at the North Lawn. Adam came up behind her and wrapped his arms around her waist. Leaning back into his embrace, she covered his hands with hers and tilted her head to the side to give his lips better access to her neck.

"I have to tell him Mandla is dead," she whispered. "Do you think the tall man killed him?"

"Most likely," he murmured against her skin. "Shaw,

too."

"If I hadn't yelled that day . . ."

"Hush," he commanded. "You know these people are a bloodthirsty bunch. Ben believes Shaw was inciting the two groups against one another, which would have led to even more bloodshed. At least now we have an idea of who the task force should be investigating."

"Mandla knew the tall man would look for me to find Ngoni."

"Mmm. He did what he could to protect you. And to protect his brother. Too bad the information died with him."

"And Ngoni is left with no one."

"The most important thing now is that he's safe." He gave her a gentle squeeze. "And the most important thing for me is that *you* are safe."

"Which means you can get some sleep." She turned in his arms and cupped his jaw. "Don't take this the wrong way, but you look terrible."

Stretching up on her toes, she pressed her lips to the dark smudges beneath his eyes. Adam threaded his fingers through her hair and repositioned her mouth, so it locked with his. She moaned her pleasure when his tongue swept over hers.

"No, Fergus! You can't have that!"

Ngoni's cries had Josslyn reluctantly pulling away from Adam's kiss.

"I should go see what that's about," she whispered. "Go get some rest. Or I'll tell Director Worcester you skipped physical therapy this morning."

With a quick kiss, she headed back into the dining room where Fergus was having a tug-of-war with Ngoni over the boy's backpack.

"Let go!" Tears were streaming down the boy's cheeks.

"Fergus!" Josslyn grabbed the wee beastie by the collar. "Drop it."

The dog's tail was wagging furiously. He was enjoying the game. But the more Fergus pulled, the harder Ngoni cried.

Josslyn reached in and grabbed the dog's snout. "Drop it," she repeated with more force this time.

Ngoni was sobbing uncontrollably by the time Fergus let go of the backpack. Unfazed, the dog barked playfully as he circled the dining room. Josslyn was unaware Adam had followed her into the dining room until he crouched beside the boy's chair.

"What is it, Ngoni?" he asked. "What's in the bag, sport?"

"Mandla said not to show it to anyone," Ngoni said through his tears. "I'm supposed to hold it until he comes back to get me."

Josslyn's heart pounded painfully in her chest. She needed to tell him his brother wasn't coming back. And she needed to do it now.

"I'll do it," Adam mouthed to her.

She shook her head. It would be better coming from her.

"Sweetheart," she began.

"Mandla is dead," Ngoni interrupted her. "Isn't he?"

Adam had the boy in his lap before the big gulping sobs resumed. The three of them sat on the floor of the family dining room in the White House with their arms around one another. Even Fergus seemed overcome with emotion because he lay down on the floor beside them, nose on his paws, quietly whimpering along with Ngoni.

"He was protecting Miss Josslyn," Adam told him once the heaviest of tears subsided. "And you."

"Adam and I won't let anything happen to you." Josslyn squeezed Ngoni's hand. "You're safe here with us. For as long as you have to stay."

Ngoni wiped his nose with his shirt sleeve. He picked up the forgotten backpack and slowly unzipped it. After digging around in the meager contents, he pulled out an expensive-looking men's wallet. Made of crocodile leather, no less.

"Here." He handed it to Josslyn.

Despite her curiosity, she opened it carefully. Her entire body began to vibrate when she got a look at what was inside.

"This belongs to the tall man, doesn't it?" she asked breathlessly.

"He dropped it in the bush when he was chasing me." Guilt tinged the boy's voice. "Mandla was going to give it to Shaw."

With a shaky hand, she gave the wallet to Adam. He whistled when he thumbed through the contents.

"There's a little notebook with names and dates of purchases here," Adam said. "This guy has his fingers in multiple poaching organizations. From the looks of it, he's trying to corner the market on animal trafficking."

Definitely worth killing for. She said a silent prayer for Mandla, his wife, and Agent Shaw.

"You know what you've done here, Ngoni." Adam wrapped an arm around the boy again. "You've solved the case. The task force will be able to stop the tall man with this. Your teacher will be so proud of you. Mandla is proud of you. I'm proud of you. You're a hero."

The corners of Ngoni's mouth turned up in a shy smile. Josslyn rubbed a hand over the top of his head.

"I'm proud of you, too," Josslyn told him. "You're so brave."

"Can I take this?" Adam held up the wallet.

Ngoni nodded.

Adam got to his feet, lifting Ngoni with him. He smiled as he reached down a hand to help Josslyn to her feet. Sensing a change in the mood of the room, Fergus scrambled to his feet with a happy bark.

"I think Fergus wants to show you the basketball court," Josslyn said. "Go grab your jacket and we'll all go."

With a subdued whoop, Ngoni scampered from the dining room, Fergus at his heels.

"Will this be enough?" Josslyn gestured to the wallet in Adam's hand.

"It's circumstantial, but from what Ben and I have un-covered, Shaw already had most of the building blocks in place to build a strong case. But I need to get it to the task force right away. I also want to make sure Shaw's son is protected."

Josslyn nodded. "What about Tseng?"

"Hopefully there's something in here to implicate him as well, but you don't need to do his bidding to out the suppliers any longer. And from the looks of it, the Twin Towers were the ones behind the violence. Now that they know we have access to the wallet implicating one of the twins, they are likely trying to regroup. It wouldn't surprise me if they run." He pulled her in for a hug. "All the same, you two stay put here today until this is all sorted out." He brushed a kiss over her forehead.

"Good, because I didn't like involving the president in any of this. I've alerted everyone at the GWC. They'll try to stop the sale of the tigers before it gets that far. Trevor is going to fill in for me at the zoo tonight. Christian will likely have a temper tantrum, but that's too bad."

"I'll be back as soon as I hear anything from the task force." With a lingering kiss to her lips, Adam headed out.

CHAPTER SEVENTEEN

HOURS LATER, JOSSLYN dropped into one of the wrought-iron chairs in the White House Children's Garden. Fergus danced at her feet, nearly toppling into the goldfish pond that was built into the flagstone patio. Ngoni whooped it up with two of the Secret Service agents at the White House basketball court just beyond the trees.

"Who knew eleven-year-old boys had so much energy?" she declared.

Her father's nurse chuckled. "I envy the kid," Marc said. "If I ran around like that, I wouldn't be able to walk for days."

"Boys are supposed to have boundless energy," her father added.

Josslyn and Marc waited for him to finish his thought but he was seemingly distracted by Fergus. Marc shot her a sympathetic look. Josslyn smiled back and shrugged. She was used to her father's foibles by now.

"These are my granddaughter's handprints." Her father pointed to one of the stones where Josslyn's niece Arabelle's tiny handprints were embedded. The pathway was lined with pavers containing hand and footprints of all the presidential children and grandchildren since President

Johnson.

"She's a bit of a hooligan," her father added. "Takes after my daughter, that little girl." His tone was affectionate. "Not the one who is First Lady." His brow creased in confusion. He glanced over at Marc. "Which daughter is that again? The hooligan?"

Marc shot Josslyn a sheepish look.

She might have laughed if the situation didn't make her so raw.

"Josslyn," she chimed in. "Her name is Josslyn Emmeline."

Her father's face relaxed until he was smiling peacefully. "Emmeline."

He whispered her mother's name so reverently, Josslyn's throat grew painfully tight. She blamed her taut nerves for making her so emotional. Until Adam returned with word on what was going on with the poachers, she wouldn't be able to get rid of this feeling of restlessness. As much as she wanted to spend time with her ailing father, she couldn't deal with his dementia today. It was too painful.

Ngoni squealed again at the sound of the basketball going in the hoop. She jumped from her seat.

"Maybe if I bribe him with lunch, he'll come inside," she suggested.

Turning toward the basketball court, she was caught off guard by the sight of Adam leaning a shoulder against the Stayman Winesap apple tree a White House groundskeeper had planted decades ago so the kids and grandkids of the president would have a tree to climb. Adam's body still bore the signs of exhaustion, but a ghost of a smile clung to his lips.

"Adam!" Josslyn didn't care who was around to see them, she looped her arms around his neck and buried her face against his freshly shaved skin. He smelled like soap and tasted like home.

Fergus circled their feet barking as Adam rubbed his hand up and down her back. The gesture did wonders to soothe her frayed emotions. Josslyn settled into his warm embrace. The sounds of the Washington traffic beyond the trees and Ngoni dribbling the ball faded into the distance until all she heard was Adam's pulse beating beneath her cheek. She could have stayed in his arms all day.

"Agent Lockett."

Josslyn started at the sound of Director Worcester's voice. Adam quickly pushed her away from him. Were it not for his career, she would have said the hell with it and stepped back beside him. But she knew how much being in the Secret Service meant to Adam. Out of respect she kept her distance. That didn't mean she had to like it.

"Doctor Benoit." The director acknowledged her with a strained nod.

"Sir." Adam practically drew himself to military attention.

"I wanted to let you know that we just heard from Interpol," the director announced. "The animal trafficking task force has already moved on the information you gave them. The Huang brothers were picked up at Taipei's

Taoyuan Airport a half hour ago. It seems both were in a hurry to return home."

Josslyn's sigh turned into a laugh she was so relieved. Adam grinned as well.

"Interpol and the task force are quickly rounding out the other suspects in Africa and Asia," the director continued. He, too, was wearing an easy smile. "Well done, Doctor Benoit. It seems you've accomplished what an entire task force couldn't do in three years."

"Agent Shaw's son?" she asked. "Is he okay?"

The director nodded. "The task force sent someone to secure him last night immediately after Agent Shaw was killed."

"Ben was able to grab video of Shaw's killer," Adam added, his expression now apprehensive. "It was one of the motorcycle guys who tried to grab Ngoni last night. We think they used the Nimba symbols on the dart to misplace the blame."

Josslyn met his eyes and knew right away what he didn't say. "The one I shot?"

He nodded.

"Well, then, I guess that worked out." She rubbed her sweaty palms on her jeans. "Were you able to pass on the information about the tiger sale to the task force?"

Adam nodded. "They already have some leads thanks to your friends from the GWC. And they're confident that once they decipher the information from Huang's wallet that will lead them to the tiger traffickers before the sale."

Josslyn allowed herself a relieved breath. "So that's it,

then?"

"For the time being," Adam said. "There was nothing we could find on Tseng."

"Aside from adultery," Josslyn quipped. "I'm just glad I don't have to see him anymore. The man gave me the creeps."

"We're still trying to puzzle together exactly why Shaw was killed," Adam went on. "I suspect it was because he wouldn't divulge where Ngoni was hidden. It turns out, Shaw was the taxi driver"—Adam made air quotes with his fingers—"who picked them up at Dulles."

"He didn't double-cross them after all," Josslyn said.

"No, the tall man Mandla and Ngoni saw at the airport was actually the other Twin Tower. They didn't know there were two of them."

Josslyn shook her head. "Which was probably lucky for Ngoni and Mandla."

Adam smiled at her. "Ngoni has had a lot of luck on his side."

"Well, if I have any additional updates, I'll let you know." The director fixed his stare on Adam. "I'm assuming you're still on leave, Agent Lockett."

"No," Adam answered.

"Yes," Josslyn said at the same time.

The director's mouth twitched, but otherwise, he remained inscrutable. Adam, however, looked like he was going to blow a gasket.

"He needs sleep," Josslyn insisted.

Adam tried to stare her down, but he should have

known by now that she was made of sterner stuff than most women. She held her ground.

"Doolittle still needs protection until all the players are accounted for," Adam bit out through his clenched jaw.

"Agreed," the director said. "There are a number of agents within the White House who will ensure her safety today."

Josslyn reached up and ran her palm along his cheek. "Go get some rest, Adam," she commanded softly. "I'm not going anywhere. You should know by now I'm not leaving you."

She thought he might have growled with impatience before he covered her hand with his and brought it to his mouth. The director cleared his throat when Adam's lips lingered. Adam reluctantly dropped her hand and followed the director out of the garden.

"I sort of figured that was the way of it."

Josslyn spun on her heel to where Trevor loitered in the shadows on the path between the basketball court and the Children's Garden. Her cheeks burned with embarrassment.

"I guess I shouldn't get my hopes up about us getting back together one day." He was teasing, she knew him well enough to know.

"We would have never worked," she replied.

Trevor wandered over to her, a wicked smile on his face. "No, but we sure had fun trying."

She glanced over to where her father dozed. Marc was doing his best not to eavesdrop but the man could probably write a book after leaving her father's service.

"How's the arm?" Josslyn figured a subject change was in order.

He jostled his sling. "Still attached."

Josslyn rolled her eyes. "It looks like Interpol nabbed the people who shot you."

"The poachers? And the suppliers?" Trevor's voice shook with excitement. "Tell me they nabbed them, too?"

She nodded and Trevor let out a war whoop rivaling Ngoni's. At the sound, Fergus began barking, startling her father from sleep. Ngoni sprinted in from the basketball court.

"Mr. Trevor!" he cried as he wrapped his arms around Trevor's waist. "You are alive!"

"Of course I am," Trevor said. "It takes more than a gunshot to bring me down. I'm a surfer superhero, remember?"

"Really?" Josslyn mouthed behind Ngoni's back.

He gave her a one-shouldered shrug.

"I hear you've had quite an adventure," he said to Ngoni. "I'm very sorry about your brother."

Ngoni cast his gaze down to the flagstones. "Adam's going to get the tall man and the other bad guys. He's a special agent."

Trevor winked at her. "Well, special agent trumps surfing superhero any day."

Josslyn held back another eye roll, wrapping an arm around Ngoni's shoulders instead. "The police already arrested the tall man," she told him. "You have nothing to worry about anymore."

He looked up at her in wonder. "Really?"

"Really." She smiled back at him.

Ngoni whooped again. "Come on, Trevor. You have to see my hook shot."

He shrugged out of her embrace and raced down the pathway toward the basketball court.

"He seems well," Trevor remarked as they followed behind.

"I'm sure he's processing things the best way he can. My sister will be home tomorrow. She's better equipped to deal with these things. Together, we'll make sure he gets the help he needs."

"As long as he has access to basketball, he'll be fine."

"Speaking of that," Josslyn chastised him. "You bribed him with the promise you'd bring him to the United States to play basketball if he gave us the names of the poachers. That was never in the cards. Since when is it okay to lie to an eleven-year-old boy?"

He stopped on the path beside her, the free-spirited, bohemian surfer nowhere to be found in his expression.

"I do whatever it takes to ensure the animals are protected," he snapped. "So did you once upon a time."

Shame bubbled up in her chest. Trevor was correct in saying she had been guilty of doing whatever it took. Even if it meant breaking the law. And embarrassing her family. But duping a young boy to save an elephant didn't feel right to her and she doubted it ever would.

"Look, we did what we thought was right," he added.

"None of that is going to matter to you any longer, though. I doubt you'll have the time or temperament to operate the way we've always done once you're linked to law enforcement."

"What's that supposed to mean?"

Trevor sighed. "Do I have to spell it out?"

"Yes. I believe you do."

"Before, when it was just your sister and her political husband you were hurting, it was exciting because you loved to antagonize them. Now, well, Agent Lockett doesn't look like the type who'll appreciate his woman running around thumbing her nose at the law."

Josslyn's cheeks burned again. "First of all, I'm my own woman," she fumed. "And neither Adam nor anyone else is going to tell me what I can and can't do."

He raised an eyebrow at her smugly. "Whatever you say." He continued down the path.

She was ashamed to admit his theory about her sister and Conrad hit close to the mark. Not intentionally, however. Despite the difference in their ages, she loved her sister. And she adored her brother-in-law. She could do without them living in a political fishbowl; that was true enough. Josslyn's ideals and causes differed from the rest of her family, that was all. And just because she was pursuing a relationship with Adam didn't mean she was giving those passions up. She stomped after Trevor.

"I can't dribble very well with my left hand," Trevor complained.

A moment later, the natural athlete launched the basketball right through the net with a swoosh.

"Wow," Ngoni cheered. "Let's play a game of H-O-R-S-E."

"Perhaps tomorrow, sport," Trevor said. "I'm headed over to the zoo to rub shoulders with the rich and famous. And the elephants."

"A zoo?" Ngoni's eyes went wide. "Mr. Shaw took us to the zoo in Harare once. They had lions and cheetahs behind fences. I prefer the game preserves where the animals can run free."

Trevor clapped the boy on the back. "Me, too, Ngoni. But we all don't live in places where the animals can roam free. The only way for most people to see an elephant or a tiger or giraffe is at the zoo. They are a necessary evil."

"There's nothing evil about a zoo," Josslyn interjected. "If they're run correctly, they are a unique way for scientists and school children alike to study animals. One of the elephants I've been studying since you were in diapers is at the National Zoo. Tonight, lots of kids will be able to see him relatively up close."

"I think most of the kids will be more excited about the candy." Trevor grinned foolishly.

"Candy?" Ngoni's eyes grew rounder if that was even possible.

"To celebrate Halloween," Josslyn explained. "It's an American holiday where the children dress up in costumes and go door to door for candy."

"Mr. Shaw told us about this! It sounds wonderful." Ngoni looked from Trevor to Josslyn. "Can we go?"

Josslyn's stomach sank. After all the boy had been through this past week, she hated to deny him.

"Pleeeease," he begged. "I want to see this elephant of yours."

Trevor chuckled. "Don't forget the candy."

"I don't know." Josslyn gnawed on her lip. "I promised we'd stay put until everything was resolved."

"Everything is resolved," Trevor said.

Ngoni nodded. "The police have the tall man. You said so."

He was right. Ngoni was no longer in any imminent danger. And if they put him in a costume, no one would even know who he was. Plus, she could help Christian schmooze the big donors he'd invited for infrastructure money that would, in the end, preserve the wildlife. He'd mentioned that his wife wouldn't be attending, so their paths wouldn't cross. It was a viable plan.

So why did she feel guilty? Trevor had it all wrong. She could still do as she pleased. It wasn't as if she was betraying anyone. She'd promised Adam she'd stay put, but that was before the Twin Towers were in custody a half a world away. Adam cared about her. He hadn't told her to her face, but he wasn't the type to curtail her passions. He'd likely agree to her taking Ngoni to the zoo if she asked. But he'd insist on accompanying them and he was exhausted. His concussion would never heal if he didn't get some rest. And the sooner he was healed, the sooner he could return to his regular duties.

There, she'd made the decision. She was doing what

was best for everyone. Besides, if they went without a crowd of agents, they would attract less attention. It was a good thing Marin had showed her how to sneak out.

"You have to promise to stay close to me and do whatever Trevor and I say," she demanded.

Trevor and Ngoni high-fived one another, both of them shouting and shuffling around the court.

She sighed. "Great. It seems I'm taking two children to the zoo tonight."

They wrapped their arms around her, pulling her into their dance until she was laughing with them.

CHAPTER EIGHTEEN

"YOU WANNA TELL me again why you're sleeping on the sofa in my lab instead of the agent's lounge at the Crown?" Ben swiped at Adam's feet that were hanging off the edge of the much-too-small leather sofa. "Or better yet, why you're not in your own damn bed?"

Adam didn't bother opening his eyes. His head hurt too much. "Lauzon was staked out at the lounge. And you know how that guy snores."

"That still leaves your bed at the townhouse. Which would be the first place I'd go to get some sleep. I don't need a PhD from MIT to riddle that one out."

The thought of a comfortable mattress minus Ben's annoying prattling almost made Adam move off the sofa. *Almost.* If only his old man had cashed the damn check.

"When does Marin get back?" Adam asked.

Ben tapped his pen against the desk. "How would I know? She's not my fiancée."

He was tempted to text Griff and ask him, but suddenly moving required too much energy. Ben ceased his tapping and the room grew quiet. The whir of the servers in the back of the lab slowly lulled Adam to sleep.

Josslyn was naked beneath him, her lips moving lower on

his body. "I'm not going anywhere. You should know by now I'm not leaving you." Adam liked the sound of her words. Especially the way she was murmuring them against his skin. He could get used to having a woman worship him. Especially if that woman was Josslyn.

"Why don't you come out and admit it?"

Ben's random question in the middle of his dream had Adam nearly jumping off the sofa.

"Shit, Ben," he yelled. "I was finally asleep." *And about to get to the good stuff, damn it.*

His friend ignored him. "You can't avoid your dad forever."

"Actually, dude, I can."

He settled back down on the sofa and shut his eyes. Thankfully, Ben was silent again. Adam dipped into his sniper training and altered his breathing to relax his body. The sooner he got back to sleep, the sooner Josslyn would be worshipping him.

Just as he dozed off, Ben was at it again. "I'd give anything to have another five minutes with my dad."

Adam gave up the pretense of trying to sleep. "Your father was a cop. Killed in the line of duty. Probably by someone just like my old man. The two aren't the same thing. I don't need a PhD from MIT to figure that out."

"You don't really believe your father is that bad."

Very slowly, he rose to a sitting position trying to tamp down on the anger building inside of him. "You're stepping perilously close to a very fine line that you don't want to cross, Bennett."

"I read the trial transcripts," Ben persisted. "The man who killed your sister wasn't the same man who served honorably in the army for twenty years. Or the same man who his friends described coaching your Little League teams with, and I quote, a big heart and the patience of a saint."

His head was pounding again. "You read the damn transcripts?" Hell, Adam had never bothered to read the stupid things. "Invade my privacy much?"

Ben sighed. "Okay, yeah, a little. But you know I have to have all the pieces to solve the puzzle. And you go to complete radio silence whenever anyone asks about your past. I was curious. It's in my DNA."

"My past is exactly that, *my* past. If I wanted to share it with people, I'd go on the damn *Dr. Phil* show! You're my friend. Correct me if I'm wrong, but I thought the basis of friendship was trust."

"It is," Ben conceded. "But as your friend, I wanted to know how this man hurt you so I could prevent it from happening again."

"If you read the transcripts, then you know exactly how he hurt me. By killing my sister. By locking me in a damn tomb and never bothering to tell anyone where I was."

"He wasn't in his right mind, dude."

Adam shot from the coach. To his credit, Ben didn't even flinch. Like any good soldier, he would take a punch if he deserved it. And he one hundred percent deserved it. But something in his friend's eyes made Adam pull back. They stood there, face-to-face for a long moment before

Ben spoke quietly again.

"Surely, there are some good memories of your dad. Or did you bury them so deep in that thick skull of yours that you've forgotten they exist?"

"Why do you care?" Adam snarled.

"Because you're like a brother to me. And brothers look out for one another. Your dad showed up for a reason. And I think you should hear him out. For no other purpose than to close that chapter in your life."

Adam shoved his fingers through his hair. Why was everyone so hell-bent on closure? His life was just fine the way it was.

"You sound like Josslyn."

"Well, we do both have big brains," Ben joked. "And we both care about you."

He fell back onto the sofa. The thought of Josslyn caring about him took the edge off his anger. But it was quickly replaced with fear. Despite all of her vows to never leave him, everyone he cared about always did. His mom. His sister. Even his old man. While Griffin was still around as one of his best friends, if Griff had to choose, he'd pick Marin any day. Eventually, Ben would find someone—or build her in his lab—and Adam would be back to being odd man out.

Josslyn cared about him, sure. And Adam was afraid his heart was already engaged in whatever was going on between them. But was it enough for him to take that giant leap of faith that she'd stick around for the long haul?

Ben's computer pinged, interrupting his thoughts.

"Hmm, that's interesting," Ben said.

"You finally found the girl who ditched you at your high school prom?"

"Screw you," Ben responded. "This is about your friend, Tseng."

"There wasn't anything in the wallet Ngoni found that would incriminate him. Hopefully, the Twin Towers are singing his song in Taiwan."

"Except this is about him and Sumner."

Adam snapped to attention. "You think she'll roll on Tseng?"

"Not the wife. Christian Sumner. The undersecretary," Ben explained. "All this time we thought the connection between the two was simply the affair Tseng was having with his wife. But it turns out, Tseng and Christian Sumner go way back. All the way to their days at Oxford together."

Ben clicked a few keys on the keyboard and an image of a class photo came up. "Do you want to know who it was that got Tseng kicked out?"

"I'll bet I can guess. Sumner."

Nodding, Ben opened an article from the university's newspaper. "Tseng didn't take it well. He claimed Sumner was the one cheating. According to this article, he promised to get even."

"When was this?"

Ben scanned the article. "Ten years ago."

"Sleeping with the guy's wife certainly counts as getting even," Adam said.

"Yeah," Ben's voice trailed off as he leaned back in his chair and began tapping his pen again.

Adam knew that look. "Where is that oversized brain of yours going with this?"

"Tseng's tech companies are all underproducing," Ben said. "So his money has to come from the animal trafficking. Right?"

"But he told Josslyn that business was his dead uncle's and he got out of it," Adam added.

"A guy with his vices doesn't walk away from a moneymaker like that." Ben shook his head. "Nor does he suddenly grow a conscience."

"Then what are you saying?"

Ben was back to furiously attacking his keyboard. "The Twin Towers want access to the poaching ring to cut out the middleman and get the animals for medicinal purposes. Once it gets out that the company is involved in poaching, their stock will take a nosedive. If I'm a majority stockholder, I'll lose my shirt." Ben sat back and stared at the computer screen. "Well, I'll be damned."

"What?"

"The Twin Towers are only minority shareholders."

Adam's heart began to race.

"The majority of the company's stock was a wedding gift to none other than Christian Sumner," Ben continued. "And Mrs. Sumner didn't like that her father put her inheritance in the hands of her husband."

"So she seeks out Tseng and begins an affair with him?"

"Or she was in on the plan from the beginning." Ben

shrugged. "The result is that Sumner is ruined financially."

"And even more damaging, he's ruined politically." Adam thought back to what Griff had told him yesterday. "He's an ambitious guy working in Africa. This will be a huge blow to his career."

"If our theory is correct, Tseng had no intention of stepping away from the animal trafficking ring. He used Shaw to set up the Twin Towers and ruin Sumner."

"As much of an ass as Sumner is, I hate to see Tseng take him down like this."

Ben grinned. "Joke's on Tseng because political appointees are required to put their investments in a blind trust. Whatever bad happens with the pharmaceutical company can't be pinned to Sumner. Besides that, he's from Texas oil. His trust fund will bail him out of anything."

"He'll still take a political hit. I think someone should at least warn the guy. Seeing how he's close personal friends with the president's family. It might reflect on them if he's blindsided."

"Hmm." Ben looked at him skeptically. "Already taking up the family mantle, I see."

"Just doing my job protecting the president." Adam grabbed his jacket.

"What, getting hit on the head with the lead pipe wasn't enough?"

"Nope." Adam headed for the door.

"Nap time is over, I take it," Ben teased.

"I'm off to the zoo. Sumner is there trying to eke out money from corporate donors interested in investing in

Africa."

"Adam," Ben called after him. "Make sure Sumner knows to watch his back. Tseng went to a lot of trouble to make him look bad. Once he figures out he wasn't successful, there's no telling what he'll do."

That man is a little unhinged. Josslyn's words echoed in his head causing a tremor of unease to run down his spine. He hurried out of Ben's lab.

❖

AS DUSK SETTLED over the National Zoo, Josslyn was grateful for the warmth of Ngoni's hand in hers. They dodged the crowds of costumed children ambling down the path between exhibits.

"Are they going to have candy everywhere we stop?" Ngoni asked as he munched on a Blow Pop.

"You betcha," Trevor answered.

They were both in costume—a one-armed Batman and Robin—and it was difficult to tell which one was having the better time. Or eating more candy.

The throng of people, coupled with the descending darkness, was starting to make Josslyn apprehensive. Logically, there was no threat to Ngoni any longer. And he was impossible to recognize in his costume. Still, she was beginning to feel guilty for sneaking out of the White House without telling anyone. Especially Adam.

"You've both had quite enough candy," she said. "Once I finish at the Elephant Trails, we're headed back."

"Of course, Mommy Dearest," Trevor joked.

Josslyn ignored him. She guided Ngoni through the front doors of the elephant house and waved her badge to the guard monitoring the backstage area.

The security guard grinned. "Evening, Doctor Benoit. Your friend Dax is having a great time tonight showing off for all the kiddos."

Josslyn relaxed. She'd missed the big elephant these past few days.

"Can we go see him?" Ngoni pleaded.

"In a minute," she said. "First I have to find someone. Has Undersecretary Sumner arrived yet?"

The guard pointed to one of the teaching platforms. "He's in the middle of that crowd. Been asking for you, too."

"Trevor, can you keep an eye on Ngoni? I won't be more than twenty minutes." She pointed to the exhibits lining the walls. "Go look at the elephant poop. That should give both you boys something to giggle about."

"Aye, aye, Captain." Trevor saluted her.

"I mean it, Trevor. Don't leave this building."

Trevor's eyes softened. "Relax, Josslyn. He's safe with me. You go and get some money to help the elephants."

Ngoni was already tugging Trevor in the direction of more candy. Josslyn nodded before heading toward Christian and his entourage.

"There you are," Christian hissed quietly when she joined the others. "I was beginning to think you didn't care about the elephants after all."

Josslyn was now really regretting sneaking out of the White House. But then one of the corporate CEO's she recognized from the Kennedy Center the other night was asking her a question about the elephants' diminishing herd size and Josslyn found her groove. She explained how she and others were working on efforts to preserve the herds both through science and by eliminating the practice of poaching.

"Many of the tribes have no other viable income stream, so that leaves poaching as the only means to provide for their family. One way to stem this problem is for economic development." She turned to Christian. "Undersecretary Sumner has some wonderful ideas on how to bring that about. I hope you'll give each of them some thought."

Donning her campaign smile, she pumped hands and posed for selfies until she felt she'd put in the requisite amount of time to make everyone happy. She caught a glimpse of Trevor and Ngoni out of the corner of her eye. They were both wrestling with the huge tractor tire trying to gauge if they had the strength of an elephant. Josslyn figured she had a few minutes to slip back into the barn and check on Dax.

She weaved through the crowd and had just reached the door to the staff area when a hand grabbed her arm. Josslyn gasped loudly.

"Dr. Benoit," Agent Groesch said. "What are you doing here?"

Josslyn silently chided herself for being so jumpy. She

turned to see the agent with two young boys in tow.

"I could ask you the same thing." Josslyn grinned. "How are you feeling?"

The agent touched her head. "No double vision. Just a little headache. But I have a wicked bruise on my hip where I went down on the pavement." Agent Groesch looked around. "Where's Adam?"

This was the tricky part. Josslyn gnawed on her lower lip, but the other woman was already narrowing her eyes at her. "You snuck out again, didn't you?"

"I'm headed back right now. Promise. I just want to check on Dax."

Agent Groesch let out a beleaguered sigh. "Let me find my sister so I can hand off these two. I'll take you back to the Crown."

"That's not necessary. Trevor and Ngoni are here with me."

"Easy way or hard way?" Agent Groesch threatened. "Easy way, you let me escort you back quietly. Hard way, I call Adam. And the director."

The other woman left her no choice. "Fine," Josslyn acquiesced. "But you're not as cute as you look."

The agent grinned broadly. "Gets 'em every time. Wait here."

"I'll just stop in to check on Dax while you drop off your nephews. I'll meet you back here in ten minutes." She pointed to Trevor. "I have to come back to get them anyway."

"Make it five minutes and you have a deal."

Josslyn nodded and slipped through the doorway into the barn. Because of the openness of the exhibit, the noise from the crowds carried throughout this part of the facility. Most of the elephants were immune to it, including Dax who was contentedly crunching on a stalk of tallgrass. He looked up as if sensing her presence.

"Hey, there, big guy." She rested her forearms on the cable fencing. "I've missed you. Have you been good while I was away?"

The elephant flapped his ears before slowly waddling in the direction of the fence. Josslyn grabbed a veggie biscuit off one of the trainer's carts and held it out to him. Dax stopped suddenly. The skin at the back of Josslyn's neck tingled. Flipping his ears out wide, he lifted his trunk and trumpeted ferociously. She scrambled out of the way as he charged the fence.

"Dax!" she cried.

"That thing is crazy!"

Heart in her throat, she whirled around to find Christian hovering behind one of the trainer's carts. She hadn't heard him arrive thanks to the noise of the party echoing throughout the barn. Josslyn shivered with relief that it was only Christian.

"Oh for heaven's sake." Josslyn drew in a deep breath to calm her racing pulse. "Dax is not crazy. He just doesn't like people sneaking up on me."

"There you go again thinking I'm following you," he accused. "You're the one who slipped away back there. I came looking for you to say thanks."

Josslyn studied his face. There was always another motive with Christian, but tonight, she only detected sincerity. That had to be a first. Dax snorted possessively when Christian moved in closer and Christian froze in place.

"You don't need to thank me." Josslyn spoke softly as much for the benefit of Dax as the man standing four feet away. "We're not enemies. I want to keep these guys alive and flourishing in their natural habitat. And now that you're working in Africa, you want to see the continent's economy succeed. Just as I said back there, the two are mutually beneficial. You have nothing but my support."

He looked at her in amazement. "That's very magnanimous of you. I can't tell you how glad I am to hear it. There are some committees I work with that could use your expertise."

Josslyn knew an olive branch when she saw one. And this one would allow her to continue following her passions without the constant embarrassment to her family. Or risk to her life. She knew one sexy Secret Service agent who would be especially happy with the arrangement.

"I'd like that," she said.

Dax snorted his approval and they both laughed. She patted the elephant. "You be good. I'll be back to see you tomorrow."

They were headed to the exit when Dax trumpeted in alarm again. Josslyn turned just in time to avoid the blade of a familiar-looking samurai sword as it slashed through the air. Christian, however, was not so lucky.

CHAPTER NINETEEN

A DAM TOOK THE metro to Woodley Park and hoofed it the rest of the way to the zoo. The event was in full swing when he arrived. Orange lanterns swung from wires suspended in the trees giving the park a festive, if not eerie, glow. He was surprised to see tables set up at all the entrances to the normally free zoo.

"Do you have a ticket, sir?" a woman wearing a Friends of the National Zoo sweatshirt asked.

Shit. He'd forgotten all about that. Adam was forced to rely on the tried and true tactic of pulling out his badge.

"I'm Agent Lockett with the Secret Service. I'd like to speak with someone in security."

One of the Smithsonian's guards was at the table a minute later. Adam was in luck. It was a guard he'd worked with when they secured the elephant barn earlier this week.

"Hey there, Agent Lockett," the guard said. "'Bout time you got here."

Adam's entire body went on alert. "Why do you say that?"

"Because Dr. Benoit arrived an hour ago—"

He didn't bother hearing the rest of what the guard said. Adam took off for the Elephant Trails exhibit at a full sprint. *Damn her.* She'd promised to stay put. Would this woman ever do what she said she would?

I'm not going anywhere. You should know by now I'm not leaving you.

Her assurances taunted him as he weaved through groups of costumed kids trick-or-treating. The Smithsonian guard called out Adam's name as he huffed to keep up. This was the reason Adam kept a tight leash on his heart. Because people always let him down.

He charged into the main entrance of the elephant house and scoured the lobby for her. Adam was surprised, and immensely relieved, to see Christine pacing in front of the staff entrance to the barn area. At least she had the good sense to bring a detail.

But there was no sign of Josslyn. Skirting the outside of the room, he tried to make his way toward Christine, but a kid dressed as Batman's sidekick grabbed onto his jacket and wouldn't let go.

"Adam!" the kid cried when Adam tried to pry his fingers loose.

"Ngoni?" Adam pulled the mask from the boy's eyes. "Sport, what are you doing here?"

"I wanted to see Miss Josslyn's elephant."

He gripped Ngoni's shoulders. "Where is she?" This time, he was really going to throttle her.

"I don't know." The tears were back in the boy's eyes. "But we have to find her. The man with the fuzzy eyes is here. He looked angry."

Adam's gut clenched. He grabbed Ngoni's hand and

dragged him over to where Christine stood.

"Ngoni!" Trevor shouted as he ran up behind them. "I told you not to leave my side. Oh, hey, Agent Lockett. When did you get here?"

"Not soon enough, apparently," Adam growled. "Where is Josslyn?"

Trevor pointed toward one of the platforms above the exhibit. "Over there," he said. "With Undersecretary Sumner." His voice trailed off. "At least they were both there a minute ago."

They finally made it to Christine.

"Where. Is. She?" he demanded.

The other agent looked at her watch. "Five minutes late. She was supposed to meet me back here. And for the record, she snuck out. I'm off duty, but I'm taking her back to the Crown whether she likes it or not."

The security guard reached them, finally.

"We need to get in there," Adam informed him.

The guard punched a code into the keypad and the door clicked. As the five of them raced down the catwalk to the stalls, the sound of an elephant trumpeting woefully could be heard above the din of the event.

"Dax," Christine said as she limped ahead.

The big elephant was pacing in front of the cable keeping him in his pen.

"Adam!" she called. "We've got blood."

The guard was radioing for backup while Adam dug down for the composure that made him the world's top sharpshooter. He couldn't dwell on the fact Josslyn was in danger. Instead, he needed to use all the skills in his toolbox to find her.

"Holy shit," Trevor whispered. "This is my fault. I should never have baited her to come tonight."

"Enough!" Adam yanked his phone from his pocket and dialed Ben's number. "You." he pointed to the guard. "Secure the area. You." He pointed at Trevor. "Keep the boy back and don't touch anything."

"Talk to me, Adam." The sound of Ben's efficient voice helped him focus.

"I need you to tap into the cameras inside the elephant barn, especially those we set up to secure the area around Dax."

He could hear Ben typing. "What am I looking for?"

"Not what. Who." Adam kept his breathing even. "Tseng was here. He has Sumner. And Josslyn. And one of them is bleeding."

⊕

KEEP HIM TALKING. Wasn't that what they did in those cop shows? Josslyn pressed her hand firmly to the gash in Christian's shoulder. That tactic worked for Alyssa when Trevor was shot. She only hoped it would be successful tonight.

Tseng had dragged them down the darkened Elephant Trails, through a secure construction site, to the empty bird house. The area was closed for renovation which meant no one would be wandering back to this part of the zoo. Agent

Groesch would come looking for her, Josslyn was sure of it. She hoped the trail of blood Christian had lost would be visible in the dark.

"What do you want, Tseng?" Josslyn demanded.

He sliced the blade through the air making Josslyn flinch.

"You have been nothing but trouble." He pointed the blade at her. "Always sticking your nose where it doesn't belong. It will give me great pleasure to gut you like one of the tigers in my office."

To his credit, Christian tried to move in front of her, but his gash was a lot wider than Trevor's bullet wound. As a result, he was losing a lot more blood than Trevor had. She could see the shock beginning to set in.

"She's the sister-in-law of the president of the United States," Christian gasped. "Don't you dare lay a finger on her."

Tseng spat at their feet.

"You are still the same old prig you always were," Tseng said.

"You two know each other?" In her surprise, Josslyn jostled Christian. He groaned painfully. She couldn't hold him upright much longer. "Why don't you lie down?" she suggested.

"Can't," he breathed, but he was already slipping from her grasp.

Josslyn knelt beside him. She frantically tore at his dress shirt to sop up the blood. Agent Groesch would call Adam. Adam would find the clue she'd left for him. The thought calmed the trembling in her hands so she could concentrate on keeping Christian alive.

Keep him talking until Adam gets here.

"You didn't answer my question, Tseng."

"Oxford," Christian breathed.

He wasn't the one she wanted talking. Tseng was pacing the dark enclosure he'd barricaded them in. Among theshadows, she could make out the trees and vines remaining. The exhibit had been built to resemble a rainforest. The only windows were skylights above, but those had been covered with thick tarps to protect them during the reconstruction. Josslyn bit back a gasp when she saw movement near one of them. She glanced discreetly at Tseng, but he was still pacing, sniffling every other step. Fortunately, he was high as a kite and likely wouldn't notice their visitors, but she kept him talking anyway.

"I take it you weren't frat brothers," she said.

Tseng turned suddenly, charging at them with the sword. "He ruined my life!"

"So now you're ruining his? Sleeping with his wife wasn't enough?"

Josslyn hoped Christian wasn't alert enough to hear her comment. She wanted to distract Tseng, not hurt an already wounded man.

"Isn't he the one who's supposed to be gunning for you?" she taunted him.

The air moved when Tseng sliced the blade again.

"He hates cheaters so I made his wife one."

Christian groaned. Josslyn's hands were growing numb

from applying pressure. The light around one of the skylights dimmed momentarily.

She needed to keep Tseng's attention on her. "Why does he hate cheaters?"

"Him and his damn honor code. Everyone cheats," Tseng ranted. "He reported me to the university. They kicked me out. My father never let me help at the company again because I disgraced him. They needed my expertise to keep those companies successful." He laughed. "But I made more money than they did. As you say, Doctor Benoit, poaching is big business."

Blood began dripping from Tseng's nose. He wobbled on his feet before righting himself. There was another noise at the roof. Unfortunately, this time Tseng heard it.

⌖

BEN SWORE VIOLENTLY. "They're five minutes ahead of you. They went out through the service entrance. I'm trying to pick them up on one of the other cameras, but the lighting isn't doing us any favors. And, dude, Tseng's wielding a lethal-looking sword."

Adam was already muscling the back door open, Christine at his heels. "What's in this direction?"

"Just the Elephant Trails," the security guard answered. "The main walkway is closed off about a hundred yards from here because the bird house is under renovation. There's no one back there."

"Which is exactly where I'd go," Christine said as she

drew her weapon from beneath her pant leg.

They made their way quickly up the trail to the bird house. Members of the zoo's security force fell in with them as they went. The sounds from the festivities at the other exhibits faded as they ventured deeper into the wooded area.

"There," the security guard whispered. He aimed his flashlight at the asphalt. "The blood trail leads to the Birds of the Amazon building."

But something else caught Adam's eye. A shiny object on the pavement. Heart in his throat, he bent down to retrieve Josslyn's medallion from the ground.

Christine must have recognized it, too, because she was suddenly radiating with anger. "How do you want to play this?"

Two guards dressed in SWAT gear charged past them.

"Not with those guys," Adam said. "Stand down, everyone."

The Smithsonian guards turned toward him.

"The president's sister-in-law is inside," he announced. "That makes this a Secret Service operation. No one takes a shot unless I give the command."

"The director is on his way," Ben said.

Adam forgot he was still on the line.

"We don't have time," Adam replied. He wasn't sure which of the two was injured, but he wasn't taking a chance on Josslyn bleeding out.

"Is there roof access?" he asked the guard.

The SWAT commander responded instead. "There is

and there are four skylights that will give my team a view of the area down below."

Until Tseng walks out of view.

"Too risky." Adam didn't bother explaining why. There was a reason he was the world's top sniper and these guys weren't. He turned to the guard.

"Is there another way in?"

"Just the sewer line. Because this is a simulated rainforest, we move a lot of water in and out of there. It's narrow but a body could get through it. And there's no water running through right now with the construction."

"How long is the path?"

"Fifty yards."

Shit, shit, shit. Fifty yards in a dark four-foot wide tunnel.

"I'll go," Christine offered.

"No." Adam reached for the SWAT commander's communication device. "I'll do it."

"Dude, are you sure?" Ben asked through the phone.

"He has Josslyn," was all Adam needed to say.

"Then do what you have to do to get her out. Let your training be your guide." Ben disconnected.

The SWAT commander handed Adam his AR15 rifle. "I'll station my men on the roof, in case this guy runs again. But they'll only fire on your go ahead."

Adam nodded, praying none of these guys went rogue on him. The security guard led him over to the sewer grate. Two of the other officers were already busy removing the cover.

"That's pretty narrow, Adam," Christine said. "Are you sure you don't want me to go?"

His throat was already growing tight at the thought of being confined in there. But Josslyn was at the other end. And she was in danger. He could do this. He *had* to do this.

"I got this," he said, hoping like hell he meant it.

One of the guards handed him a headlamp.

"Nobody fires unless I say so," he repeated before he shimmied into the tunnel.

The stench of stale water and bird shit assaulted his senses before the dark, tight walls did. Clutching Josslyn's medallion in his hand, Adam belly crawled to the middle of the tunnel on adrenaline alone. Sweat began to pool on his brow as he propelled himself further. He estimated he was at the twenty-five-yard mark when his chest seized and his body froze.

"Damn it!" he wheezed before his airway squeezed shut.

Gasping, he struggled in the close confines of the sewer line to bring his hands to his neck so could loosen his suddenly tight collar. But it was no use. He was stuck. Of all the ways Adam thought he would die, this wasn't one of them. Parts of his life flashed in front of his eyes. All of them featuring Josslyn.

I have a feeling the best is yet to come.

She'd whispered those words to him that long-ago night on the ocean. Adam gripped the rifle tighter. He wanted a better life. And he wanted it with her. But first, he had to save her from that idiot, Tseng.

Once again, Adam relied on his sniper training to focus all of his energy on the task at hand. Ignoring the tightness in his chest, he convinced his body to inch forward. Then another inch. Then another until he could barely make out a brightening at the end of the tunnel.

He heard voices, too. A wave of relief washed over him when he recognized Josslyn's. She sounded healthy. The thought of holding her in his arms spurred him onward. He crawled the last twenty-five yards without incident. When he reached the end of the line, he was happy to see the space widened so he could move his arms. Dousing his headlamp, he ever-so-gently jiggled the grate leading into the exhibit. It squeaked slightly.

Damn it. Any sound would alert Tseng to his presence and he'd never get a shot off in time. Josslyn was still talking. Questioning Tseng about his motive. Adam didn't hear Sumner's voice. Not a good sign. He had to move quickly.

"I need a distraction," he whispered into the comm unit.

"Ten-four," the SWAT commander replied. "On your count."

Adam readied his body. Gripping the rifle in one hand, he wrapped his finger around the grate.

"Five. Four. Three. Two. One."

A boom sounded on the roof at the same time Adam opened the grate. He hoped its squeak sounded loud to him because he was so close to it.

"What was that?" Tseng asked as Adam slowly crept

from the tunnel.

"Just the fireworks from the Boo at the Zoo," Josslyn quickly responded.

She was remarkably poised and astute for a woman trapped in a room with a man brandishing a samurai sword. Not for the first time he thought she'd make a kick-ass agent.

"You gave up your poaching business, remember?" She continued to distract Tseng, her voice assured as if she was somehow aware of Adam's presence.

His legs tingled with pins and needles when he crouched behind one of the tall banana trees of the exhibit. Once his eyes adjusted, he could make out Josslyn on the floor, her hands compressed on Sumner's chest. Tseng anxiously circled them while slashing his sword.

"That was all for show. Those fools deserved to get caught."

He swung the sword again. This time nearer to Josslyn. Adam crept closer.

"But Ting Wei is angry now. She only wants her shares in her father's company." He pointed the blade at Sumner. "You are such a fool. She only married you so her father would give her the shares. But he gave them to you instead."

Tseng's anger seemed to be escalating. His movements became more frantic. Adam aimed the rifle, patiently waiting for a clear shot.

"I wanted to ruin you," Tseng yelled. "But you are protected by your friend the president. Well, won't your friend be sad when you are both gone?"

He raised the sword over Sumner's head.

"No!" Josslyn cried.

Adam broke with protocol ingrained in him. "Get down, Joss!"

Tseng froze long enough for Adam to pin him with the red beam. He squeezed the trigger just as the other man was bringing down the sword. The clang of metal meeting concrete echoed throughout the exhibit.

"I knew you'd come," Josslyn cried out.

The sound of her voice unlocked his frozen body. So did the smile he heard in her words.

"Situation neutralized," he barked into the comm unit as he scrambled to where she was still hovering over Sumner's body. She was covered in blood.

"It's Christian's," she said as if reading his mind. "He needs help."

Someone was battering down the dead bolt on the door but Adam ignored it. The only thing he wanted to do was wrap his arm around Josslyn.

"You're okay," he whispered as he knelt beside her and gently replaced the medallion around her neck.

"Of course I am," she replied, her eyes shining. "My daddy said that medallion meant he was always with me. And he led you straight to me. I told you I'd never leave you. And I meant it. Because I love you."

Emergency responders fanned out throughout the room, but the only thing Adam was aware of was Josslyn's warm lips on his.

Two hours later, he finished his shower in the agent's lounge before creeping up to the second floor of the residence. Josslyn was asleep in the giant bed. Christine had returned her to the Crown as promised, while Adam dealt with the director and Metro PD. Her hair was fanned out on the pillows like a halo. He nearly laughed, because this woman was no angel. She had a heart of gold, though. And a fierce will that he had no intention of subduing.

Best of all, she loved him. Flaws and all. His life just got a whole lot better.

He crawled into the bed beside her and gathered her in his arms. She murmured something unintelligible as she snuggled against him. And then he slept.

CHAPTER TWENTY

T HE NEXT MORNING, Josslyn couldn't contain her goofy smile as she sipped her tea. Ngoni was tossing the ball down the long Center Hall while Fergus yapped happily as he chased after it.

"He seems to be doing well in spite of all the trauma," her sister remarked as she settled onto the sofa next to Josslyn.

Harriett and Conrad arrived back at the White House just as Josslyn was being escorted from the zoo. To her sister's credit, she hadn't flinched at seeing her covered in someone else's blood. Or at the fact that the stray Josslyn had brought home this time was an eleven-year-old boy from Zimbabwe.

"I appreciate you examining him," Josslyn said. "He's a good kid with an uncertain future. I'd be scared, too."

"He's a typical boy. All it took to get him to open up was a bowl of macaroni and cheese."

Josslyn laughed. "You're the only pediatrician I know who prescribes mac and cheese for every ailment."

"Not every ailment, but it works for most. As for the rest, we'll figure it all out." Harriett squeezed her hand. "What's the fun of having the president as a husband if you can't do some good for people?"

Josslyn grinned at her sister, squeezing back.

"I haven't seen you this happy in years. You're practically glowing." Harriett lowered her voice. "It wouldn't happen to do with the man you left sleeping in your bed, would it?"

"Oh, my gosh." She could feel her cheeks burning. "There *are* cameras in the bedrooms!"

It was Harriett's turn to laugh. "I should hope not! Although now you've given me cause to wonder. I see an awkward conversation with Director Worcester in my future." She glanced around the room, but Ngoni was busy with the dog and Daddy was tinkering at the piano. "I was checking on Father last night when I saw Agent Lockett sneaking in there." She smiled slyly. "And here I thought you two hated one another."

For the first time in her life, Josslyn couldn't meet her sister's eyes. Adam was indeed still in the Queens' Bedroom. Just thinking of the things they'd done to one another last night made her blush more deeply. He'd been sleeping so peacefully this morning that she'd left him in bed to get the rest he desperately needed.

"You know what they say; there's a fine line between love and hate," Josslyn quipped.

Harriett's eyebrows were in danger of shooting off her forehead. "The *L*-word, too. Well, color me surprised but delighted. He's a decent man. But I've often sensed he's lonely. Just like you. It's nice when two kindred souls find one another."

Josslyn scoffed. "I'm not so sure about the kindred-souls mumbo jumbo. Remember that fine line I mentioned earlier? But I do think we will have an interesting relationship."

Her sister leaned in to hug her. "You can't have passion without a little bit of fire."

"Hey, guess who I found?" Trevor entered the Center Hall followed by another man.

Fergus greeted them with a series of barks, each one shriller than the last.

"Mr. Shaw!" Ngoni cried as he dashed into the open arms of the man accompanying Trevor.

Josslyn and Harriett got to their feet.

"It's good to see you, Ngoni," Mr. Shaw said. "How's my star pupil?"

"I'm good," Ngoni glanced shyly at Josslyn. "Miss Josslyn, this is my teacher, Mr. Shaw."

"What wonderful manners you have, Ngoni," Harriett complimented him. She marched across the hall with her hand extended. "I'm Harriett Manning, Mr. Shaw."

"Uh, it's just James," he stammered, obviously flustered to be shaking hands with the First Lady.

"James," Josslyn said extending her hand as well. "We are delighted you're here. Although I'm so sorry for the circumstances that brought you back to the US." She swallowed roughly. "I'm very sorry about the loss of your father."

James blinked a few times before meeting her gaze. "Thank you," he said. "My dad lived to serve his country.

He would consider dying while breaking up an international poaching ring to be an honor."

"Are you staying in America, too?" Ngoni asked.

"I am." James rubbed the boy's head. "Which means I need to find a place to live. I understand you need a place to live, too."

Ngoni nodded. Josslyn's heart thundered in her chest.

"Mandla gave me papers stating if anything happens to him, I would take care of you," James said gently. "Would you like that? You could go to school in the United States. Maybe we can find a place near a basketball court."

"One like the court here," Ngoni exclaimed. "It's awesome. Come on." He tugged James toward the stairs.

Trevor laughed at the boy's enthusiasm as he followed them out. James hesitated at the top of the steps. He looked back over his shoulder at Josslyn. She smiled warmly and nodded.

"I'm hoping you'll be staying in the DC area," she said.

James smiled. "That depends. Does this court he's about to show me have public access?"

"No," Harriett answered. "But you're in luck. We know the guy who lives here. We can work something out."

Laughing he waved goodbye as he chased after Ngoni.

Josslyn wrapped an arm around her sister's shoulder. "Thanks."

"Anything for you, little sis. Besides, we miss having young people around."

One of the butlers came from the kitchen carrying a

mug of coffee. "You asked for this, Miss Josslyn?"

"Yes. Thank you."

Her sister shot her an impish smile before wandering over to the piano. Josslyn headed toward the Queen's Bedroom only to stop at the other end of the Center Hall when Adam emerged. His hair was still wet from his shower.

"Good morning, sleepyhead." She handed him the coffee. "How are you feeling?"

He took a long pull from the mug. "Much better now."

She wrapped her arms around his waist. "You look much better without dark circles."

"I think this is the first time in weeks I've woken up without a headache."

"Well, that settles it then." She nuzzled his jaw. "You'll just have to sleep with me every night."

"I can get behind that." Adam's eyes spoke of a lot more than sleep.

"Ahem."

Adam went to pull away but Josslyn held him tight. She glanced over her shoulder at her brother-in-law.

"Sir." Adam wanted to struggle out of her embrace, but if he did so, he'd spill the coffee on one of them. She'd pay for her antics later. At least she hoped so.

Conrad wore a strained expression. "I just spoke with Christian Sumner. By all accounts, his surgery went well. He'll make a full recovery."

"That's wonderful," Josslyn said.

"Sumner seems to think I should award you with the

Medal of Honor or something like it, Agent Lockett." Conrad pinned Adam with the same look he used on members of congress when they didn't see eye to eye. "But I see you've chosen a prize that is much more precious." His face softened when he looked at Josslyn. "Assuming that's what she wants?"

Josslyn nodded.

Conrad sighed. "That's settled then." He turned back toward his bedroom.

Adam blew out a breath. "Well, that was all kinds of awkward."

"You're telling me," Josslyn quipped. "I was the one who held the compress on Christian's wound. If anyone gets a medal, it should be me."

He laughed before leaning down to kiss her thoroughly. It wasn't lost on her that he hadn't told her he loved her. But he didn't have to. She felt his love with every fiber of her being. Even before Agent Groesch told her what he had done to rescue her.

◈

ADAM AMBLED INTO the opulent hotel lobby of The Chevalier's Georgetown location. The exclusive chain of boutique hotels catered to the world's wealthy elite. After nearly two decades spent in a twelve-by-twelve cinder block cell, his old man was likely enjoying the luxury of the five-star hotel's owner's suite. No wonder he was taking his sweet time cashing the check. But Adam was done with his father taking advantage of Marin's family's hospitality. This game ended today.

As he rode the elevator up to the top floor, he tried to tamp down on his restless emotions. Adam didn't like that his father was forcing his hand. He couldn't have cared less if he ever saw the man again. But watching Josslyn with her father yesterday at the Children's Garden, seeing the sorrow and regret in her eyes every time Dr. Benoit looked through her, had cut Adam to the quick. He was doing this for her. Because for some reason it was important to Josslyn that Adam get the closure she couldn't.

If anyone had asked him days ago whether he'd ever subject himself to the whims of a woman, he would have laughed out loud. But love made him do strange things, apparently. And right now, knowing Josslyn loved him for who and what he was made Adam believe he could handle confronting his father once and for all.

And, after that, he'd let the woman he loved know it. Speaking the words tonight and every day of their lives.

The elevator doors opened on the penthouse floor. Adam shook his head when he pressed the doorbell. He could hear it echoing throughout the suite. A moment later, a freaking butler answered the door.

"May I help you?" the man asked.

"I have to be in the wrong place," Adam said more to himself than the other man.

"You came," a gravelly voice bellowed from within.

The relief he heard in his old man's words made Adam's throat tight. Clenching and unclenching his fists, he reminded himself that, after today, he'd never have to see this man again. *This is for Joss.* He repeated the mantra as he strolled into the spacious living room with its panoramic views of Georgetown and the Potomac River beyond.

Suddenly, the shock of a butler was nothing compared to the appearance of the man who greeted Adam. He had assumed that nineteen years of prison would not be kind to the sixty-year-old. But the man leaning a hip on the baby grand piano wasn't nearly as diminished as Adam expected. The thought fueled his already festering anger.

Chet Lockett's green eyes homed in on Adam, seeming to drink him in. As if sensing his son's raising annoyance, he called out to the butler.

"Stephen, can you bring some whisky for my son."

"I didn't come here to drink with you," Adam choked out around the tightness in his throat.

"I've been sober since the day they put the handcuffs on me."

"Not hard to do when you're behind bars."

His father chuckled. "You'd be surprised the things you can get in prison. I just never acquired a taste for rubbing alcohol. And now that I'm out, I don't have much of a taste for the good stuff anymore. I prefer a clear head instead."

The butler came into the room carrying a tray loaded with a single cut-crystal glass and a bottle of Glenlivet. A tall tumbler of something resembling a vegetable smoothie was also on the tray. Adam's father chugged the remainder of a bottle of water before taking the smoothie from the butler.

"If you don't mind," his father said as he took a seat at one of the two sofas dominating the room. "I'd prefer to have this conversation sitting down."

Adam didn't honor his request. "I'd 'prefer' we didn't have this conversation at all. In fact, I'd 'prefer' you stop taking advantage of the generosity of my friends. Take the money I gave you and head out of Dodge."

His father's nose wrinkled as he sucked the smoothie through a straw. "You have nice friends," he said once he'd consumed half the glass.

Swearing under his breath, Adam clenched and unclenched his fists a few times more. "One word from me and my 'nice' friends won't hesitate to put you out on the street."

"I'm glad," his father surprised him by saying. "It means you are a good and honorable man to be surrounded by such loyal people."

"No thanks to you," Adam snapped.

Setting the smoothie down on a side table, his father scrubbed a hand down his face. "No, of course not. I know I can't take credit for the man you've become. But in spite of that, I can still be proud of you. Maybe even more proud than if I hadn't screwed up your life. Because you succeeded in spite of me."

Something unsettling fluttered in Adam's gut.

"Not only that," his father continued, "but you're an officer." He stood resolutely, saluting Adam with a beaming smile.

"Stop it," Adam ordered. "I don't want any of your parental accolades. Not now. Not ever."

His father's smile dimmed as he retook his seat. "You always did want to be a soldier. Do you remember when you were little and you used to stomp around in my boots? Your mom would chew me out whenever I let you help me polish them. You'd get more of the polish on you than on the boots." He laughed to himself softly.

Adam's head began to pound. That same recollection had come to him unbidden the other day. He didn't like it any more now than he did then.

"I didn't come here for some stroll down memory lane," he bit out.

His father lifted his eyes to meet Adam's "You're so tall. You get that from your mother's side. Your pappy is still a tall man, even in his eighties."

"You've been in touch with them?" Adam rocked back on his heels slightly. There didn't seem to be an end to the surprises.

"Of course," his father admitted. "They've kept me updated on you. Your mother's people are good people."

As he rubbed his temples, Adam suddenly felt a little betrayed by his grandparents. This man had killed their granddaughter, not to mention their great-grandchild. They should be solidly in Adam's camp, not sharing information with a man who didn't deserve a son after what he'd done.

"Don't take it personally."

Adam hated the way his father could so easily interpret his emotions.

"I don't care what Meemaw and Pappy told you," Adam lied. "I don't care if they sent you my damn report cards. All I care about is you taking the damn check and getting the hell out of my life."

"Why is it so important to you that I take the money?"

Nothing about this encounter was going as Adam planned. "Isn't that what you're here for?"

A sad smile settled on his father's mouth. "No."

Damn it. Ben was correct. This was one of those twelve-step things. His old man wanted some sort of absolution. Adam would rather drain his entire bank account than give him that.

"You had three life sentences. Why didn't they just let you rot in there?"

His father sighed. "That's easy. Try not to be too disappointed, but I'm dying."

Adam suddenly felt a little woozy. He reached down and grabbed the bottle of Scotch off the tray. Not bothering with the glass, he took a hefty swallow. It burned as it went down. Too bad it didn't burn out the tightening in his chest.

"I was a model prisoner. I earned a college degree and a master's degree." His father winked at him. "I told everyone inside that I got my smarts from my boy. Based on that and my diagnosis of pancreatic cancer, I was offered a compassionate release."

"What is this about then?" Adam croaked. "You want my forgiveness before you die or something?"

He felt like an ass just saying the words. Josslyn would

be so disappointed in him. But it would take the entire bottle of scotch and then some before Adam could likely get any words of absolution out.

"No," his father shot back at him. "I'm not fool enough to think you'll ever give me that. But I can't leave this earth without telling you my side of things."

Adam suspected this was his father's end-around way of obtaining forgiveness, but he let him have his say.

"I wasn't in my right mind after my third deployment, but I ignored it. Your mother begged me to get help. It got worse when she died. I foolishly assumed she was the one good thing to ever happen to me and that I had nothing to live for. She left me two precious gifts to remember her by and I thoughtlessly threw them away. I have no excuse for what I did that day. None. Every day I have to live with how I destroyed our lives all those years ago."

Sliding onto one of the sofas, Adam glared at the man before him. "You didn't destroy my life. So please don't try to take credit for that. Go in peace."

Adam let himself think it was the whisky talking, except the bottle in his hands was still full.

His father's rich laugh filled the room. "You always were a stubborn one. Don't worry, with death will come peace, especially now that I've seen for myself how well you have survived."

"So that's it?" Adam refused to acknowledge the feeling of disappointment that flared in his gut. He replaced the bottle of Scotch. "You'll take the money and go?"

"I don't need your money, Son."

Adam flinched at the word "son." His father pulled the check from a tattered billfold Adam recognized as one his mother had given him for Father's Day all those years ago. He placed it on the tray without reluctance.

"How will you live?" he asked, angry at himself for even caring.

"The VA has a network of care facilities. I'm headed to one in Florida. It was all arranged with my release. After so many winters in Kansas, I want my last days to be spent in the sunshine."

There was that kick in his gut again. "How long?"

"A couple of months." His father dragged his palms across his jeans. "Let's not dwell on that because there is another reason I came to see you."

Adam knew there had to be a catch.

"I know I have no right to say this, but I want you to know that I love you. You don't have to love me back and I certainly understand if you don't. But I wanted to tell you not to let our relationship color the other ones in your life. Life is too short to hold back on love. You should always let the people you love know it."

"Did you develop clairvoyance while you were in prison?"

His father's eyes were damp but smiling. "No. But I hope that means I'm preaching to the choir and you have someone special in your life."

Adam swallowed roughly before nodding. "I do."

"Good. She's a lucky girl."

Now Adam was even angrier at himself for not saying

those three little words to Josslyn when he had the chance. But she knew how he felt. Her eyes told him so every time he looked at her. Still, he was going to tell her the first chance he got. Of course, now every time he told her he loved her, Adam would hear his old man's voice.

Damn it.

He lifted his gaze to meet the green eyes of his father's, a mirror image of his own. They weren't mocking. Instead, they were filled with pride. It was the same look he'd given Adam when he'd scored the buzzer beater in rec league, basketball when he was ten.

Adam sat forward on the sofa and rubbed at his temples. That was the second good memory of his dad that week. Was Ben right? Had Adam buried any recollection of all the good times?

"No, I'm the lucky one," Adam said.

The apprehension that had been lurking in his father's eyes seemed to ease. "I'd love to hear about her."

❖

TWO HOURS LATER Adam's step was much lighter as he emerged from the elevator into the lobby of The Chevalier. He and his father would never have the relationship Josslyn wanted for them. Instead, they'd both agreed to start fresh from right now and see where it took them during the last days of his dad's life. It would have to be enough.

Adam did a double take when he passed the hotel's signature fountain. His jangled nerves relaxed at the vision of

Josslyn seated on one of the sofas. She was doing her best to look cool and collected, but the agitated swinging of her booted foot let him know she was as anxious as he'd been when he walked through the hotel doors hours earlier.

Unable to contain the smile just looking at her brought to his face, he sauntered over to where she sat. "Fancy meeting you here."

She fiddled with the zipper on her leather jacket. "I wanted to make sure you didn't need backup."

He laughed. "As good as you are with a gun I'll take you as my wingman any time. But that's not necessary today."

"Too bad. I told you I'd never leave you."

"Mmm. So you did. A couple of times now, as I recall." He reached down and hugged her to him. She sighed contentedly when their bodies made contact. "But you might want to hold onto that thought because I'm going to take you up to meet my old man."

She shook her head. "You're stuck with me no matter what. That's the way this works."

Adam's heart felt like it was beating outside of his chest. "Good. But before we go up, there's something I need you to know. I love you, Doctor Josslyn Emmeline Benoit. Very much."

Josslyn's lips curved into one of those saucy smiles as she wrapped her arms around his neck. A throat cleared beside them. Adam looked over to see Christine giving him the side-eye. She blushed as she did it.

"I told her I don't need a detail any longer, but I can't

seem to shake her," Josslyn complained halfheartedly. "She seems to think I'm destined to walk into another dangerous situation."

He shot his fellow agent a knowing grin. Given Josslyn's reputation as the She-Devil, it was highly likely she was going to find herself in numerous close calls in the future. But Adam had no intention of taming her. He loved her just the way she was.

"Thanks, Christine," he said. "But I'll take it from here." He pulled Josslyn in closer. "In fact, I'll take it from now on."

Christine might have sighed or scoffed. Adam wasn't sure. Nor did he care. He was too busy kissing Josslyn.

"Keeper," he murmured against her lips.

She pulled away, fixing him with a questioning look.

"Your new code name," Adam explained. "At least in private."

Josslyn threw her head back and laughed. And then, to his vast relief, she kissed him again.

THE END

FROM THE AUTHOR

Despite worldwide efforts to ban the sale of elephant tusks, demand for ivory remains high. This, unfortunately, leads to the continued poaching of elephants. Tens of thousands of elephants are killed each year and their ivory tusks sold illegally on the black market. There are many organizations out there devoted to helping save the elephant from extinction. One in particular is the David Sheldrick Wildlife Trust. You can foster an elephant or donate to their mission at their website www.sheldrickwildlifetrust.org.

The elephant, Dax, is based loosely on Spike, the big bull living at the Smithsonian's National Zoological Park in Washington, DC. I'm grateful to the friendly docents at the Elephant Trails exhibit for providing background information for this book. Any mistakes I made are totally my fault! One factual error was intentional, however. The zoo's Front Royal facility does not house animals for quarantine. Elephants are routinely held in quarantine within the elephant barn for thirty days before being allowed to interact with the other elephants. Because I couldn't pause the story for that long, I needed Dax to arrive at the zoo having already gone through quarantine. Therefore, I played with the facts a bit. This is a work of fiction, after all!

As Josslyn points out in the book, the National Zoo belongs to all of us. It's staffed by professionals and knowledgeable volunteers alike. If you'd like to contribute to the zoo's educational efforts, please contact the Friends of the National Zoo (FONZ) at this site nationalzoo.si.edu/membership/about-fonz.

Finally, thanks to loyal reader Denise Stout who gave me the name Fergus for Dr. Benoit's dog. I hope you enjoy this little glimpse inside the White House and Washington, DC. I love to hear from readers. Email me at tracy@tracysolheim.com. Or find me on Facebook at Tracy Solheim Books (facebook.com/TracySolheimBooks). Happy reading!!

THE MEN OF THE SECRET SERVICE SERIES

Book 1: *Recipe for Disaster*

Book 2: *Shot in the Dark*

Book 3: *Between Love and Honor*

More fantastic reads by Tracy Solheim

Smolder

Holiday at Magnolia Bay

Available now at your favorite online retailer!

ABOUT THE AUTHOR

Tracy Solheim is the international bestselling author of the Out of Bound Series for Penguin. Her books feature members of the fictitious Baltimore Blaze football team and the women who love them. In a previous life, Tracy wrote best sellers for Congress and was a freelance journalist for regional and national magazines. She's a military brat who now makes her home in Johns Creek, Georgia, with her husband, their two children, a pesky Labrador retriever puppy and a horse named after her first novel. Her fifth book for Berkley, Back To Before, will be released in January. She also has a digital holiday novella for Tule Publishing's Southern Born Books coming October 20. See what she's up to at www.tracysolheim.com. Or on facebook at Tracy Solheim Books and Twitter at @TracyKSolheim

Thank you for reading

SHOT IN THE DARK

If you enjoyed this book, you can find more from all our great authors at TulePublishing.com, or from your favorite online retailer.

TULE
PUBLISHING

Manufactured by Amazon.ca
Bolton, ON